The Pirate of Panther Bay

SR Staley

Published by:
Southern Yellow Pine (SYP) Publishing
4351 Natural Bridge Rd.
Tallahassee, FL 32305

www.syppublishing.com

This is a work of fiction. Names, characters, places, and events that occur either are the products of the author's imagination or are used fictitiously. Any resemblance to actual persons, places, or events is purely coincidental.

The contents and opinions expressed in this book do not necessarily reflect the views and opinions of Southern Yellow Pine Publishing, nor does the mention of brands or trade names constitute endorsement.

ISBN-10: 1-940869-17-X
ISBN-13: 978-1-940869-17-9

Front Cover Design: Jim Hamer

Printed in the United States of America
Second Edition
July 2014

Dedication

To Claire & Evan, without whom the inspiration for this novel never would have happened.

Acknowledgements

Second Edition

The publication of the second edition of *The Pirate of Panther Bay* is also an opportunity for reflection. As a writer, I am humbled and gratified by the staying power of the lead characters, Isabella in particular, and the inspiration they have given to readers over the years. The tagline about the 18th Century girl pirate captain who kicks butt as she grapples with betrayal, survival, and romance on the high seas continues to capture the imagination of readers. The ability to keep her story alive in this second edition as well as the sequel, *Tortuga Bay*, is a gift.

This edition and the series, however, might not have survived if it weren't for the enthusiasm of Terri Gerrell, my publisher and owner of Southern Yellow Pine Publishing. Terri not only agreed to publish *Tortuga Bay*, but embraced a new edition of *The Pirate of Panther Bay* as well. Terri's commitment to the series has significantly ratcheted up its quality and given me breathing room for fleshing out the characters and their stories in even more exciting ways. So, a big shout out goes to Terri and her team for putting together a first-rate second edition (including the engaging and exciting new cover).

Of course, the second edition would not exist at all if not for the enthusiasm and support from all the people that provided advice, counsel, and badly needed constructive criticism during the writing, publication. and marketing of the first, including: Claire and Evan Staley, Carly Jay (Weng), Gloria Jaspers, Gary and Heidy Simon, Alex Carmoega, Morgan Finkelstein, Bob Breen, Tim Bete, and Mike Sprout. The comments provided by the students at the Miami Valley School helped shape the new edition and the course of the characters in the series. Mike Rienke, my business partner for the first edition, provided invaluable assistance in putting the original edition together, and Len Gilroy was essential in creating the web platform we needed to market the book and the series.

I would like to thank my former literary agent Mary Sue Seymour. A query back in the late 1990s led directly to the creation of the characters and plot in the Panther Bay series. While she could not place that early draft of the manuscript, her early support, combined with the discipline required to sell the manuscript, gave me the confidence to continue as a fiction author and ultimately ensured Isabella, Jean Michel, and Juan Carlos would see their lives play out in published books.

Finally, I need to give a shout out to my peers and colleagues in the Tallahassee Writers Association and my Tallahassee-based critique group. Their insights and experiences are a daily inspiration, and I may well have abandoned this journey without their support and dedication to the craft. TWA is one of Florida's largest and most active regional writers groups, and their inclusiveness and support is a testimony to their commitment to writing as a powerful and constructive part of the everyday lives of regular people.

SR Staley
Tallahassee, Florida
July 4, 2014

1

Isabella stormed into the cramped cabin of the *Marée Rouge**, letting the door thump wildly.

How could this have happened? Everything seemed lost, and she hadn't even begun. Her first command of a pirate ship and she let her first prize blow up out from under her! She needed to do something… fast.

Isabella began a frantic pace before the powder-stained windows, carved out of the ship's stern.

Two bodies tumbled into the room just seconds behind her. A short, gangly man looked around as if expecting someone to jump or bludgeon him. A larger man discretely latched the cabin door shut. The closed door seemed to give him confidence. He straightened his shoulders and lifted his face forward. The short one stood, holding a jumble of papers and envelopes. Unsure of what to do, he glanced nervously from place to place. The two men stood, quietly, watching Isabella pace.

The *Marée Rouge* heaved over the afternoon swells. The ship's wake churned any remaining links to her prey, the 32-gun frigate *Ana Maria*, off into a fading horizon. How could she have let this prize slip away? God, what would Jean-Michel think?

Isabella ran her fingers through locks of hair matted by salt water and smoke. She looked out the window as white caps rose and fell outside her cabin. Isabella smirked at the thought of how well they seemed to match her mood. The sea always seemed to rise and fall with her moods. She felt free—liberated—each time she cast her gaze into the swells.

"Where is he?" Isabella barked.

The two men standing anxiously in front of her exchanged surprised glances.

* *Translation (from French): Red Tide* 1

"Mr. Stiles," she asked again, looking menacingly at the short one, her frustration feeding a new wave of impatience. "Where is he? Where's the boy?"

"Err... boy?" the gangly man sputtered. If Isabella had cared to look closely enough, she would have seen his indignation. After all, Stiles, like the rest of the crew, knew Isabella wouldn't be commanding this pirate ship if she hadn't inherited it from her lover. Stiles bristled at her attitude.

"The prisoner!" Isabella demanded, impatience mounting with the spray on the cabin windows. "Where is he, Stiles? You're the quartermaster, right? Aren't you keeping track of our prisoners?"

Stiles shifted thin, oblong feet uneasily. "Below with the spare shot," he said finally, lifting his chin from his chest. His British accent was unusually thick. Exhaustion was eating away at him as he tried to collect his thoughts. "We've got him bound up good; he ain't goin' nowhere soon. Let the sergeant o' arms take care o'im."

"Don't let him nod off," Isabella ordered, still looking out the window. "I'll want to talk to him."

Isabella took a deep breath, hoping to ward off a shudder creeping up through her legs. She needed to control her emotions—she couldn't show weakness. That's what Jacob had taught her. She couldn't let Stiles—or Jean-Michel—consider the thought that she couldn't lead this crew, this ship, to victory. She could. She had to. She had her destiny. Her mother had told her the prophecy. She remembered the night she heard it—near the fields, the smell of sugarcane sifting like perfume through the small cluster of wood huts on the plantation. It seemed like yesterday in her dreams. How could she doubt it? Still, the *Ana Maria* was lost....

Isabella absorbed the roll of the sea. It was soothing now, a quaint antidote to the death and mayhem of the past few hours. God, she needed someone to talk to. How could Jacob have left her with this ship so unprepared, so vulnerable?

"Why did we lose the *Ana Maria*, Mr. Stiles?" Isabella asked. "What caused the explosion?"

"Don't know ma'am," Stiles said, struggling to keep calm.

"Hah," she smirked, still looking out the windows. "Some quartermaster! Aren't you in charge of the cargo?"

"Aye, ma'am," Stiles stammered. "But, I'm not the ship's boatswain. We barely had time to get the manifest and charts." A stack of papers and envelopes fell from his arms to the thick oak tabletop, separating Isabella from her ship's officers. The desk provided a welcome buffer.

Isabella turned and found herself lodged up against the desk. Seized from an America-bound slave ship, it consumed the room. The side drawers held the ship's manifests and stationery. A stark, wood-frame chair served as a captain's chair—her *throne* according to Jean-Michel. Two smaller chairs, stools with backs, sat idly between the men and the desk.

The space was suffocating, but its meager privacy somehow gave Isabella a workable distance from her new job. Compared to Jean-Michel's quarters—a hammock strung across a cannon, separated from the crew by a thin wood screen—her cubbyhole was a palace.

Isabella thumbed through the stack deposited by Stiles, as the larger man patiently studied her. She paused at a formal set of papers and glanced at a royal seal on the envelope. She slapped them together angrily and threw them down to the desktop. "Just as I thought," she muttered. Isabella turned toward the windows again and pulled in a deep breath.

"Qu'est-ce que c'est, mon capitaine?" the larger man asked after a few more awkward moments.

Isabella looked at him as if about to say something, and then stopped. *"Rien,"* she said, shaking her head. "Nothing."

"The *Ana Maria* was an unfortunate loss," Jean-Michel continued, this time in English. Even after two decades at sea, his southern French drawl coated his words.

"Aye," Isabella responded, still deep in thought.

Stiles and Jean-Michel waited another minute that seemed like fifteen. Isabella finally turned. Stiles looked disheveled and a bit off. His mood lacked the cool efficiency she saw on the deck of the *Ana Maria*, before the explosion, before her swim back to the *Marée Rouge*.

"What's on your mind Stiles?" she asked matter-of-factly.

Stiles hesitated. Her mood ebbed and flowed faster than a duel of equals. The quartermaster uneasily pulled his shoulders up, putting his head at risk in the low-hung ceilings. "Nothing ma'am," Stiles said quickly. Too quickly, for Isabella's taste.

The humidity in the cabin was almost unbearable. Isabella turned and pushed open the windows. A breeze cleared the cabin. She drew in a deep breath. Even the smallest puffs of fresh sea air seemed to calm her, just like the fields of Hispaniola. Then, she couldn't wait to break out of the huts and rush into the openness of the fields. Isabella smiled as she remembered how her mother would shake her head with the other elders. That seemed so long ago. She had come so far. Yet, now, she felt lost. The prisoner didn't help matters. Pirates didn't take prisoners, only hostages for barter, ransom, or *entertainment*.

Isabella placed her hands on the window frame and looked down at the swirling water. The ship was steady now, cutting cleanly into the waves. The rudder shuddered against the stiff current, its rhythm kneading Isabella's tired arms as it accented the gentle creak of the ship. She was home. Why did she feel so alone?

Isabella turned back to Stiles and Jean-Michel. "We've sailed together for two years." The comment raised an eyebrow from Jean-Michel. "Two and a half," she corrected. Her fingers browsed the pages of the manifest and unconsciously directed her eyes away from Jean-Michel. "Something's on your mind, Mr. Stiles. Out with it."

"Nothing, Captain," the quartermaster said.

"You doubt me."

"No! No, ma'am. It's a bit different, but we're... I... I'm... fine with it." Stiles shifted his weight. "This battle was different," he added, as if he knew his first response wasn't enough. "It was harder." Stiles seemed incapable of stopping his free fall. "Odd in some ways." Isabella looked at him puzzled.

"Our crew fought well," Jean-Michel interrupted. "We captured the prize. That's the important thing."

"It's a pity we couldn't bring the *Ana Maria* home," Isabella said, hoping a new tone might put Stiles at ease. She sensed some truth behind Stiles' bumbling speech. "The crew put up a good fight."

"Aye," Stiles acknowledged. "But, she didn't carry much bounty."

"Some prizes are richer than others," Jean-Michel reminded him.

"There's hardly anything in the manifest," Stiles persisted. Jean-Michel looked at Isabella expectantly.

"We don't know what she had on board," Isabella noted. "She sank too fast."

"She sailed from Cadiz four weeks ago," Stiles said, as if reading from the ship's log. "The manifest lists dry goods, powder, guns, and a few packets for Viceroy Rodriguez. No gold or coin."

"The best treasure is not always in the manifest," Isabella pointed out. "We've found hidden gold, diamonds, and doubloons on these ships before."

"Aye, Captain." Stiles paused, as if that were the end of it. "The men'll be disappointed."

"Maybe so, Mr. Stiles," Isabella said. Was this all he was worried about? "But that's why I have you. You keep things in perspective for the men, don't you?"

Stiles opened his mouth to say something, but a glare from Jean-Michel gave him the discipline to stop. "Aye, Captain."

Isabella and Stiles looked at each other, trading awkward stares.

"So, Mr. Stiles," Jean-Michel said finally. "What do you think caused the explosion? What sent our esteemed captain into the drink?"

The quartermaster shifted his weight again. His eyes darted about. "It was most likely a spark in the powder room."

Not good enough, Isabella thought. "Were any of our men below deck at the time?"

"Don't know for sure. We only have a count for the ones wounded in the battle."

Isabella nodded. She was sure there was more to Stiles' strange line of questioning. What was it?

"The *Ana Maria* would not have been much use anyway," Jean-Michel observed. "We wouldn't have been able to repair her forward mast. Besides, we seized two eighteen-pounders. They'll be fine additions to the cliffs over Panther Bay."

Isabella thumbed through the manifest again. How many times was this? Three? Stiles stood patiently. Why didn't he just come out and say it?

Isabella asked again, "What else, Mr. Stiles?"

Stiles paused. He shook his head, avoiding Jean-Michel's eyes. He suddenly seemed to lose his self-discipline. "It's the crew; they ain't sure what's goin' on."

"What do you mean?" she prodded, startled.

The quartermaster hesitated.

"Speak your mind. You've a witness here in Jean-Michel. There will be no retribution." That's another valuable lesson Jacob taught her.

Stiles looked at Jean-Michel. "The men don't understand why you took the prisoner." Isabella sensed Jean-Michel's eyebrows rise in silent agreement.

"That's a fair concern," Isabella admitted. How could she explain this? She wasn't sure herself. She followed her gut, and it said this was an exception. She didn't have time to think. The ship was sinking, and she had to salvage what she could. She just knew she should save this man… or hold him. After all, he single handedly rallied the Spaniards in a counter attack. His presence was unmistakable. He had a power, a character, she had not seen among the Spanish before. He was a key. She just didn't know to what.

"First," she began, "as captain, I set the rules and enforce them. You know that; this is not an ordinary pirate ship. You are not an ordinary crew. You were hand-picked. We operate under the shadow of Jacob. I am the captain. Jean-Michel is my lieutenant. I'm not elected by you or anyone else. Neither is Jean-Michel. You choose to follow or leave. So, you accept my decisions, whether you like them or not."

Stiles winced at the sharpness in her tone.

"Second, this prisoner is not ordinary. He was a civilian on a Spanish warship. Don't you think that's odd? We're at war with the Spanish Crown. It's a fight we can't afford to lose. We have our goal, but not a map. It's a puzzle, perhaps even a riddle. This man is an important clue." The explanation was unsatisfactory, but the best she could muster. She needed time to think. She was drawn to this prisoner—his courage, his purpose, his determination. He intrigued her. He frightened her. And she felt guilty. What would Jacob think? So soon after his death?

Stiles looked puzzled. "Why him?" he said at last. "He's a boy."

"I'm a girl," Isabella retorted. She looked into his eyes as if challenging him.

"No," Stiles said. "You're my captain."

She felt her face flush. She hoped her skin, darkened even more by the sun and open sea, would not betray her. She dared not show him how she felt. Not now. Especially not now. "Some things are more important than bounty," she said in a quick, steady voice.

"What's more important than gold?" Stiles scoffed.

Isabella looked at him, unsure if he was serious. The quartermaster shifted his feet again. "The Spaniard's taking up space and rations. He ain't signed on. We ain't sure o' his future disposition."

Isabella let the tension mount before answering. "Mr. Stiles, the boy's disposition is my affair, and Jean-Michel's. He's secure below deck. Isn't he? Saint John is less than two days sail with these winds. Our rations are rich enough for one more mouth. We'll decide what to do with him when we get to Panther Bay." She stopped, and then added, "The gallows still work, don't they?"

"Aye, ma'am," Stiles responded, clearly surprised at the suggestion the prisoner might be hanged.

"This civilian was given a special escort in the Navy of King Charles III," Isabella continued, hoping finally to satisfy Stiles. "I suspect the Dagos'll make another attempt to secure their trading routes. The British and Americans are squeezing them even with the so-called revolution in the colonies. Criminals, such as us, costs Spain far more during competitive times like these."

The quartermaster still wasn't convinced. She could tell.

"Fifteen more minutes on the *Ana Maria's* deck, and the prisoner wouldn't be here." Her tone carried a finality that neither challenged. "That's all for now, Mr. Stiles. Come back when you have a complete report from the boatswain. I want to know how and why the *Ana Maria* sank. I don't care much for swimming in these waters. I want a complete report on our stores, munitions, and battle capabilities. Two days is long enough to meet another ship, and we need to be ready."

"Aye, Captain," Stiles said crisply. He turned and walked out the door.

2

"I don't like him," Jean-Michel said, moments after the door had shut.

"Maybe not, but he's the best quartermaster I've seen."

Jean-Michel shot a piercing glance toward Isabella. She smiled.

"You know who I mean," he said, clearly irritated. "This isn't the time for jokes." He slumped into a chair opposite the desk. "The Dagos'll back stab you faster than you can blink."

Jean-Michel's beard consumed a taught face, far thinner than his body, and it still glistened from the sweat of the afternoon's battle. His skin, deeply marked by years of sun and salt, barely held the hints of the Old World features that could still reveal his noble family roots. Nights inside the fortress walls of Puerto Rico's El Morro had distanced him from his family history long ago.

"We've taken on new crew from captured ships before," Isabella said. Her voice was tired and weak, now that they were alone.

"*Oui,*" Jean-Michel acknowledged, "but ten? I don't like the way they jumped at the chance—a little too eager for my taste." He looked at Isabella with a fatherly tenderness.

"And the prisoner—your *boy*. He showed more courage than all the Dago captain's officers put together did. He rallied those marines when we had them down. He's probably responsible for most of the dead and half the wounded."

Isabella looked at Jean-Michel, comforted by his tone but surprised. Jean-Michel had an unusual, English-like hatred for the Spanish. He almost always objected to bringing Spanish crew on board, claiming their seamanship was so poor they would run a dingy aground. The Spanish prisoner worried him, and that betrayed a respect she had never seen before. Of course, Isabella had never taken an interest in a prisoner before either. Six months. Was it too soon to put to sea after Jacob's murder?

Jean-Michel looked around at the cabin, giving Isabella a few moments to collect her thoughts. The ceiling was low, forcing everyone except the cabin boy and Isabella to duck. On the port side, a small, deep washbasin filled with fresh water stood ready, cleverly suspended in a wooden frame to keep the water from spilling in rough seas—pirate ingenuity. Above it, a frugal mirror hung securely to the ship's plank siding. A small bureau on the starboard side held whatever clothes Isabella felt she would need on the voyages—usually just a few shirts and a spare pair of breeches. A strategically placed small cot between the bureau and hull was in a corner nook below the aft windows. Her carpenters had re-cut the windows to widen her view at Panther Bay, a comforting gesture after Jacob's murder.

"We can deal with the boy," Isabella reassured him with a reluctant smile. "Besides, we can use a few more tars scrubbing the decks." He looked at her unconvinced. "We've seen this before, Mick. We offer adventure and excitement. We promise bounty. Only fools prefer the yardarms and cat-o-nine tails of a European man-o-war."

"Bounty's been scarce."

"If they can't claim loyalty to me—to us," she said testily, "we'll send the Dagos on their way. They wouldn't be the first."

"And the crew?"

She looked at him startled.

"And the boy?" Jean-Michel continued, interrupting her thoughts.

Why would he ask that?

"That's trickier." Isabella started to thumb through the folders again.

Jean-Michel closed his eyes and shook his head. "We should have let the *Ana Maria* go."

"Let her go? If anything would set the crew off, letting a prize go would have."

"We should have discussed it."

"I didn't have enough information."

"You had enough to commit this ship." Jean-Michel's tone was disciplined and authoritative. "You had enough information to risk almost two hundred men, to sacrifice at least fifteen of them. You had enough to commit me."

Isabella stood dumbfounded. He was right. How had she not discussed this with him? How could she have been so foolish? Did her destiny—her mother's prophecy—so consume her that she had stopped all logical thought?

"Isabella, *mon cher*." Jean-Michel's voice became low and urgent. "Times are different. The *Marée Rouge* has a new captain. Dissension is in the crew."

Was this what he meant when he referred to the crew earlier? Jean-Michel hesitated before saying anything else.

"What do you mean? What have you heard?"

"Nothing's been said to me," he said. "They know better. They move differently at their tasks. They talk. They worry. I see it; I feel it. It wasn't there on Saint John. I saw it on board when we left Panther Bay. It was on board before we engaged the *Ana Maria*. I feel it. On deck. At night most deeply."

"When they move," Isabella asked, trying to manage the fear bubbling inside her, "When they worry, what do they say? What do you feel? Who are the leaders?"

Jean-Michel leaned forward in his chair. "Isabella, it's hard enough for them to obey a man, but a girl? Jacob gave them everything they could ever dream of. He's the only pirate captain I've ever sailed with who didn't need the Articles; they didn't worry about their captain because they knew they would always elect him again. You inherited this ship, its crew, and their goodwill. But, things are different since Jacob's death."

"We can keep their stomachs full. We give them wealth, just like when Jacob commanded the *Marée Rouge*."

"Logic and reason protect your mind," Jean-Michel said, his forefinger pointing to his head "but not our command. Today should have been their first taste of victory and wealth under your command. What did we end up with? A victory? Not by their standards. Fifteen men are dead. Another score wounded. Ten prisoners. Our prize? Two eighteen-pound cannons, some extra shot, clothes, a few small gems, and... papers! How do you split that up? That's not what they signed up for."

Isabella sat, thinking quickly, almost desperately. What would Jacob do? He was so confident; he always had a plan. He seemed to make the big decisions effortlessly. That was part of her attraction to him, more than two years ago, once she got past his blue eyes and sun baked, dirty-blond waves. "I've got gold saved. I can compensate them from my account."

"You'll need to do that if you want them back. And keep Rodriguez off your back."

Isabella hesitated, as if pondering whether she needed to tell Jean-Michel something else. Something important. Jean-Michel waited, curious. "The viceroy's not our only worry," she said, after several minutes.

Jean-Michel's eyebrow turned up. "The only threat in these seas right now is Yellow Jacket. I don't think he's strong enough to take us on. He's got the attitude, but not the crew. Even with a frigate of 30 guns, he can't match our nimble little brig of 22."

Isabella nodded. "Aye, but he's a rogue. He senses weakness. If our men are vulnerable, he'll figure out how to use them. I swear he was behind Jacob's murder."

"You may be right, *mon cher*," Jean-Michel said. "But we don't know for sure. The privateers are an odd lot. They have their own rules. Can't trust 'em. At least I know what the Dagos and Brits are up to. The Americans? Only God knows."

Perhaps Jean-Michel would add some gold to the pot to keep the crew in line. No, she wouldn't dare ask him for help. This was her mistake, not his. Giving out gold was a small price to pay for their loyalty. "We can't promise success each time out. I don't have enough gold to compensate them for every failure. How many ships have we captured together?"

"With Jacob?" asked Jean-Michel. "More than a dozen. Sold some off to the Americans. Two we crewed as privateers. I don't know how many we let go. Are you serious? You expect me to keep count?"

Now, Isabella raised her eyebrows: "Isn't that the point? We've captured our share of ships and bounty; we'll do it again. Under Jacob, we captured more than any other pirate in fifty years."

Jean-Michel looked at her poker faced. "A pirate crew is not patient. They can't remember much further back than their last tin of rum. And, you're not Jacob."

His point sucked the air from her lungs. She shuddered at a sudden longing for the familiar sweet smell of the sugarcane fields of Hispaniola. Each passing month made the fields seem less harsh, less evil.

"Six months," she said wistfully, "and his death still haunts me."

"His death haunts us both."

Isabella looked at Jean-Michel, tears lending a sad sparkle to her tired eyes.

"*Mais, ma petite,*" Jean-Michel said, interrupting her thoughts, "battle and loot are not the only things on your mind." He leaned across the desk and took her hand. "You're not alone."

"Now you sound like my mother," Isabella said quietly, letting her hand rest in his as a small smile broke through. "In the evenings, after we came in from the fields, she would talk about the spirits. The spirits would work with us in the fields, and protect us." She left out what the spirits had told her mother about Isabella's future before she was even born. She had only trusted two people with that information. She couldn't help but think it led to their deaths. She couldn't afford to lose Jean-Michel now. Not so close to losing Jacob.

"I don't know about spirits or other gods," Jean-Michel said. "But I'm sure one God—my God—is with you."

"Your God? I don't know about your God," she scoffed. Her voice hardened again. "I'm not even sure I believe the spirits protect me anymore."

"You're not alone," he repeated, stroking her hand. "Jacob saw to that. He had vision, as all great leaders do. That's why we have the *Marée Rouge*, and a pirate crew more seasoned than any frigate in the West Indies. In time, his memory will fade, and you will find your own peace with his death. Your place with this crew will be firm. But, beware of the Dago prisoner. This is a difficult time. Resist him. Be strong!"

Isabella's back tightened. She pulled her hand from his and crossed her arms close to her chest, as if the balmy breeze through the windows chilled her. How could he know so much? She didn't dare confess those feelings, not even to Jean-Michel. "What do you mean?"

"You know what I mean," he said, his tone noticeably transformed.

"Don't play games!"

"*Les jeux?*" Jean-Michel said, mocking surprise. "I don't talk to ghosts before sending my men to their deaths."

How dare he! Isabella's eyes hardened. "*Our* men. Be careful where you tread." Besides, what were those prayers he recited? What was the trinity he traced by using his fingers to cross himself?

"Don't pull rank on me!" Jean-Michel rasped angrily, but carefully, keeping his voice low and disciplined. "Twenty years hunting these waters gives me rights… and privileges."

"Rights and privileges that I bestow at my pleasure!" she blurted, instantly regretting the outburst.

Isabella stood, tipping the chair backward as its legs scraped against the floor. She closed her eyes and inhaled deeply. How could she say that to him? The crew depended on him as much as her, especially now. She leaned over the desk, her palms bracing her. She looked into his eyes. His eyes were calm, even caring.

Isabella looked apologetically down toward the desk. She slammed a fist into the wood. What was she doing? They didn't have time for this! She needed to keep the crew focused. She knew Jean-Michel was loyal to her. Jacob never doubted Jean-Michel. They earned each other's loyalty in this spit of watery hell, fighting dozens of battles never recorded in books or histories. How could she doubt Jean-Michel now? She needed him now more than ever. Indeed, especially now that she knew—she suspected—the viceroy's plan. Why did these thoughts of betrayal consume her? Self-doubt? Guilt? Destiny? Damn Jacob for leaving her so soon!

Jean-Michel sat, his face reddening. "Don't forget my loyalties, *mon cher,* Jacob was like a brother to me, not a lover. My commitment to him goes far beyond his death, or you."

Isabella's face flushed. "Do not underestimate me!" She closed her eyes again to regain her composure.

She opened her eyes, redirecting them into his. Isabella relaxed her hand, opening her fist to let the palm brace her on the desk.

Jean-Michel's stare was disciplined and compassionate. "I don't. Not only that, I won't. You're little more than a child, but the fields hardened you more than any battle could ever pretend to… or the walls of San Cristobal's cousin, El Morro. I know."

Isabella paused. She took in a deep breath. Calm began to cloak her mood. "Jean-Michel, I need you. You know that, don't you?"

"We need each other," Jean-Michel insisted. "Jacob's death gave both of us opportunities. Your courage keeps them fighting."

"You keep this ship afloat."

"We need each other."

Isabella chuckled at the futility of their argument. She shook her head softly. "A child and an old man. What a pair we will make in the history of this God-forsaken blister on the world. One of these days the prison walls of El Morro will protect us from all of them!"

"Bold ambitions," Jean-Michel smiled. "Worthy of Henry Morgan, even, although I hate to credit an Englishman with anything so rich! Jacob left you a hearty, committed crew. It's up to you to lead them. So far, we are not scoring well on that account."

Isabella bristled at the thought the crew would abandon her. "A little gold will help." Why would they abandon her, anyway? Because she was a woman? Anne Bonny was a pirate at 16, as old as Isabella was when she met Jacob! She paused, opening her mouth as if to say something, but stopped. "I'm not the first woman to command a pirate ship."

"You are the first girl—not even twenty," Jean-Michel pointed out. "No woman older has lived long as a pirate. None by themselves."

"But I have you."

"Aye, but they follow your courage, not my command."

"Calico Jack provided men and a ship," Isabella said quickly. "Anne Bonny and Mary Read carried them to victory."

"Legend, not history."

Isabella suddenly felt vulnerable again. "I'm not alone," she said doubtfully, feeling her hope ebb with the cresting waves.

"No, you aren't." Jean-Michel was at least trying to reassure her, but the pit of her stomach knotted.

"But I'm not Anne Bonny either. I don't have a wealthy father to whisk me away if I lose. My gold can't buy a plantation... yet." Her shoulders straightened, as she seemed to gain resolve. "The plantations seasoned me well enough to take anything this life can throw at me."

"I'm betting on that. Jacob hoped for it."

"If anyone questions my skills," Isabella continued, renewed resolve thick in each word, "or my courage, let them challenge me. I'll put my command on the line." She grabbed the hilt of her sword still at her side. "A fight to the death."

"And if they take you up on the offer?"

"Set it up."

"Choice of weapons?"

"Saber, cutlass, foil, pistol—their choice," she said confidently.

"Daggers?"

"Yes," Isabella confirmed unflinchingly, "even daggers."

Jean-Michel nodded. "Jacob would be pleased. Your skills may finally match your courage."

Isabella let a sheepish smile break through. Would a duel be enough? Isabella sorted through papers on her desk while her mind raced. "It's a shame the Spanish captain had to die."

"No Dago is worth such thoughts," Jean-Michel said bitterly.

"Mick, respect the dead."

Jean-Michel tapped his fingers on his thigh. The dead officer. The unusual interest in the prisoner—her *boy*. These were unsettling. Isabella, like Jean-Michel, hated the Spanish more than any other race. The mere mention of King Charles or his lap dog Rodriquez in San Juan was enough to send her into a brood. Her hatred dogged the Spanish trading routes. Los conquistadores had a black, unfathomable place in her soul. Jean-Michel didn't fully understand it, but he respected it. Her hatred was so close to his own feelings, it seemed to bind them together. Why the interest in the boy?

"The captain was Spaniard filth," Jean-Michel spat.

"He fought well. It was his chosen life. Besides, aren't you French brethren now, allied with Charles III in aid to the Americans against the British?"

"He's still a Dago, in service to the Court. My values don't shift with politics... or Royalty."

"Most of us have Spanish blood," she reminded him.

"You are Creole. Your Spanish blood did not come by your will. Or your mother's."

"True. Nor does my British blood. Only Africa's blood is true."

"Jean-Michel, *mon ami,*" Isabella said abruptly, pushing the manifest aside, "bring the prisoner to my cabin."

"That's not a good idea, *mon cher,*" he said, invoking a fatherly sternness.

"Why Mick!" Isabella exclaimed, the flicker of a cagey smile evident once again. "I'm shocked. What are you thinking? That I would fall for a Dago royal? Don't worry. The overseer's whip is still fresh on my back." She looked at him again and rolled her eyes. "He's only a boy," she insisted, although she wasn't so sure herself.

Jean-Michel sighed. What could he do? He turned, ducked under the beams, and squeezed himself through the doorway. The door closed respectfully as he pulled it shut.

***

Isabella sat slumped in the rough wooden chair, legs sprawling under the desk, grateful to be alone. The sudden silence sent her head spinning. Even the steady creaking of the beams and hull didn't seem to soften the effect. The loss of the *Ana Maria* weighed heavily again, thickening her brain. What was so different about this ship? She struggled to understand the emptiness pitting her stomach. Was it the prisoner?

She sat, feeling isolated and distant. Jean-Michel even seemed like a stranger now. How could that be, after all they had been through? Did he think she was losing her grip? Was she losing her edge? She longed for someone to talk to. She needed to talk about the ship, Rodriguez, Jean-Michel, the prisoner—everything. She closed her eyes and rested her head on her forearms.

She smiled as she remembered Jacob, sitting in a rickety old chair in their room over Carl's pub in Charlotte Amalie. It was their safe haven. They could be together without worrying about soldiers or privateers. He would wrap his arms around her as they lay together in bed, letting the breeze cool them at night. If they were lucky, the moon would brighten the room just enough that they could make out every crease of their faces, every curl of their hair.

Carl complained because he could never rent their bed when they were in port. He wouldn't take their money, either! "Cursed pirate treasure," he would spit, although he never seemed to have trouble taking buccaneer gold at the bar.

The room was the first place they were alone after four weeks, running from Spanish pirate hunters off Hispaniola. He had taught her everything that mattered—how to use a sword, how to live as a freedman, how to command the respect of rogues and ruffians like the ones they seemed to fight in the streets of Charlotte Amalie. He was her world, her future, for two years. "Jacob," she whispered. "Why did you leave me so soon? We had so much to do, so far to go."

A tear grew and began a slow, searching journey down her face. For an instant, it tickled her cheek. Then, it dropped. She saw it fall—painfully, slowly—its smooth oval shape splattering onto the tabletop. The tear had fallen onto the Royal Seal. The letters began to dissolve.

Isabella blinked. She lifted her head swiftly and surely, eyes wide and determined.

"Enough" she insisted loudly, bringing the palm of her hand down on the desk with a crack. She straightened herself, forcing energy through her arms and hands. She picked up the letter that should have introduced Juan Carlos Lopez de Santa Ana to the colonial viceroy of the West Indies. What role did her prisoner play in this game? She folded the letter and put it back down on the desk.

She stretched her arms, shaking them out of a slumber. She was stiff. She walked awkwardly over to the washbasin. Isabella stared into the mirror, transfixed, as if captured by a ghost. Her hair was wild and matted. Soot from spent gunpowder and the smoldering deck fires stained her face with long, dark streaks, making her eyes seem like deeply recessed holes. The desperate swim from the *Ana Maria* had dissolved the edges, giving the lines a pattern resembling Carib Indian war paint. She unbuttoned her silk blouse, and let it silently slip from her shoulders. Years climbing rigging gave her arms a crisp definition. The sun had deeply tanned already dark skin. Her shoulders and breasts, protected from the weather, remained strikingly clean and smooth. The contrast was surreal.

She dipped her head over the basin and splashed warm water over her face and neck. She rubbed vigorously, buffing the streaks from her skin. She lifted her head, half-afraid, half hoping the person in the mirror had disappeared. She let the water bead comfortably on her skin. The tint of gunpowder was gone. Droplets cooled her as they dripped from her forehead, down her cheeks, off her chin, onto her breasts and stomach, and gently soaked into the waistline of her breeches. Destiny. How could she think she was destined for anything? She was a slave, freed by bizarre events beyond her control.

Isabella pulled her arms close to her chest, eyes closed, hands kneading her shoulders. Familiar warmth overcame her as she remembered her nights with Jacob in Charlotte Amalie. Her fingers worked rhythmically toward her shoulders. The tension in her muscles evaporated with each rolling fingertip. Is this what Jacob's embrace felt like? How could she have forgotten?

Isabella's fingers jerked her from the fantasy. The scars! Even the calluses earned daily on the *Marée Rouge* could not deaden her fingers to the legacy of the overseer's whip.

"Damn Spain!" she spat, violently shaking the last drops of water from her hair. "Damn their kings. Damn their God. I will not stop until they are purged from these seas and these islands."

Isabella looked into the mirror again. Her vulnerability was gone, replaced by buccaneer determination. She had a destiny. She was sure of it. She couldn't let anything—anyone—get in her way. She would soon deal with the dissention in the crew. Her prisoner would be the key.

She blotted away the last drops of water and pulled a clean shirt from a rack in the corner. The oversized sleeves billowed in the cross breeze, as she clasped the cuffs closed. The pleats would have framed a similar man's body perfectly. They conveniently hid Isabella's femininity. She smiled as she remembered the surprise in her prey's face—they always underestimate her. Twenty-two guns and a two-masted boat against a 32-gun frigate? They never counted on pirate bravado and 200 souls with nothing to lose! She tied a scarlet sash securely around her waist.

Isabella reached into the breast pocket of her overcoat and pulled out two brass buttons. Any human signs of the Spanish captain and his lieutenant had been buffed cleanly away in the pocket. More casualties of her destiny. How long would their faces haunt her? One night? One week? One month? At least the boatswain played the game smart. Allowed to live, he led the remaining tars to safety, and will serve the Empire on another day.

Isabella opened a small drawer underneath the washbasin. She let the buttons fall haphazardly into the drawer. Jiggling brass filled the room as the newest markers joined more than a dozen others. Isabella locked the drawer, and walked over to her chair. She was ready.

3

Three crisp, hard knocks announced the *boy's* arrival. Isabella's heart quickened. She forced steady, normal breaths. How could she let anyone, let alone a Spaniard, seize her so powerfully? She lifted her right hand inside her shirt tenderly to feel the scarred skin covering her shoulder. She relaxed. Her resolve stiffened. Nothing could forgive King Charles, or his underlings.

"Entrez."

Jean-Michel pushed the prisoner violently through the door. He ducked but cracked his head against the bulkhead anyway. Jean-Michel smiled. Isabella calmly watched the prisoner adjust to the cabin light from her throne.

"He didn't make it easy," Jean-Michel said as he muscled his way in next to the young man. Isabella glanced at the ropes binding the prisoner's hands and nodded. Jean-Michel looked at her disapprovingly but untied them.

She was startled by how handsome he was. His Latin features were almost elegant. On the deck of the *Ana Maria*, they seemed hard and cold. He had bent his head to avoid the beams in the cabin, so he must be about five feet, ten inches, perhaps an inch taller. His black hair was long, with a natural wave, uncharacteristic of officers in the Royal Army or Navy. It gave him a flamboyant air, even playful. His trim physique was unmistakable, even in the relatively dim cabin light. Isabella was intrigued, despite her best efforts—again.

"Buenas tardes, Señor Santa Ana," Isabella said politely. The prisoner ignored her. Isabella gestured to one of the small chairs. *"Sientese, por favor."*

She rose from her desk and stared directly into his eyes. "I assure you, your neck and back will praise you for accepting my offer."

Santa Ana looked at her, paused deliberately, and relented. Isabella fumed—how could she let him take the advantage like that? He needed to come to her.

She looked at him carefully, taking stock of his clothes, face, and hands. His clothes were decidedly civilian—European. He was young, perhaps as young as she was, but less grizzled by battle. He carried the marks of the duel with the *Ana Maria*. His eyes betrayed character unlike anything she had seen on the merchant ships plying the West Indies. His well-tailored coat had torn, shredded really. A slice across his soiled white shirt revealed a cut very similar to the deadly one she had administered to the young Spanish lieutenant in the heat of the battle. His boots were fine leather, probably Italian. Only the Court would bestow authority on someone so young she thought. Isabella felt her enthusiasm wane at the thought that this man could be from the Court of Charles III. How could she let him overwhelm her like this? He is the enemy.

Isabella sat down again, perplexed. She leaned back, folding her arms across her chest. They looked intently at each other for several minutes. Not many men, she mused, would put up such resistance in the hands of a pirate. "Do you know where you are?"

"*Si,*" Santa Ana said tartly.

"I don't think so."

"What makes you so sure?"

"Well," Isabella said, clasping her hands behind her head, "it could be you're just stupid." Santa Ana's body hardened at the slight. Isabella relaxed, pleased. She was in control again.

"I assure you," Santa Ana said in a measured response, "I am not stupid."

Isabella lifted a letter from her desk and unfolded it. "Juan Carlos Lopez de Santa Ana," she read. "Dispatched by His Most Catholic Majesty Charles III to Roberto Maria Rodriguez, Viceroy of the West Indies." Santa Ana's right eyebrow ticked up as she read the words. Isabella shifted her eyes to another stack of letters. "Your papers are dated May 5, 1780," she continued. "You embarked from Puerto Cadiz on June 1, 1780." She looked at him. Aside from the eyebrow, Santa Ana's face showed no emotion. The eyebrow was enough.

"Senor Santa Ana, the information is here," she said, pounding the papers with her index finger.

"You know I set sail from Cadiz. You know I am loyal to my King."

"You're not just a civilian," Isabella retorted. "Your background is military. Your commission is not from the navy. You are, or were, army, and your civilian rank is senior despite your youth."

"We both rank beyond our birth."

"Aye," Isabella acknowledged, allowing herself a tempered smile. How did someone so young become a senior advisor to the viceroy? Surely, the King could not trust the security of an economic empire to someone so inexperienced about the New World.

She stood, letting the chair scrape against the wood floor. She paced toward the washbasin, and caught her image briefly in the mirror. Her waves were tame, and her face clean of the marks of battle. She looked like she was fifteen again, even though she carried herself with the seriousness of someone much, much older.

She turned to face Santa Ana squarely. "My rank is earned. It's not the bounty of privilege."

The prisoner bristled.

She moved to the edge of the desk. She sat upright, one leg hanging comfortably over the corner, shoulders hunched toward him. In a low, provocative voice, she said, "We both know who the vanquished is on this ship." Santa Ana shifted his weight angrily, clenching his fists. Jean-Michel stepped forward.

"I earned my rank! I have been tested!"

"You seem to have fallen short at sea," taunted Isabella.

"Underestimating me or my King is neither virtuous nor wise."

Rage rippled through Isabella. How dare this man—this boy—a prisoner on her ship, say such a thing.

Isabella pulled her head back and raised her eyebrows half-heartedly. "I'm afraid you are the one who underestimates the power of his opponent."

"I've seen your crew," scoffed Santa Ana, his shoulders falling as he seemed to relax, "and their captain. A crew of coal can't withstand the gold of the Spanish Navy."

Isabella turned sharply. "My crew is African gold. I know their loyalties. My treasure sowed the fields of your plantations. These men are spurred by the bitter taste of coffee and sugar harvested from their backs. Their bodies were enslaved to you, not their spirits. They didn't sip the fruits of their labor during an afternoon *siesta*."

"Pirate crews do not last more than a few years," Santa Ana said, a calculated revelation that piqued Isabella's interest.

"Half my crew has sailed with me for two years or more. None were driven to this ship by a whip or club. They fight for no one but themselves. They fight for the most precious thing they know: freedom."

"Only one pirate captain in the West Indies has commanded such loyalty," Santa Ana said.

Isabella felt her resolve weaken. Did he know about Jacob? Jean-Michel watched her intently. "Your information is not what you think," she said, not believing her own words.

Santa Ana detected her weakness.

"A girl captain?" he smirked. "The only criminal of the high seas that has commanded the loyalty of pirates was Jacob the Red." Isabella froze, grasping at any way to check her emotions. She couldn't break. Not now.

"Jacob the Red?" she said with a false calmness.

"Jacob the Red," Santa Ana confirmed. "But, he's dead." Santa Ana studied her. He had hit on something important. "Privateers ambushed him last winter," Santa Ana continued, as if circling his prey, waiting for the right moment to attack. "The Spanish Crown has reasserted its authority in the West Indies. Whatever pirates remain in these waters sail on borrowed time."

Jean-Michel looked at Isabella. He too, sensed her struggle, but couldn't decide what to do. They should have let this one go.

Curiosity suddenly calmed Isabella. How did Santa Ana know so much about Jacob? Did he know about her? About Jean-Michel? "You don't know as much as you pretend," she said quietly, looking away from him. Her tone hardened. She turned to look directly at him. "Pirates care about results, not proclamations."

She spoke with such decisiveness Santa Ana hesitated. He shifted his weight again, as if suddenly feeling the closeness of the cabin air for the first time. The tiny room weighed on him. He suddenly longed for the chains in the powder room.

Santa Ana's eyes shifted to the oak tabletop; he spotted the *Ana Maria*'s manifest. His eyes darted to the charts propped up against the wall. They were labeled and marked in English, French, Spanish, even Portuguese—the languages of the Old World. "Perhaps I misjudge," he said, shaken by the revelation. "Few rogues and wenches read their native tongue, let alone the languages of their prey."

Jean-Michel shifted his weight angrily, like a boy ready to join a schoolyard brawl, and upset it had started without him. He started toward Santa Ana. He opened his mouth to upbraid him, his fist rising to his shoulder, but a twitch from Isabella's hand stopped him.

Isabella's eyes drifted to the charts. "It's a necessity," she pointed out. "Charts are more than a compass."

"Of course," Santa Ana nodded respectfully, "the notes."

Santa Ana's quickness surprised her. "A captain or quartermaster's quill is far more valuable than the ink on a map." Despite every ounce of resistance she could muster, her respect for him was growing. She had no way of knowing that Jean-Michel saw the same thoughts in her eyes, and that worried him more than anything else she had done since Jacob's death.

Isabella turned to walk around the desk. "What was your destination?"

"You have the manifest," Juan Carlos said stiffly.

"San Juan is an important port."

"That is what I've been told."

"Surely you're going to do more than warm the overstuffed chair of a governor's assistant."

"I've been dispatched by my King at the request of His Excellency, Viceroy Roberto Maria Rodriguez. I will get my orders when I arrive in San Juan."

Isabella laughed. "When do you think you will get to San Juan?"

Santa Ana's face went flush. He hadn't considered that possibility! What confidence. What arrogance! "I'm a man of my word," Santa Ana said unconvincingly. "I serve my King, my Country, and my God."

Isabella's joy was obvious. She looked expectantly at Jean-Michel. He was looking cautiously, almost fearfully, at Santa Ana. Isabella dismissed his look. Santa Ana was key to the Spanish plan, dispatched at the request of the viceroy. What was the plan? Perhaps the connection was to the trade routes and the American revolt against the British.

"Senor Santa Ana," Isabella prodded. "Why did the *Ana Maria* engage me? It was foolish."

Santa Ana's face dissolved. "Hindsight doesn't do justice to the decision at the time of battle."

Isabella seized her opportunity: "It was careless. The captain was experienced. He wouldn't risk his ship with those odds. Where was he stationed before?"

Jean-Michel sensed his opportunity. "Of course, Dago seamanship and resolve doesn't count for much in these parts."

Santa Ana's jaw grew rigid. "The captain was assigned to the coast of Spain," he snapped. "Perhaps the Mediterranean."

How could Santa Ana, an officer in the Royal Army and Emissary of the Royal Court, spend four weeks with a sea captain and know so little? His papers and diplomatic rank confirmed he knew far more than he would admit. She looked at him again. His features were calm. His eyes were deep, distant. He blinked incessantly. He was hiding something.

"The captain had not sailed in the West Indies before?" Isabella asked again, knowing Santa Ana would lie.

"No," Santa Ana said, diverting his eyes to the tabletop.

Jean-Michel cast a skeptical glance toward Isabella. Experienced officers and tars on any man-of-war—especially Spanish seaman—knew the West Indies and South America as well as anywhere along the coasts of Europe.

"And your role on the ship?" Isabella continued.

"You have everything you need in the papers," Santa Ana said, anger rising in his voice. "I serve my King, my Country, and my God."

"Your God!" Isabella blurted. She stood abruptly, letting the folder clap loudly onto the table. A sleepless night with pirate rations should soften him.

Isabella walked around the table, signaling Jean-Michel to take Santa Ana away. Santa Ana lifted himself from his chair. A puff of air gently passed through the cabin windows, causing Isabella to pause. She looked up and was transfixed for the instant their eyes met. There was something soft behind the determined military face. Calm suddenly sapped the frustrated energy from her legs. She closed her eyes, hoping, praying, they hadn't already revealed too much. She pulled back, letting the table support her as she leaned against it. Could he know how she felt? She opened her eyes an instant longer than a blink as Jean-Michel shoved Santa Ana out the cabin door.

4

Isabella's head was spinning. How could she be attracted to this boy? Santa Ana symbolized everything she fought against—slavery, privilege, plantations. What was she going to do? He was a prisoner, but she didn't have a prison. She let her head sink into her hands. Were the gallows her only choice?

Jean-Michel looked at her across the desk, hands grasping the back of one of the small chairs. "Well?" he said finally.

"Well, what?"

"What were you thinking?"

Isabella looked up at him, eyebrows furrowed. "What do you mean?"

"What do you think?" he said, leveling his voice. "*Señor* Santa Ana!"

"I was interrogating him."

"You were toying with him."

"I got what I needed." Jean-Michel looked at her suspiciously. His beard sparkled in the heat.

A slight breeze puffed through the windows again, but seemed to stop grudgingly at the front of the desk. She sighed, disappointed it wouldn't sweep the cabin.

"Then tell me. What did you find out?" Jean-Michel sat down in the chair, crossed his legs, and waited for her answer. "Nothing from what I saw."

"It was obvious," Isabella said, her defensiveness betrayed only by lifting her head defiantly to meet his eyes.

"Don't toy with me," Jean-Michel interrupted. *"Ne fait pas les jeux."*

She looked at him again, quickly realizing his seriousness. "Jean-Michel," she said in a light girlish tone, "I'm not toying with you."

She looked into his eyes. They carried an unusual hardness. She sighed; he needed to know everything. Perhaps she could wait until she questioned Santa Ana again.

"You knew he was on the *Ana Maria*," he said accusingly.

"What? Of course not!"

"I don't believe you."

"How could I have known? I don't have spies in the viceroy's office."

"You knew what the *Ana Maria* carried." Jean-Michel didn't hold back the hurt created by the secret. "How did you know? Why didn't you discuss it with me?"

Beads of sweat formed on her forehead. She couldn't afford to keep Jean-Michel in the dark any longer. Where was that breeze?

"It was a mistake," she confessed. "I should have trusted you. I'm sorry."

Jean-Michel let his eyes fall to the desk, casually looking over the letters and envelopes still stacked in front of Isabella.

"I'm disappointed," Jean-Michel admitted. "Remember our last night with Jacob?"

Isabella opened her mouth, but couldn't speak.

"He thought you could do great things."

Isabella turned toward the windows, struggling to hold back tears. Jacob believed the prophecy. He believed in her. Did Jean-Michel believe in her that much? Could anyone?

"What would Jacob think?" Jean-Michel continued.

How cruel! How could Jean-Michel use Jacob's memory like this? She clenched her fists, grinding her teeth. *No,* she ordered herself. *Don't let him manipulate you this way. Your destiny is yours, not his.*

"Charlotte Amalie," she said without looking at him.

"Carl?" Jean-Michel asked, his suspicions deepening. "When did you talk to Carl?"

"You know we see him every time we make port."

Jean-Michel looked at her even more suspiciously.

"Carl suspected Rodriguez requested reinforcements from the King," Isabella continued in a calm and deliberate tone. "They've lost a lot of cargo since the first of the year. Rodriquez is concerned about his status with the King. Carl has a *friend* who reported more activity in San Juan harbor—sloops mostly, lightly armed, for quick raids.

However, more may be coming; heavily armed brigs or even a frigate, like the *Ana Maria*. I heard they may even send a ship-of-the-line."

Jean-Michel stared at her. "Why didn't you tell me?"

"I needed to confirm it. It was just rumor."

"Isabella!" Jean-Michel barked. "Am I worth nothing? Jacob would have asked for my advice. Twenty years! Fifteen on a ship-of-the-line— those years count for something."

She looked at him, her eyes softened by shame. "They do! Mick, it was a judgment call. It was wrong. It won't happen again."

"It better not," he warned. "There are 200 men on this ship who won't stand for it."

He paused, and then looked at her. His eyes twinkled. "You can't afford it. You don't have that much gold!"

Isabella laughed grateful he wasn't abandoning her. "If only they knew where it was!"

He smiled at her, satisfied, for the moment. They both relaxed.

"How does the Dago boy fit into the plan?" Jean-Michel asked, getting back to business.

"I don't know." Isabella tapped the letter with the royal seal on her desk, the carefully scripted words blurred by her tears. "His papers are a simple letter of introduction."

"Maybe he's on vacation."

Isabella chuckled. Juan Carlos Lopez de Santa Ana lounging on the beaches of Puerto Rico? "He's too serious—a man of action. Didn't you see him on the *Ana Maria*? He had purpose. Disciplined purpose."

"A man with a destiny," Jean-Michel pointed out. "But, if he doesn't have papers...."

"My experience counts for something, too," Isabella said proudly. "The fact the letter says so little, says a lot. Rodriguez already knows Santa Ana's mission. How else would Santa Ana know about Jacob's death?"

Jean-Michel nodded. "What does that mean for us?"

Isabella's eyebrows furrowed. "I'm not sure." She began a slow, thoughtful pace in front of the windows.

Jean-Michel lifted his hands, as if begging for an explanation. *"Je ne comprends pas."*

"I reckon the Spaniards have lost more than a dozen merchant ships full of gold, sugar, cloth, spices, and cotton in just the past three months," she recounted. "The ports are overflowing with seized goods. I saw some of it in Charlotte Amalie. Carl said much more was in Kingston."

She paused, as if expecting Jean-Michel to acknowledge some divine revelation. "Rodriguez probably figured we disbanded when Jacob was killed. That would normally be expected from pirates. He probably increased the number of ships and trade thinking they would be safe. After all, Jacob died off Saint Thomas six months ago. But, he didn't expect something... someone...."

"Yellow Jacket!" Jean-Michel exclaimed in sudden recognition.

"Exactly," Isabella turned back to face him. "They figured with Jacob out of the way, they could clean up the trade routes quickly. All they needed were a few more ships—fast gunboats—to finish us off. Yellow Jacket raised the stakes, taking advantage of Jacob's death, too."

"Yellow Jacket would make mincemeat out of any Spanish frigate within range of his twenty-four pound cannon," Jean-Michel sneered. "He don't take prisoners."

"All the more reason for them to go after him now, before he masters the West Indies. The British already control Jamaica. Rodriguez has ships patrolling Tobago, Trinidad, Dominica, and the other southern islands."

"But," Jean-Michel reminded her, "they can't find Yellow Jacket, let alone beat him."

"Not with sloops," Isabella agreed. "But, how many *Ana Marias* could do the job?"

Jean-Michel's eyes opened with understanding. "Do you think Yellow Jacket's figured this out?"

"I don't know. He's not acting like it. I heard he threw a party after Jacob was killed."

"Not willingly," Jean-Michel said skeptically. "I'm not sure working a yardarm for Yellow Jacket is any better than scrubbing the sandstone of a Spanish prison."

"Aye," Isabella said. "But, he makes promises."

"Promises that he keeps?"

Isabella's glanced over to him. "Our crew will get their reward."

"We hope," Jean-Michel said. He paused. "If Yellow Jacket is trying to build a fleet, we better stand guard. Especially now."

"Aye. We'll have enough trouble keeping the crew together without his empty promises."

"If I didn't know better, I would have thought the *Ana Maria*'s sinking was his doing," Jean-Michel concluded. "I can't think of a more difficult alliance—Rodriguez and Yellow Jacket?" Jean-Michel shook his head. "What about Santa Ana?"

"You saw him on the deck of the *Ana Maria*," Isabella said. "His actions speak for themselves." He and Yellow Jacket can't be allies. He had discipline and loyalty—two things Yellow Jacket used but did not respect.

Jean-Michel looked at her nervously. "What are you going to do with Santa Ana?"

Isabella shook her head, slumping down into her chair and turning toward the windows again. The sun was fading. The sky was overwhelmed with red, yellow, and orange layers. Wisps of ragged, blue-gray streaks stretched across the horizon. Its beauty was calming. "I don't know," she admitted. An unwelcome emptiness overcame her. She could use another breeze. She admired Juan Carlos Lopez de Santa Ana—his determination, skill, intelligence. Jacob excelled in those traits, too. She fell in love with those parts of Jacob as well as the spark in his eyes and his overwhelming sense of purpose. He was here to accomplish bold things, he would tell her. He didn't know what they were, but he was a good pirate, and plundering Spanish merchantmen had a naturalness he couldn't resist. His commitment to his destiny kept her by his side for almost two years. Two years, until....

"Isabella!" Jean-Michel said, almost yelling.

"What?" she sputtered.

"What is it? The Dago has done something to you." He looked at her earnestly. "You've taken an unhealthy interest in him."

"Jean-Michel! I haven't... I won't! I have no interest in keeping him around. But, we can learn from him."

Jean-Michel looked at her doubtfully, agitation sweeping over his face. "Then, we can send him to the gallows, or into the sea," she said authoritatively.

Jean-Michel walked over to the washbasin. "I don't understand it," he finally admitted, looking into the cloudy water. "Your courage on the *Ana Maria* was wondrous. The men were inspired. I was inspired. I can't remember taking a ship so quickly. I thought we had finally defeated Jacob's ghost."

"Maybe we did," Isabella said without thinking. Her heart seemed to stop when she heard the words. What was she saying? Did she believe it?

"If it weren't for Santa Ana," Jean-Michel said, looking at her in the mirror, "it would have been almost bloodless. We would have had a prize; a trophy for Panther Bay. A second ship."

Isabella looked out the windows. The sun—her sunset—was almost gone. She wished it would stay longer, remain just like now, lighting up the sea. Just a few hours longer. For the first time since she had met Jacob, the darkness unnerved her. Was it the crew? Jean-Michel? Jacob's memory seemed misty since her talk with Santa Ana. The ship and its crew felt strangely distant. Why did she feel this way? She pulled her arms close, hoping her own embrace would comfort her. Such a silly reaction, she scolded herself, trying to push away any thought that her shivers might be a clue to the prophecy.

Jean-Michel turned toward Isabella. "I knew bringing him on board was a mistake."

"You're overreacting," Isabella said dismissively. Was he? She couldn't be sure, at least not in her heart. Something about Santa Ana was different. She was afraid. He seemed to be pushing Jacob's memory further and further away. Like her sunset. Another shiver shimmied up Isabella's spine.

Jean-Michel walked over to Isabella and put his hand gently on her shoulder. He seemed to sense a deep unease. His breath felt comforting on her neck. She let her cheek rest on the back of his hand. She was tired. He moved closer, putting his hands around her waist, holding her. She relaxed, comforted by the warmth of his body.

A swift row of powerful knocks thumped at the door, pushing Jean-Michel and Isabella apart.

"Come in," Isabella said embarrassed. Jean-Michel quickly retreated to the front of the room. Their eyes met briefly. "We'll take this up later," he promised. Before she could respond, the door swung open. Stiles stepped crisply into the room.

"Your report, Mr. Stiles," Jean-Michel said gruffly, still looking at Isabella.

"Twenty-six men out of action, unless someone else ends up missing," Stiles reported, looking at a scrap of paper in his hand. "Eight killed in action; eighteen wounded; five laid up bad enough they won't make it to Saint John. Clean dressings will keep the others alive."

"And the Spaniards?" Isabella asked.

"Ten joined us. Forty-seven cast their lots with long-boats when the *Ana Maria* sank." He looked accusingly at Isabella. "The boatswain was the highest ranking officer."

"Your assessment?" Jean-Michel ordered.

"Six are solid, eager enough to join. The other four? I'd send 'm off as soon as we make port."

"Bon," Jean-Michel said. "I want their names and birth place as soon as you can."

"And the *Marée Rouge*?" Isabella asked eagerly.

"She's tight," Stiles reported more happily. "The boatswain reports no serious damage. But, we weren't able to unload enough powder and shot to restock what we spent during the battle."

"That's unfortunate," Isabella said, thinking uncharacteristically aloud. "Our dry goods and rations are enough, but not as plentiful as I would like. Three months at sea and the salt pork and lemons are holding up. We'll have to set sail again—soon. We need something to trade in Charlotte Amalie. Thank you Mr. Stiles. Give the crew an extra ration for a good day's work. They'll get more from the stores when we make Panther Bay. That's all."

Stiles saluted, turned, and left the room, leaving Jean-Michel alone with Isabella once again. He stepped toward her.

"No," she said, raising her hand. He stopped, as if blocked by an invisible wall. *"Merci, mon ami,"* she said, smiling. Isabella looked at him, lifting her palm softly to his cheek. She needed to think alone. *"Je vient de penser. Seulement."*

Jean-Michel looked at her and understood. He nodded and pulled the door shut as he left the room.

Isabella walked over to her cot, and stretched herself over the worn mattress. Soon, the only things left were the dark gray shadows of the desk and the glitter of the stars against a darkening sky. She listened to the sea's spray, and let go.

5

Isabella was confused. No. Torn. How could this Spaniard draw her in like this? She knew it was wrong. She had to get him out of her head. If she didn't, her days as a pirate captain would surely be over.

She couldn't beat down the presence she felt in her chest every time he was in the room. Her heart wouldn't let him go. His very existence seemed to suck her closer, in some vague new direction, toward a place bigger and more embracing than her life now. The embrace seemed dark and overwhelming, like El Morro. Would this Spaniard break her, like El Morro had broken so many of Spain's enemies? Like it almost broke Jacob and Jean-Michel?

Isabella opened her eyes. She usually cherished sunrises from her perch, sitting one hundred feet atop the aft mast of the *Marée Rouge*. Now, she cursed it.

Isabella lifted her head from her knees and thumped it against the wooden mast. She closed her eyes again, hoping to extinguish Juan Carlos...Santa Ana...from her thoughts. If she could just blot out the rest of the world, she could think clearly. Couldn't she just think of El Morro instead? After all, Santa Ana and El Morro were the same. Weren't they? Isabella just wanted to go back in time. Forty-eight hours. That's all she needed to set the right course.

At least she was alone. The lookouts had learned long ago that the crow's nest was her space when dawn approached. She listened for the familiar, soothing sounds of creaking timber and the gentle flap of the sails in the night breeze. High above the deck, sitting on the ragged platform, she could usually relax. Not today.

Isabella lodged her foot between a rope and the oak planks to secure herself. She pulled her knees to her chest and rested her chin, deep in thought. She took another deep breath to try to relax. She felt so young and inexperienced. Her emotions seemed to ride with the swells. Why did Jean-Michel put up with her? Especially after she snapped at him so viciously. He was a saint. Maybe there was something to that religion of his.

She needed to think. The crew was restless. Jean-Michel didn't trust her. Moreover, she was drawn, for some bizarre reason, to a Spanish prisoner, an officer of the Royal Court! Jacob must be turning in his grave. Isabella let out a low moan.

Another day and a half of sailing and they would be in Panther Bay. Isabella would have to decide soon. Santa Ana was a mistake, she tried to convince herself, but she couldn't fix it. A few hours of sleep weren't enough to clear her **head.** The sun peeked over the horizon as the *Marée Rouge* pushed toward Saint John. That didn't help either. The darkness seemed like a friend now. The sun vanquished the darkness, even with her eyes closed tight. Isabella began to fidget, drumming her fingers on her knees.

Finally, she gave up and opened her eyes. A sailor stood on the forward crow's nest. He dutifully watched the horizon, telescope sweeping the surface. Thoughts seemed to dart through her head randomly. She almost hoped the watchman would find something, anything that might give her an opportunity to correct yesterday's mistakes. Jean-Michel and the crew would expect a decision by the end of the day; she couldn't avoid it. She would have to interview Santa Ana again.

She looked down to the deck. A few pirates milled about in the bow. Some of the more energetic had slung their hammocks above the gun deck, letting the roll of the ship and the salt air lull them to sleep. Even the occasional spray was a welcome reprieve from the stifling heat below deck.

The forecastle hatch swung open and the distinctive shape of Stiles appeared. Another figure emerged awkwardly. His outline was ragged and hunched as a third swarthy man pushed him forward. The crisp, erect shadow of the third man hovered close, a firm grip on the second man's arm. Isabella heard the soft clink of shackles. Santa Ana was on deck. Isabella felt her heart pound as she watched Stiles and the guard take Santa Ana to the rail.

Santa Ana's head and shoulders bowed over the railing. The third man slapped the back of his head. Isabella instinctively clenched her fist. She breathed deeply to control herself. Stiles was probably justified. Santa Ana was a prisoner—a slap on the head was hardly out of line. Who knows what vile thing he had said? He probably deserved a harder hit.

She sighed, leaned back against the mast, and let her hand rest on her forehead. She couldn't go on like this. She couldn't let him grip her this way. He was a Dago, loyal to Charles and Rodriguez—King, God, and Country. He didn't deserve her compassion. He couldn't get in the way of her mission, her destiny.

"Sail!"

The warning boomed across the deck. Isabella scrambled to her feet, grabbing the ropes. She leaned toward the warning.

"Sail! Off the port bow!" The watchman pointed leftward in the direction of his telescope. The sun crested the horizon, rays giving the mysterious topsails a bold, unmistakable glow. The hull was still well below the horizon, but she was moving quickly. Close hauled, she was taking full advantage of the revived wind. The darkness had covered her approach. Surely, the ship had spotted them; the *Marée Rouge*'s masts at full sail would have been visible in the pre-dawn light. Another half hour and they would be within cannon shot and sniper range. An hour and a half would find them engaged in a full fight. Isabella's mind raced.

"Colors?" she yelled to the watchman.

"None yet," he called back, his eyes intent through a telescope.

"Mr. Stiles," she called down to the deck. "Clear the decks! Beat to quarters!"

A ship's bell clanged loudly as the men, already awake, scurried to their stations. Others tumbled on deck from below, preparing cannon, readying shot, and checking the powder tins. A group of sailors began assembling muskets and sabers in the bow and stern of the ship. Isabella marveled at the order and deliberateness of their work. This was a good crew, well drilled, and focused. Not many pirate captains could count on this kind of discipline. She was fortunate. Jacob was an excellent captain—and teacher when he wanted to be.

"Captain!" the watchman yelled. "She's still not running her colors, but she ain't run her guns out."

Isabella looked toward the sails again. The ship was moving toward them at full sail, enslaving every possible puff of wind. She acted as if the *Marée Rouge* was her target. Only one person could be so bold; only one person knew these seas well enough to hunt at night.

Isabella hopped onto the rope ladder leading to the main deck. She lowered herself quickly, letting the ropes slide smoothly through the nook of her knee. Her hands checked her speed expertly at each rung. Within seconds, she was on the main deck, firmly planted next to the helmsman. Sand, spread across the deck to dampen fires and soak up blood, forced deliberate steps.

"Nothing like a dawn surprise to keep you on your toes," Jean-Michel said energetically, handing Isabella her saber and pistol. She strapped the blade to her sash and looked at Jean-Michel anxiously. "Relax," he reassured her. "He won't try anything foolish."

"Only Jacob kept him in line," Isabella muttered, checking her pistol, and lodging it uncomfortably in her breeches.

"Now, he has to worry about us," Jean-Michel said, a hint of anger in his tone.

They moved to the portside railing and surveyed the approaching ship. "Her gun ports are still closed," he noted.

"I don't trust him," Isabella said.

"Neither do I," Jean-Michel admitted. "We've primed the guns."

The ship had closed within sniper range. A well-rifled cannon could easily pick at the *Marée Rouge*'s rigging. Isabella's left hand tapped the railing rhythmically, her right hand resting on the heel of the saber. She looked nervously at the crew. The men were huddled below the gunwales, careful to keep out of sight. They could run the cannon out at an instant's notice, if needed.

Santa Ana was on deck too, just a few feet away from her with his guard at his side. He watched the approaching ship intently. She studied him. Did he still hope for a rescue? He was calculating. She could tell. Occasionally, Santa Ana would glance around at the *Marée Rouge*'s crew and deck. Content, he would turn back to the approaching ship. In another place, on another ship, he could be its captain. However, this was not his ship; he was her prisoner. Isabella smiled at the thought; Santa Ana might have thought the approaching ship was a Spanish brigantine or frigate. She would have liked to see his dismay and disappointment when he realized he was now in an even thicker den of West Indian pirates. What was he thinking? Was he plotting? She found herself wanting to know everything about his thoughts; indeed, everything about him.

Jean-Michel leaned over the rail, letting his forearms prop him up as he sized up the approaching ship and its rigging. Its lines and armaments were all too familiar now, and he knew that meant trouble. He nudged Isabella, pointing to the distinctive yellow stripe running along the outer gunwales. A single line of squared black gun ports gave it a checkered motif, easily identifying an array of cannon that could levy a crippling broadside. The line, however, cleverly obscured another set of smaller cannon and swivel guns that added up to more than thirty in all. Combined with the hull's dark brown primer, the ship looked almost festive with its satin-like white sails.

"Only one captain dandies his ship up like a carnival," Jean-Michel said.

"A carnival of blood," Isabella said.

"Aye," Jean-Michel said. "But you can't argue with results."

Isabella looked at Jean-Michel, but he pointed back to the approaching ship. It continued to close on the *Marée Rouge* but was now tracking an almost parallel course after heaving to. The captain had brought her across the wind—a good sign, they hoped. Seamen scaled its masts and began trimming sails.

At the stern, on the quarterdeck, a figure stood resolutely near the helm. His tri-corner hat capped unkempt black hair and a full beard and mustache. A bright yellow overcoat, tails dipping to his knees, gave him a deceptively clown-like appearance—an obvious target in battle, although both Isabella and Jean-Michel knew well enough his catlike qualities. This captain had more than nine lives. Black breeches billowed from the cuffs of jet-black deck boots. He seemed arrogantly calm and unconcerned as the two ships drifted within one hundred yards of each other. The letters W.A.S.P. were now clearly visible near the bow. Isabella shuddered—to think she could have been attracted to him! That was before Jacob, before she knew what he was capable of doing.

"What does he want?" she wondered out loud.

"We'll know soon enough," Jean-Michel answered, turning to the helmsman. "Stand down!" he called to the gunners. "Boatswain! Trim the sails and heave to. Looks like we're going to have company."

The two ships slowed to almost a dead stop. The topsails remained unfurled, catching the breeze to steady their course with a slight headway to keep the ships from drifting too close to each other. Isabella thought they were close enough anyway; she thought she could smell its crew and captain.

"Ahoy, *Marée Rouge*!" yelled the man under the tri-corner hat.

"Ahoy," Jean-Michel called back, through cupped hands. "It's a beautiful day for cruising the West Indies."

"Aye!" the man replied. "Do ya have time for a cup of tea?"

Isabella rolled her eyes. "Can't he leave us alone?"

"It's against his nature," Jean-Michel quipped, "but, we can't risk turning him down." Jean-Michel looked toward the main deck. "Mr. Stiles, ready the deck for visitors. It looks like we're not in for a fight today." At least not the kind Jean-Michel thought.

***

The entire day seemed to pass before the deep-hulled long boat rowed up alongside the *Marée Rouge*. A half dozen men scaled a rope ladder slung over the gunwales down to the water. The captain's boots soon swung over the railing, thumping to the deck with both feet and the full weight of his body and clothes. Heaving over the railing, the yellow long coat and tails billowed around him. His quartermaster followed close behind. Isabella couldn't help but be drawn to the snakeskin whip hanging from the quartermaster's yellow sash—Yellow Jacket's "trademark"—as he dropped to the deck. She tapped the handle of her saber.

"I finally get to meet the now great Pirate of Panther Bay," the captain said as Isabella and Jean-Michel approached. His hat remained lodged on his head.

"No different than before," Jean-Michel said, unable to contain his annoyance. "Just now she's got a command." Isabella shot a scolding look toward Jean-Michel.

"Good day, Captain Smith," Isabella said far more politely than she intended. Why couldn't she muster a grittier tone, for Jean-Michel's sake if no one else? "Or, should I address you as Captain Yellow Jacket?"

"Such courtesy," Smith said, nudging his hat respectfully. "The pleasure is all mine."

Smith turned to face the crew. "Looks like they weathered the battle well enough." He scanned the railings and decks. "Ship's held up well, too."

"What do you mean?" Isabella asked, feigning ignorance.

"Oh, please. I know everything." Smith looked at Isabella with a catty look that reminded her of his deviousness. "You should know that better than anyone, my dear Isabella." Isabella mustered all her strength to keep her eyes trained on Smith and not to look toward Jean-Michel.

Smith looked over to Santa Ana. He was still standing at the railing, next to his sentry, watching the verbal sparring. "Who, or what, do we have here?"

"If you know everything," Isabella chided, "you don't need an answer."

"Aye," Smith acknowledged. "I don't."

Jean-Michel looked at Smith. "Did they survive?"

"Survive? Who pray tell?" Smith raised his hands in mock surprise. He glanced greedily over to Santa Ana.

Jean-Michel's eyes narrowed. "You know who I mean. You're nothing more than a blood-sucking eel. You don't care where your next meal comes from, or even if you need it."

"My, my," Smith clucked. He walked up to within inches of Jean-Michel. He looked squarely into his eyes, hands resting on the blunt handle of his saber. Isabella looked for a pistol, but didn't see one in his sash or boots. She instinctively inventoried the weapons of his quartermaster and the other four hands. Surely, Smith wouldn't try something here, on the deck of the *Marée Rouge*. That would be suicidal.

"Aren't we a bit uppity for a frog," Smith grumbled, all signs of playfulness or humor gone. Jean-Michel's muscles tensed. He dropped his hand to a cutlass, fastened snugly to his hip belt. Smith's fingers danced on his saber's handles. Isabella walked up to Jean-Michel and touched his elbow. He instantly relaxed.

Smith's eyes twinkled. "Not in command yet, eh Jean-Michel?" he taunted, loud enough for the *Marée Rouge*'s crew to hear. Jean-Michel's hands folded over the cutlass handle again, staring coldly at Smith.

"Everyone on board has their responsibilities and duties," Isabella said. "Everyone knows their place. Jean-Michel's duties are clear to all. They don't need you to remind us."

Smith swiveled effortlessly on his heels to face Isabella. "The cat wakens!"

Isabella remained calm, calculating. Something about her confidence riled Smith. He hesitated. She could see the anger build in his cheeks. "Bridle your confidence," Smith growled. "Don't forget the alleys or inns of Charlotte Amalie so quickly!"

A fire seemed to light up Isabella as she gripped her saber. This time, Jean-Michel moved forward. Smith smiled and opened his mouth to say something else when a voice interrupted them.

"Captain!" Smith's quartermaster had managed to slink up to Santa Ana. The quartermaster was watching him, oblivious to the scene unfolding between his captain and Isabella. A playful spark twinkled in the quartermaster's eyes as his hands played with his whip. "Look what we have here."

The quartermaster pulled the whip from his sash. Its tip dropped menacingly onto the deck. He took the handle and pushed it into the crook of Santa Ana's neck.

"It's a Dago. An awfully pretty Dago, too. He would be a fine addition to our mess." The quartermaster snapped the whip. "I think we can give'm his first lesson about living under the command of a Yellow Jacket." The quartermaster stepped back and cocked the whip.

A blinding heat surged through Isabella. She lunged past Jean-Michel, drawing her saber, forcing herself between Santa Ana and the quartermaster.

"Let him be!" she barked. The quartermaster let the whip fall obediently, startled by her quickness and determination.

"What?" Smith elbowed his way through what had now become a crowd. He looked at Santa Ana. "He's just a Dago. Why can't we have a little fun with the Spaniard? The only thing more entertaining would be a frog." Smith winked at Jean-Michel. "I'm sure he would be far more entertaining on board the *Wasp*. My quartermaster would make quick work of those clothes. I'm sure he feels bound up in those fancy shirts and breeches. After all, what use could he possibly be to a bunch of runaway slaves and Old World outcasts?"

"He's my prisoner," Isabella said. "I'll decide what's done with him."

"Pirates don't take prisoners," Smith retorted. "Real pirates don't." Then, he smiled. "But, I forgot. A girl runs this ship!"

Isabella and Jean-Michel raised their swords.

"I know what that means in this case," Smith said, a smirk breaking through his beard. Smith's sailors pulled pistols from their belts. The quartermaster coiled his whip, and pulled his sword.

"I don't need pirates to defend me," Santa Ana said. "I fight my own battles."

Smith laughed. "Spoken like a royal!" He turned to Isabella. "Give him a weapon," he ordered. "I want to see what he's made of."

"He'll take up weapons when I give the order," Isabella said. "He's not your boy, Smith."

Smith turned and leaned toward Isabella. In a low hoarse voice, he said, "I wonder why you are taking interest in this prisoner. Oh, but he's a pretty boy, ain't he? Can't take the girl out of the alleys, can we?"

The prisoner and his purpose are no business of yours," she said again, anger seething through each word.

"Perhaps he can tell us about the Court's newest fashions," Smith bellowed, satisfied he had rattled Isabella. He flipped his wrist uncontrollably and pranced across the deck with glee. "Or perhaps," Smith said, turning his eyes back to Isabella, "you want him for your own devices."

Isabella raised her saber, cutting a wide, precise arc through the air.

"Enough!" Jean-Michel said. "You've overstayed your welcome, Smith. Tea is over. Take leave. You're lucky we don't blow you, your ship, and your little boys out of the water now."

"Hah!" Smith said, whirling to his quartermaster. "Your brig against my frigate? I've got ten more cannons than you have. You wouldn't survive our first broadside." The quartermaster smiled. Smith's crew closed ranks.

Isabella extended her tip in warning. "Take leave, Smith. You're not welcome on this ship."

Smith's quartermaster shuffled over to the prisoner. "Come now, ma'am. Won't you let us take the Dago with us? He'd be a nice prize for the crew. We've needed a bit of entertainment." He lifted his blade to Juan Carlos's neck, letting the tip rest just above the artery. Isabella drew her saber up swiftly and instinctively, pushing its tip up in a circular arc, and then pulling it down to beat the quartermaster's blade into the deck.

The quartermaster brought his blade up angrily. Embarrassment fueled his fury as his tip clanged against the top of Isabella's blade. She parried, deflecting the blow. Smith stood nearby, amused by his quartermaster's instincts.

"Don't start," Jean-Michel warned the quartermaster in a measured tone. He looked at Smith. "You don't want this."

"I'll not have anyone throw my blade," the quartermaster scowled. His eyes deepened. His eyebrows narrowed his eyes to slits.

"I would take Jean-Michel's advice," Isabella counseled. But her tone seemed to send Smith's quartermaster into a near rage.

"I think my man knows how to handle himself in battle," Smith prodded. "I'll bet he knows the stakes. I'll let him make the decision."

What was Smith doing? Smith knew what she could do; he'd seen it in the streets of Charlotte Amalie.

"Don't push," Isabella warned. "Pride muddles the head."

"I'll push as far as I want, when I want," the quartermaster said. The tip of his saber carved a tight circle in the air. He wasn't going to let anyone challenge him in front of his captain. Besides, how could he go back to his ship if he had backed down from a girl?

"Don't expect quarter," Isabella warned, letting her tip drop inches below his, challenging him to make the first move.

"I don't ask," the quartermaster said, letting his anger become even more obvious, "and I don't give."

He lunged. Isabella parried, and he lunged again. She deflected the blow low, and swung her blade up, ticking a hole into his shirtsleeve.

"No blood!" the quartermaster said gleefully, mistaking her move for a miss. Isabella stood silently, keeping her eyes trained on the tip of the quartermaster's blade.

He brought his blade up and pulled it down in a wide arc. Isabella lifted her blade, deflecting the blow expertly. It was a hard blow, but she let her blade absorb its energy. She moved forward, tip down, challenging him to make another arcing cut. He raised his sword up and pulled it forcefully down again. She parried, letting her blade absorb the blow's force again.

Again and again, the quartermaster attacked. Isabella parried, and then thrust her tip forward in a feigned riposte, lulling the quartermaster into another powerful cut. She deflected each cut. First up, then down, then to the side. She watched him as the blade sliced through the air. Each arcing cut weaned a little more strength. She marveled at how he took the bait, time and time again. When he slowed to regroup, she would riposte or lunge, drawing him into another aggressive cut.

Isabella wondered at his strength. She didn't dare test her opponents in a contest of strength—it would kill her. *How long are we going to go on like this?* She asked herself impatiently. *Calm yourself,* she thought, taking deep breaths. *Wait. Patience. Your turn will come, any moment.*

Several minutes passed as their swords clanged and chinged, the only noises drifting over sparkling blue waters. Small clouds provided momentary relief from the rising heat, but the respite was all too brief.

Isabella retreated strategically with each powerful cut, giving the quartermaster hope. Smith's crew cheered, only to be silenced by one of Isabella's ripostes. Sweat streamed down their faces, soaking into their shirts, then their breeches, and into their boots.

The crew of the *Marée Rouge* watched, content to accept whatever outcome emerged. Jean-Michel was too experienced to ignore the subdued response of his crew. He watched the duel, one eye looking for any sign of weakness from Isabella, the other sizing up the crew. He could see Santa Ana watch each move, like a schoolboy eagerly learning a new lesson. He seemed to be logging each cut, each riposte, each lunge, and each arc. *What was he doing?* Jean-Michel wondered. A resounding clang pulled him back into the fight.

The pace quickened. Isabella parried, but her ripostes came fast and often. She was pushing the quartermaster back; he was tiring.

Isabella stepped forward, her blade darting from point to point. Each flick of the wrist cast aside another threat from the quartermaster. Finally, she began edging her blade closer to his arms, his chest, and his thighs. The quartermaster's movements weakened and became defensive. He seemed to sense defeat, but he refused to ask for quarter. Isabella pressed, back straight, blade disciplined.

"Quarter?" she said a few cuts later, sweat flowing through her curls.

"He don't need quarter," Smith growled from the sidelines. Resentment built inside Isabella: How could he say that? Were his men worth so little?

The quartermaster, sensing a mental lapse, lunged. His blade tore through Isabella's sleeve, drawing a crimson line across her upper arm. Surprised by the turn, Jean-Michel straightened, pulling his sword from its sheath. Before he could advance, Isabella riposted, throwing the quartermaster back against the gunwales.

Focus! She screamed to herself. How could she let Smith distract her like that? How could she underestimate him so fatally? She needed focus. Blood soaked through the cotton slit as she forced herself back into the fight, oblivious to the pain. She had to end this—now. Her blade seemed animated with its own purpose. Isabella stepped forward, effortlessly cutting, thrusting, and arcing.

She advanced again. She lifted her blade in another arcing cut. The quartermaster's parry was too late. Isabella's blade looped cleanly and purposefully, undercutting his blade. She thrust her tip deep into his arm. The quartermaster's sword clattered to the deck as the force of her lunge tacked his arm to the gunwale. She pulled the blade, letting blood gush from the open wound. The quartermaster wavered, stunned by the wound, and groggily fought to clamp the cut with his good hand. He sank to the deck, expecting the inevitable.

The intense sun gave the blood an eerie sparkle along the steel of Isabella's saber. She thrust it toward the quartermaster's neck, but stopped before it pierced his skin. She let the tip rest in a deeply depressed circle of skin. The quartermaster stared at Isabella, his eyes vacant and wandering, dumbfounded by how quickly the fight had turned. Panic consumed his eyes; he sat helpless, a nervous twitch from death.

"Quarter?" she mouthed silently.

"No," he said, loud enough for Smith and the others to hear.

Isabella hesitated, tip steady against his neck. She should kill him. No, she needed to kill him. She began to turn the blade. The quartermaster closed his eyes.

Isabella gripped the saber's handle firmly, preparing for a final thrust. Suddenly, she felt the crowd around her: Jean-Michel, Smith, Stiles, and the crew. They were watching, waiting; expectation stifled the air on deck. Would she have the guts to follow through? What of Smith's crew? Santa Ana?

She started to laugh. Her blade dropped from the quartermaster's neck, and she turned to Santa Ana.

"How was the show?" she teased, lifting her blade toward his chest. She let the tip dance at random points, ticking pin-size holes in his shirt without breaking the skin. "What?" she asked. "No words from the warrior? I thought we were beyond this." Santa Ana looked at her with steel-like hardness.

Isabella leaned toward the wounded quartermaster and tore his sash from his waist. She wiped her blade clean and then threw it back into his lap.

"Captain Smith," she commanded, "high tea is over. Return to your ship. We have no use for you or your crew here."

Smith approached Isabella, contempt rippling through his body. His hands twitched with anger. "This isn't over."

"It is today," Isabella responded victoriously, turning her back on him. "Get your crew off the *Marée Rouge*. We have work to do."

Smith started toward Isabella, but Jean-Michel stepped firmly in front of him. "You heard the captain," he said. Smith turned toward the ladder leading down to the long boat and motioned toward his crew to follow.

"Don't forget your garbage," Jean-Michel called. Stiles and another crewman scooped the quartermaster up, dragged him to the railing, and dropped him into the boat below. In seconds, Smith had swept his crew from the deck of the *Marée Rouge*.

Jean-Michel turned. "Come now, mates. We've got work to do before we make Saint John. Mr. Stiles. Get someone to swab the deck. We don't need blood to attract more vultures." The men scattered, looking for chores and securing cannon, shot, and powder.

6

Isabella stood, hands resting on the railing, watching Smith and his crew row back to the *Wasp*. Smith was animated, his hands moving wildly. His arm swung what looked like a cane or a thin-bladed sword and pointed it haphazardly toward the quartermaster. The quartermaster lay motionless, leaning against another seaman. He seemed alone. Isabella grew angry. She wanted to dive into the water, swim out to the boat, and slash Smith's neck. Her knuckles grew white as she gripped the railing. "Damn him," she murmured.

"He won't last the night."

Startled, Isabella turned. Santa Ana had moved close to her. His hands rested on the railing, relaxed but fighting against the weight of the chain links.

"You don't know Smith," she said. "His crew won't dare mutiny. They call him Yellow Jacket because his sting is quick, powerful, and painful."

"I wasn't talking about Smith," Santa Ana corrected, amused.

Isabella shifted her weight. "The quartermaster's wound wasn't fatal," she said, knowing that wasn't Santa Ana's point. How did he get so close? Where was his guard?

"That's true," Santa Ana admitted, "physically." He turned to look at Isabella. "I expected better leadership."

"What?" she sputtered. How dare he reprimand her this way?

"You were weak," Santa Ana said. "You let the quartermaster live, here, on your ship. You knew Smith would do your handiwork, finish your job. That's cruel. Cruelty is the sin of a leader."

"Who are you to lecture me about leadership?" She hated the feeling Santa Ana was playing with her, like a cat with a mouse.

"You're young, but you can learn."

Arghhh! Isabella wanted to smack him. "You're forgetting your place," she warned, "boy."

"I know my place," Santa Ana said with the smoothness of a boy fresh from the Court's tutors. Isabella's rage bubbled again. "Your courage was obvious on the decks of the defeated *Ana Maria*," he continued. "Your skills with the sword are quite well developed. Everyone saw that here. I've schooled with the best. Your instincts, your skills, would put you—"

"The Court," she interrupted. "Your precious King; he would never allow a woman or slave to learn from the great masters of Toledo."

Santa Ana stopped in mid-breath. How did she, a slave from the West Indies, know about the master swordsmen of Toledo? "You are no longer a slave, correct? Slaves cannot command others, let alone a pirate ship. Your thinking was confused by the duel."

"My head was clear," she insisted. How dare he talk to her like this? How condescending. Why was she letting him get away with this? "It's obvious you haven't grown up on these waters." She paused before using her most sarcastic tone to add "Your Excellency."

"He challenged your authority," Juan Carlos persisted. "There was only one proper end to that fight."

Isabella turned to her prisoner, still shocked by his forwardness. Even chains and a night deep in the bilge hadn't softened him.

She looked at him. His hair was mussed, slickened by the heat. His face was dirty, but his Latin features were still clean and obvious. His eyes were softer than she remembered, but their softness wasn't from lack of resolve. He was talking to her, not at her. His words reminded her of Jean-Michel, but Santa Ana was sharper—his mind raced, thinking, analyzing, finding, fitting parts of the puzzle. His voice was smooth and his tone calm, almost as if they were discussing the day's strategy. Perhaps they were, but the thought made her nervous. He was experienced. She couldn't help but feel intrigued, still drawn to him. She felt so young. Just like when she met Jacob two years ago. Then, she was young. Too young.

Isabella leaned against the ship's rail, and let the breeze blow through her blouse. Her sleeves ballooned as the air cooled her arms and cheeks. Her anger melted under the mid-morning heat.

"Tell me something," she ventured, a hint of a challenge in her voice. "What do you think would have happened if I had killed him?"

Santa Ana looked at her as if the answer were obvious. "You would have gained the respect of your crew."

"What about Smith's crew?"

"Why is Smith's crew your concern?"

"Who do you think my enemy is?"

"Spain, of course," he said, sensing that his answer—the obvious one—must be wrong.

Isabella shook her head. "That's why you will lose the West Indies."

Santa Ana stood, unsure of how to respond. Isabella hid her smile, entertained by the image of Santa Ana's mind flip-flopping over different ways to figure out what she meant.

"Spain against the world?" she said.

He looked at her, confused.

She shook her head again. *How delightful*, she cackled inside. *He really was clueless.*

She leaned close, as if telling him a secret. "Spain is the least of my worries," she whispered. "Smith can do more to destroy me and my crew than a squadron of Spanish men-of-war."

Santa Ana looked at her, scowling. Isabella laughed. "*Señor* Santa Ana, you have confirmed my prayers. Spain has no chance. Your presence will ensure my destiny."

Santa Ana turned back toward the sea, embarrassment welling inside him. She could see it; he knew it. The mighty Spanish advisor, dispatched by the Royal Court, was unable to understand the simple logic underlying the war he was to wage.

Isabella couldn't resist. "Let me give you another hint." Santa Ana continued to stare into the swells. The waves had grown, fed by a stiff breeze from darkened clouds, gathering on the horizon. "What if my goal is not to throw the Spaniards out of the colonies? What if it's personal? What if I want to go after another captain? Nevertheless, let's make it interesting. We're equals, matching, cannon for cannon, and sword for sword. Do you rush into battle with even odds?"

Santa Ana remained silent. Isabella continued, answering her own question; "Of course not. You attack when you have the advantage. So, if I can't out shoot him, and I don't have more men, what do I do?" Santa Ana's expression began to soften.

"Now you see," she said. "You go after his men. You work their hearts and minds."

Juan Carlos lifted his head. "You showed weakness."

"Perhaps," Isabella said. "But whose weakness? Mine or Smith's?"

Juan Carlos turned his head. Score! Isabella turned back toward the sea, concerned that sudden pride might make her blush.

"I don't care about his quartermaster," she said, trying to keep her voice even. "Every captain expects his crew to do two things: fight for him and win. Smith went in thinking he had the advantage. He misread the hand of his enemy. He played the wrong cards, and his men suffered for his arrogance. Smith's quartermaster was simply foolish; he didn't understand the odds or the game. It was Smith's gamble. He needed his quartermaster to win, or die trying. The benefits of the win are obvious. The benefits of his death are not. In these waters, a sacrifice for the cause can rally a crew to victory. Smith needed a martyr. Martyrdom comes with death. Surely, you, a Christian, should know that. Wasn't it your Christ's death that created the Christian spirit?"

Isabella looked at Smith's ship as it tacked toward the horizon. Why didn't Smith play his hand better? He had stronger cards to play. He must have something up his sleeve. Was he expecting another fight? Another meeting at Panther Bay?

"The quartermaster lived," Isabella said, satisfied. "Now, Smith's in his cabin, figuring out how to save himself. He doesn't have a prize. He doesn't have a martyr." Isabella smiled, pleased at the thought of Smith racking his brain alone in his cabin. He was probably hacking uncontrollably at the walls of his cabin. It was a wickedly, delightful image.

Joy overtook Isabella. She could feel the truth of her mother's fireside prophecy. Her confidence gave her renewed strength and focus. Isabella would stand over the gates of El Morro victorious. Would Santa Ana be there?

Santa Ana's brain seemed to spin as he tried to absorb Isabella's explanation. "So, he's done," he concluded.

"Smith's never done," Isabella warned. "His ambition is too great. Much like your King."

Santa Ana's body tightened. His knuckles whitened. "Smith isn't the only one on this sea with ambition."

"Aye," Isabella acknowledged. "But my ambition is simple. I have one goal, shared by many." Isabella was sure Santa Ana didn't understand. He didn't have the wisdom of knowing the prophecy and her destiny. He didn't have the benefit of knowing slavery.

"What do you think Smith will do?" Santa Ana asked.

"They call him Yellow Jacket because of his sting," Isabella pointed out. "But they're wrong. He's a phoenix."

They stood, watching the swells and feeling the soothing roll of the ship.

"You were right in one respect," she said after another moment. "The quartermaster is dead."

"Why?" Santa Ana asked, confused. "His wound wasn't fatal. How does his death help Smith's cause?"

"Smith's crew serves his ambition." Isabella turned back toward the deck. "The quartermaster will be dead by the evening. Smith still needs a martyr. That's my gamble."

"You want the quartermaster to die?"

"I don't want anyone to die," she confessed, her eyes glancing to the deck. "All I had to do was win the duel. Death may or may not be necessary. My gamble was that, today, his death on my ship was not necessary."

They stood next to each other deep in thought as the sails ballooned with the quickening breeze. She wasn't nervous about his presence any longer. Somehow, this scene, this picture, seemed to fit. She relaxed. "Whether the quartermaster lives or dies is a decision Smith will make, not me."

"You could have kept him here as a prisoner."

Isabella looked at Santa Ana and remembered Jean-Michel's warning. "No," she said shaking her head. "I couldn't. His loyalty was to Smith, not to me. Losing a duel to a girl?" She smiled sheepishly as if saying, "Surely you know that is an unthinkable crime."

Santa Ana nodded. "Your crew doesn't seem to mind following a girl." Santa Ana suddenly seemed like a boy, not the army officer she saw rallying the marines on the decks of the doomed *Ana Maria*. She couldn't help but turn a small smile as she looked into the waves. She thought, for a brief moment, what it would have been like if they had met under the palms of Cinnamon Bay. The early afternoon sun would have soothed their muscles as they relaxed together on the white sands.

"Pirate crews are an odd sort," she said admiringly. "They are individuals with their own souls and conscience."

A ghost's presence seemed to stir the air around them.

"Where's the guard?" Jean-Michel's gruff voice said.

Isabella shook herself from what seemed like a daydream. She saw the agitated face of Jean-Michel and looked sheepishly toward Santa Ana. She was a girl again. The guard was nowhere around.

"Excusez moi," Santa Ana said. Jean-Michel looked at him suspiciously.

"Don't worry," Isabella said, ignoring Santa Ana's French. "What was he going to do? Kill me?"

"Yes," Jean-Michel said.

"That's not a good survival strategy," Santa Ana quipped.

"Guard," Jean-Michel called. A bare-footed seaman padded up to them. "Take the prisoner below."

The sailor grabbed Santa Ana by the arm and pulled him toward the forward hatch. Santa Ana resisted, walking confidently on his own. The fresh air, and his talk with Isabella, seemed to energize him, but, for what purpose?

"What were you talking about?" Jean-Michel demanded.

Isabella looked at Jean-Michel. "What do you think? I gave him the plans to the ship, a map to Saint John, and a complete inventory of our cargo and gold." His stare was hard and cold. "Oh," she said as if remembering one last detail. "I also marked our secret route to Cruz Bay on the map. I used the special black ink and wrapped it up nice and tight. It shouldn't take him more than three days."

Jean-Michel scolded her with another look. "Do you want to do this here?" he asked like a parent upbraiding a child.

"Where else?"

"Perhaps your cabin would be more appropriate."

"I don't think there's anything we need to talk about," she retorted, but she knew that was a lie.

"Everything you tell him he will use to destroy us."

"I didn't give him anything." She hoped this was true, but now even she wasn't sure. "We talked about the fight." She looked at him irritated. "He thought I was weak!"

"You are!"

"I'm not," Isabella objected, her voice rising. "It would have been easy for me to kill Smith's idiot. I didn't. I didn't give Smith the martyr he wanted."

"I wasn't talking about Smith!" Jean-Michel said. He moved close, lowering his voice. "Isabella, be careful," he pleaded, "the Dago can kill you as easily as Smith can hire a privateer to do his dirty work."

"I have yet to see anyone surpass my skills," she said. "Jacob was the best swordsman in these waters."

"And he's dead," Jean-Michel said. "You're one of the best; not *the* best." He turned and paced the quarterdeck. "That's beside the point. I'm not worried about your skills in battle, or your courage."

She looked up at him, surprised. "What else is there to worry about?"

He looked at her, his eyes sensitive, almost tearing. He clenched his fist, and pulled it to his chest. Isabella looked away, embarrassed.

"Don't worry Jean-Michel. Jacob is still here."

"He's going to leave sometime. This is not the time to open your heart—to anyone. Stay the course."

She turned away, frightened by what he might see. Why was she becoming so comfortable with Santa Ana? She yearned to be with him, to talk to him. Jean-Michel was right. She had to stop this. She couldn't open her heart, especially to someone as dangerous as Juan Carlos was.

Jean-Michel stood beside her as the *Marée Rouge* gained speed in the rising wind. Isabella couldn't see Jean-Michel's arm move up behind her back, as if attempting to embrace her, and then falling softly back to his side.

They were moving swiftly. If the breeze stayed with them, they could make landfall by morning and anchor in Panther Bay by dusk. Neither Isabella nor Jean-Michel could know how fate and destiny were about to play out under the seductively placid shadows of Saint John's cliffs.

7

Isabella was exhausted; she reckoned she had slept just four hours—damn Juan Carlos Lopez de Santa Ana. The muggy afternoon seemed to be pulling her into a half-trance. She could feel the bay—the placid waters—but she didn't seem to see it. She drifted... focus! She shook her head violently, as if throwing tangled ropes off her mind. For a twisted moment, she yearned for the adrenalin of battle and the acrid smell of spent gunpowder to keep her senses sharp.

"She's beautiful," Jean-Michel said, "and deadly."

"Aye," she said to Jean-Michel with false confidence, "but the eighteen-pounders from the *Ana Maria* will give us comfort."

The cliffs sprouted above the cove, higher and higher, as the *Marée Rouge* slipped under their shadows. Lush green palms traced maze-like corridors up the mountainside, sometimes disappearing behind giant boulders, like a game of hide and seek. A waterfall glistened as its white froth cascaded halfway down a cliff, feeding a small stream protected by the bay. Only a handful of sailors on the beach betrayed the presence of the buccaneer village cleverly hidden in the jungle.

The scene was deceptively tranquil, and Isabella knew it. She couldn't afford to forget. Her crew seemed to disintegrate into reckless abandon each time they returned from a hunt. Now, the imprisonment of Juan Carlos haunted her and the *Marée Rouge*. She closed her eyes. Her decision was close.

She couldn't relax, not until she rested comfortably in her *bohio,* nestled safely under the palms halfway up the mountain. The flowers would be beautiful—a menagerie of blues, whites, yellows, and red.

A softening sun slipped below the horizon as the *Marée Rouge* nudged into the harbor. Isabella turned to the helmsman. "Running rum taught you a turn or two, eh?" she joked, tipping her hand respectfully.

"Thank you, ma'am." The helmsman kept his eyes trained on the ship's last few yards. Isabella wondered if he would torture himself over a person like Santa Ana. Could he hang him without thought or guilt?

Seamen darted about, running yardarms, flying through rigging, scurrying to secure the last sails. A handful were untying the long boats, readying them to ferry sailors to shore. Several had ditched their drab deck clothes for brightly dyed island shirts and trousers.

The festive colors reminded Isabella of the stories Jean-Michel told her of growing up in southern France. Gypsies would travel through town with bears and bright uniforms in a feast of music and activity. Jean-Michel reverently retold the stories of children like himself, gathering around the animals, hoping to get close to legendary beasts. Isabella was never quite sure whether to believe his tales, but she enjoyed them.

The ship coasted to a stop. The anchor dropped, shattering glassy, smooth water. Isabella relaxed, finally letting herself succumb to the calm of the bay. Was she the Gypsy or the child? For some reason, she thought it mattered now.

"Mr. Stiles," she called, spotting him at the bow as the anchor dropped loudly into the blackening water.

"Aye, cap'n?"

"Is the watch schedule ready?"

"Aye, cap'n. Gave it to Jean-Michel before we came into Panther Bay."

That was prompt. Unusually so. Stiles must want to get off the ship quickly. What does he want to do on shore? Where was Jean-Michel, anyway? He had disappeared.

Isabella walked the quarterdeck's railing to give her a better view of the ship.

"*Mon capitaine,*" came a familiar voice behind her.

"Jean-Michel?" Isabella said, twirling to face him. "Where were you?"

"A bit jittery for being in your home port," he teased.

Isabella struggled to keep her composure. "When will the ship be secure?"

Jean-Michel smiled. "In a few minutes. I've already got the roster and shifts for the crew; Stiles was efficient today."

She looked at him expectantly. "Well?" She lifted her hand, palm up.

Jean-Michel rolled his eyes. "*Pardon, mon cher.*" He slapped a crew roster into her hand. "Don't trust me?" The tone was goading, and Isabella struggled to keep her emotions from flaring up through a loud, verbal rebuke.

"Jean-Michel," she said, "you know me better than that." Jean-Michel couldn't read, but he painstakingly worked to memorize the names of the crewmen. How could he know if someone tampered with the roster?

Isabella looked over the columns. Stiles had categorized each crewman with obvious, careful precision. She paused and studied the list. His schedule had almost the entire crew leave the ship during the first watch. "That's odd," she said. "Why does Stiles have so many leaving the ship?"

"He was smart. A lot of 'm think they came home with nothing to show for it. They're better off getting off the ship and dip'n a little rum before they stew on it."

"He's keeping six on board, plus three more on shore, to watch the ship tonight," she said, trying to keep her brain focused. "That seems like a light crew." Maybe that was to her advantage. She could interview Juan Carlos again without suspicion.

"Appropriate, given the circumstances," Jean-Michel said. "Most won't be going to Cruz Bay til morning. If we need 'm, we can get them back on board soon enough. Some will be watching Panther Bay from the batteries in the cliffs, too."

Isabella nodded. Jean-Michel looked at her, this time with a more searching eye. "Isabella, *mon cher*, get some sleep," he ordered in a soft, gentle tone. "Go down to the cabin for an hour or two. The men have about another thirty minutes of work. Then it will be quiet—perfect for a few extra minutes of sleep. I can get you in a couple of hours."

"What of Santa Ana?" she asked wearily.

"Humph," he snorted. "We ought to tie him up, keel haul him, and throw him to the sharks." Isabella scowled. "Well," he said, "you better decide soon, or the crew will. I'll keep him down below. We can decide when I wake you."

"Make sure he's alive when I wake up," she joked. Isabella turned clumsily to walk below the quarterdeck and into her cabin. She didn't remember anything once the door shut, but she felt the comforting blankets around her, as she lay fully clothed in a deep sleep.

***

Isabella's eyes shot open. Darkness surrounded her. The blankets rested, crumpled at the end of the bed. A thick web seemed to ensnare her thoughts. Her body felt heavy, as if chained to the bed and weighed down with shot, but she wasn't.

She lay on her cot, letting the grog seep away. Her eyes began to focus. Slowly, the moon seemed to invade the cabin through the stern windows; she recognized the shadows of her desk, washbasin, and chairs. A small light reflected off her mirror, swaying with the gentle role of the bay. The window was still open; a delicate breeze meandered its way through the cabin, glancing over her body. Small waves lapped at the hull.

Isabella suddenly realized she was warm, but resisted an instinct to tear off her shirt. Why was she awake?

A muffled voice eeked through the door. Boots clapped against the wooden deck above. What had happened? She hadn't heard the ship's bell. Isabella lifted herself, still dull from sleep, and rested her head in her hands. She listened. More boots, more muffled voices.

SLAP!

Someone must have slammed open a door to the main deck. Why? There wasn't enough wind to push it shut.

SPLASH!

More hurried steps. Boots of several men stomped on wooden planks, and then seemed to climb up a ladder.

SLAP!

"Where is he?" cried a voice through the wooden ceiling.

"What do you mean you don't know?"

That was Stiles' voice. She heard it clearly this time through the open stern windows. What was he doing on board? He was supposed to be off the ship on the first watch. Jean-Michel was supposed to command the watch. Isabella stood up, adrenalin clearing her mind. She walked over to the desk and picked up her saber. The blade hardly made a sound as she pulled it from its sheath. She strained to hear. Had the Spanish found them? Had someone boarded?

Isabella pulled the saber to her side. Her free hand glanced across a pistol lying awkwardly on the desk. She picked it up and rammed it into the back of her breeches. She walked carefully, silently, to the window.

"We've got to find him," Stiles said from the deck above.

"Aye," said another unfamiliar, gravely voice. "He seems to have disappeared."

"He couldn't have disappeared!" Stiles grumbled.

"Forget him," said a third voice. "Let's get the captain."

Whose voice was that? One she knew, but the tone made her brace.

"No!" Stiles said quickly. "Not yet. Find'm first. You two look in the foc'stle. You three; search below deck; work at the bow and move toward the stern. Don't forget the hold and bilge. I'll wait here with the rest o'ya to see if we can flush'm onto the main deck. Then we can take care of 'm and get the captain."

Juan Carlos must have escaped. He must have been the splash she had heard. Isabella barely noticed the sense of relief she felt as she stepped back to lean against her desk. Then, she grew angry. Santa Ana—escaped? How could those idiots have let that happen?

Isabella swiveled noisily and started to walk toward the door. The voices above hushed. She stopped. She listened. Why weren't they talking now? Were they embarrassed that their captain may have overheard their negligence? Jean-Michel must already be plotting their punishment. Where was he? He was supposed to wake her. Surely, he hadn't gone on shore, leaving Stiles in command, or had he?

The questions gnawed on her insides. A sense of dread overcame her. Fear began to tickle her stomach. Something unpleasant was beyond her cabin, but she knew she had no choice. She had to find out what was happening to her ship.

Isabella slowed as she reached the door. She listened for signs above her. She listened for sounds outside her cabin. Nothing. She put her hand on the brass handle and gently turned it. The door unlatched, but she kept it from opening more than a crack. A dim light flickered into the room. Someone had a lantern on.

Isabella pulled her saber close, re-checked the pistol lodged in her back, and opened the door a few more inches. Nothing.

She peered around the door and looked into the hallway—nothing.

She slipped through the door, carefully keeping it from opening completely, and waited again—nothing.

Isabella pulled the cabin door shut behind her and started down the hallway. A lantern's light defined the outlines of the lower deck—the ladder leading to the main deck on the right; the passageway to the main crew's quarters running to the left. Jean-Michel's cabin door was on the left. Isabella inched forward, making sure each heel landed softly and silently.

She lifted her saber's tip in front of her, and focused on the ladder. Surely, she could hear someone on this level. The saber's tip lifted to the top of the ladder. She was at the end of the passageway now. She still couldn't hear anything. Where was Stiles? Where was Jean-Michel?

An invisible force seized her sword's tip and pulled it downward. Isabella pulled at its handle, refusing to let the force take it. Something thick and round wrapped around her neck. A hand closed over her mouth. Her head twisted violently as she struggled to loosen the arm's grip. She clawed at the flesh; she tried to bite its fingers. The arm pulled her neck tighter, pulling her firmly against a body, a man's body, deep in the corner of the deck.

She struggled; she kicked. The arm lifted her above the deck and her boots thrashed about harmlessly. Her attacker neutralized the saber by hugging it to his body. She couldn't move; she was helpless. Air! She couldn't breathe. She needed air.

"Silence, *mon cher,*" a voice whispered in her ear. "Silence."

Isabella fought his arm, instinctively, desperately.

"Silence, *mon cher,*" Jean-Michel insisted. "They're coming. Our only chance is silence."

What was going on? Jean-Michel didn't want her dead. If he wanted to kill her, she would be dead. She would have been dead as soon as he had grabbed her, but she was alive. She relaxed.

"I'm going to uncover your mouth," he informed her. "You have to stay quiet." He relaxed his hand just enough for her to nod through the fingers.

"What's happening?"

"Stiles," Jean-Michel hissed.

"Where's Santa Ana?" Isabella felt Jean-Michel's critical glare in the darkness. "I heard a splash in the bay from my cabin," she blurted defensively, half apologetically.

"Santa Ana's resourceful; I'll give 'm that," Jean-Michel said. "Stiles was going to cut him."

"What? On whose orders?"

"Apparently, he doesn't need orders. At least no orders from you or me."

The pieces began to fall into place. "That's why he sent most of the crew on shore."

"Aye, that's what I think." Jean-Michel's face was now an outline.

"Why are you here, hiding?"

"I'm a fool," he said bitterly. "I fell right into his trap. Santa Ana was a ruse. Stiles pulled Santa Ana onto the main deck. He was toying with him, using a cutlass to slice up his shirt. I tried to stop him; we were saving him for the crew, I said. Stiles must have figured I would do this, so he trumped up a charge that I wanted to save the Dago, playin' as if he was rousting up the crew. Me? Save a Dago?"

She could hardly believe it. Mutiny. She gripped her sword, anger rising through her body. "What happened to Santa Ana?"

"Hah," Jean-Michel whispered. "Stiles didn't count on him being so quick. Spanish Army's always been a rung or two higher than the Navy, and it showed tonight. Santa Ana figured out what was happening. Stiles was going after me, so Santa Ana bolted below deck after tossing a couple of Stiles' henchman. The commotion gave me time. Stiles and the others took off, and I came down here to wait it out. I still wasn't completely sure of Stiles' plan. I heard a pistol go off in the bow. A bunch of men ran onto the main deck. I heard a splash. Then, they were shouting at each other. Then you came out of your cabin."

"So, you just happened to be outside my door?"

"I knew they were coming for you."

Isabella's mind raced—what were they going to do now? They stood for a few moments, listening for more footsteps and voices.

"How many men does Stiles have?"

"At least six," Jean-Michel reported.

"Too many."

"Can't tackle that many out in the open," Jean-Michel reasoned. "We might be able to get onto the main deck to one of the long boats. We could make it back to shore, rally the crew."

Boots clacked on the deck above. They were running toward them from the bow. Isabella grabbed Jean-Michel's shirt and tugged him toward her cabin. In moments, they were through the door. "Lock the door," she ordered even though she knew Jean-Michel had already secured it.

Isabella strode to her desk. She pulled a match from a drawer, struck it against the tabletop, and lit the lamp. A dull light flooded the room. She looked around, half expecting to see mutineers crouched in each corner. She turned to Jean-Michel. "Where are your weapons?"

"Stiles cornered me on deck," he confessed, his embarrassed face hidden in the dim light. "I couldn't get to my sword and pistol."

What were they going to do? Isabella looked at the charts resting loosely against the wall. She walked over and kicked them with her boot. Paper scattered across the floor in a muffled roll, exposing a sword stowed neatly against the planks. Isabella hooked its handle with her saber and flipped it into her free hand.

"Here," she said, tossing the orphan sword to Jean-Michel. "This will have to do."

Jean-Michel tested its balance and inspected its blade. "It'll do." He looked at Isabella. She seemed calm. Unnaturally calm. What happened to her temper? She should be livid with anger.

Isabella walked over to the open windows. Silence from the deck above told her that they had just a few more minutes at most. She looked into the water. A smooth black satin sheet seemed to cover it. Shore was a few hundred yards. Its white sand gleamed in the moonlight. Surely, she and Jean-Michel could swim it. Abandon her ship? What would Jacob think? Jacob could never run. How could she abandon him? She suddenly wished Juan Carlos had found them below deck. They had a common enemy now. She closed her eyes, trying to squeeze his Latin face and dark eyes from her mind. He was still the enemy. Stiles was treacherous scum, but Spain was worse.

"We wait," Isabella said.

Boots thudded against wood outside, the dull sound sifting through the door. Jean-Michel looked at Isabella uncertainly. "Are you sure? We could swim...."

"And leave the ship to Stiles? I'm not going to let that idiot have the pleasure of chasing me off my ship." She looked at Jean-Michel: "Our command."

"There are at least a half dozen of them," he reminded her.

She glared at him. "I'm not leaving this ship. Not without taking them with me. If you want to leave, the window is open."

Thump, thump, thump. "Captain?" said a voice outside the cabin.

Jean-Michel looked at the window. He looked at Isabella. Isabella stared at the door, lifting her saber's point.

Thump, thump, thump. "Captain?" came the voice again. "I need to report on the status of the prisoner."

Jean-Michel walked over to the desk, never letting his eyes stray from Isabella. She looked older, more seasoned. He paused by the window. A breeze puffed in from the bay. A strong odor of dead fish and salt dizzied him. Jean-Michel rested his hand on the sill and looked into the murky, black bay.

"Captain!" came the voice from outside, its tone more insistent. THUMP! THUMP! THUMP!

Jean-Michel turned toward the cabin door. Isabella watched him, saber ready. He walked to her, bringing his face within inches of her lips. He leaned toward her and kissed her softly on the cheek. "You know where my loyalties are," he whispered. Isabella closed her eyes, desperately trying to keep tears from bleeding onto her cheeks. She wanted to grab him; hold him; hold him closer than she had held anyone, but she didn't.

The knocks grew violent. Isabella's judgment hour had arrived—again. Jacob was gone. Santa Ana was gone. Jean-Michel remained. How could she have doubted his loyalty? She drew a deep breath, refocusing her thoughts. The door, and what was behind it, was all that mattered now.

"Six?" she asked.

"Six."

They looked at each other as if for the last time.

"I slept three hours," she said casually.

Jean-Michel laughed. "Six mutineers is nothing to the Pirate of Panther Bay." He raised his sword in a sweeping arc, cutting into the beams above, where the blade stuck. Isabella laughed at the sight of

Jean-Michel pulling at the blade just seconds before they would be fighting for their lives.

He finally jerked the sword from the beams, and smiled sheepishly. He looked at the blade approvingly one last time. Then, he looked at Isabella: "*Je t'aime, mon cher.*"

She smiled warmly. "*Je t'aime aussi, mon ami.*"

CRASH! The cabin door ripped from its hinges. Three pirates hurled into the tiny cabin, two of them rolling forward onto the floor. They quickly scrambled to their feet as Stiles leapt over them, cutlass in hand. He looked at Isabella and Jean-Michel, startled. His face calmed once he recognized them.

"My," he taunted, walking toward them, "Look what we have here." He stopped when their blades rose to meet him. "Why the hostility?" Stiles raised his cutlass, cutting an arc swiftly through the air in front of them.

The room's temperature thickened around Isabella and Jean-Michel as six mutinous pirates closed on them. Sweat beaded on their faces; their shirts instantly darkened with moisture. Their blades wavered at the mutineers. The cabin was too small for them to charge all at once. Stiles' swagger told them they didn't have a chance... unless he made a mistake.

Stiles brought his sword up, beating Jean-Michel's aside. "A bit testy tonight, ain't we?"

Jean-Michel held his blade steady, bringing his tip back in defense.

"Stiles," Jean-Michel warned, "you don't want this fight."

Stiles laughed. "You? Warn me?"

Stiles swung his blade again, beating Jean-Michel's down to the deck, but he didn't attack. Jean-Michel brought the tip up again—precisely, calmly, and deliberately.

Stiles looked at Isabella. She stood patiently, despite the perspiration soaking into her shirt. The fabric clung to the pistol lodged in her back. She straightened her shoulders, trying to pull the shirt away from the flintlock—it would be useless if it were wet. She eyed Stiles and the other mutineers, searching for any opportunity to turn the tables.

"Where's the prisoner?" Isabella asked.

Stiles hesitated in mid-pace. His eyebrow curled. "No need to worry you're pretty little girl head about that."

Arghhh! Isabella screamed to herself. Her eyes sparkled. She brought her blade up and lunged toward Stiles. Another pirate beat her blade down as Stiles jumped clear.

"Foolish girl!" Stiles yelled. He lunged. Isabella pulled her blade up in a defensive arc, deflecting Stiles' cut into the hardwood table. A foot long gash splintered across the top. He pulled his sword up again, slicing another arc through the air wildly, narrowly missing her face. Isabella pulled her blade up again in a parry, avoiding another cut, but didn't attack again with a riposte.

"I'm warning you Stiles," she said, bitterness building in her voice. "Stop this, now. Or, else!" The force of the order rattled the mutineers. They hesitated, almost as if they expected Stiles to call off the mutiny.

"You seem to forget what ship, you're on," Jean-Michel said, sensing an opportunity. "The captain of the *Marée Rouge* serves at her own pleasure, not the crew's—"

"A mistake," interrupted Stiles. "A mistake we plan to correct."

Isabella's hand began to twitch with anger. "Jacob would have cut you down faster than grapeshot for words like that!"

"Precisely," Stiles said. "Jacob is dead. The Creed says no woman or child is allowed on a pirate ship. It's about time we enforced that law."

Isabella stumbled through her thoughts. How clever: Stiles was using the Pirate's Creed to rally her crew to mutiny. Jean-Michel would surely have an answer to Stiles' challenge. Jean-Michel remained silent, seemingly as baffled as she at Stiles' tactic.

"That law has never applied to the *Marée Rouge* or its crew," observed Isabella.

"Another mistake," Stiles growled. His voice carried a force she had never heard before.

"Jacob left the command to Isabella," Jean-Michel said coldly.

"Jacob is dead!" Stiles voice rose to a half-crazed shout.

"He is alive in the spirit of the *Marée Rouge*," Isabella retorted.

Stiles fumed. "Pirate ships aren't handed down like property."

"What makes you think the crew will follow you?" Jean-Michel prodded.

Stiles straightened his shoulders with confidence. "I can deliver bounty. That's something this wench can't do. This sortie showed that, and the crew knows it."

"You treacherous liar," Jean-Michel growled.

"Enough *Lieutenant*. This ship has had enough of a girl captain. We ain't goin' to follow no more orders from a girl." Stiles glared at Isabella. "You got only one place on this ship," he spat, "and that's tied to my bed!"

Isabella exploded, lunging at Stiles with a fury that Jean-Michel had never witnessed. Stiles stumbled out of the way, letting Isabella's tip slip deeply into the belly of a sailor behind him. The mutineer screamed as his blade rattled helplessly to the floor. The seaman's eyes glazed instantly; he looked confused and dazed, and fell weakly to his knees. Isabella pulled the blade out as blood spewed onto the floor.

Stiles struggled to pull his cutlass around in the cramped space, pulling it up over Isabella's head. Jean-Michel lunged, blocking Stiles' cut, forcing him into the corner. The mutineers rallied chaotically as the wounded mutineer moaned in a widening pool of blood.

Isabella retreated to the side of the table. Jean-Michel pulled back to the other side. They held their ground, ready for another attack.

"That's one down," Isabella counted coolly. "It won't take long for us to get the rest."

Isabella started forward, but the remaining pirates rushed them. Three slashed and cut at Isabella as Jean-Michel defended himself against the other two. The table kept the mutineers from working together; a tactical stroke of luck that might give Isabella and Jean-Michel the edge they needed. Isabella parried left, then right. A riposte into the arm of another mutineer sent another scream ringing through the cabin.

Isabella yelled to herself. *Three blades, three tips. Follow them. Know where they are. Arc, cut, parry, riposte. Lunge!* Jean-Michel must hold them off; she could feel the strength of his fight just inches from her head. Grunts followed slashing cuts as the pirates poured all their strength into beating down Jean-Michel and Isabella's blades. Parry, arc, cut....

"Ahhhh!" gasped Isabella as a mutineer's blade finally found its mark, steel surging into her left arm. Her knees began to buckle as the mutineer pulled his blade from her shoulder. An overwhelming fatigue gripped her body, paralyzing her every move. She struggled to lift her blade to thwart another lunge. She tumbled backward, retreating behind the captain's desk. She looked up. Victory twinkled in Stiles' eyes. She hesitated. Had the end finally come?

Silence invaded the room; everyone seemed to know what was about to happen. Stiles pulled himself erect, looking down into the defiant eyes of his former captain. "Now," he said, his voice calm and hardened. He drew his sword up, pointing its tip at Isabella's throat, daring her to continue.

"I'll see you in Hell," Isabella rasped, wincing with each throb of her wounded arm.

"No, deary," he sneered, advancing toward her. Jean-Michel retreated to Isabella's side, trying to keep the mutineers at a blade's distance. He reached down to Isabella's shoulder, grabbed her shirt, and pulled her to her feet. Isabella seemed to draw strength from Jean-Michel's effort. They stepped back, the windowsill against their thighs. The air was refreshingly cool against their backs.

Stiles signaled with his hand. A tall, lanky pirate jumped onto the tabletop, pushing his blade toward Jean-Michel. Isabella summoned all her strength. She reached around her back, pulled her pistol from her sash, clicked the flint back, and aimed it squarely at the bearded figure. CRACK!

The pirate screamed, clutching his face. His cutlass clattered to the floor, tripping another pirate, who fell into Stiles. The wounded mutineer fell to the tabletop, writhing back and forth. Stiles lost his balance. He fell toward Isabella, blade forward, but Isabella couldn't move. The edge of Stiles' blade pushed against her belly, slicing through her shirt. A blinding pain pierced through her body. She buckled forward. Her stomach bound up, and she felt like she was going to throw up. Dizzy, weak, and no longer able to stand, she drifted toward the deck as her knees gave out.

A hand grabbed her shoulder and whipped her head back. This was it. Stiles blade would cut cleanly through her neck. This was how it would end: She had failed. She had let Jacob down. Juan Carlos was right. She closed her eyes as her head whipped backward, arching her back. Pain barreled through her body. Everything went black.

8

Isabella's body seemed to defy any sense of gravity. She felt weightless, unable to move her arms or lift her feet. Jacob's face appeared, disappeared, and then reappeared. Jean-Michel was now holding her hand on the deck of a magnificent Spanish man-of-war. Juan Carlos smiled softly at her, sitting on a cliff nestled in the snug jungles of Saint John. She drifted. An endless current swirled around her, tiny bubbles grasping at her hair and arms. Blackness surrounded her, like a cocoon. Was this what her mother had meant about the *middle place*? Where worms became butterflies? The place you waited for death? Where the spirits judged your life and all that made up you as a person?

Isabella floated aimlessly, aware of nothing but an overpowering emptiness. Hours seemed to pass before her senses began to revive. Coldness began to nag at her, first her toes, then her fingers. The cold began to spread into her legs and arms. She felt it close in on her chest. Clothes clung to every curve and bump on her body. Her pants and shirt were heavy, pulling at her. Now, her feet seemed oddly warm. Heaviness settled into her chest. Her arm throbbed painfully. Her stomach ached. She didn't dare breathe. Why?

She was under water. My God! How did she get here? She didn't remember the water close over her. Her chest seemed tight, bound like the chains on an executioner's block. She had to get to the surface; she had to breathe. Her chest tightened even more, screaming for air. Isabella began to thrash. She had to get to the surface. Swim. She had to swim, but, which way? Was she going down or up? She couldn't tell! The water churned around her like a maelstrom, tugging, grabbing at her. Which way? Was she being pulled toward the surface or deeper into the bay?

Think, she cried to herself. *Calm down. Don't let the water fool you.* She kicked and stroked wildly, frantically, trying to ignore the rising ache that clutched her lungs with each move. Her boots seemed to weigh her down, like slick weights, unable to grip the water and push her forward. Her lungs seemed to close in on her like the thick wooden doors of a prison cell as she pulled and stroked. How long had she been underwater? An hour? It couldn't have been more than a minute. Maybe this wasn't the end. Maybe something, someone wanted her to live. How long could she hold her breath?

Another panic robbed her of precious strength as she stroked and kicked, kicked and stroked. *The pain! Open your eyes. Look around. Darkness. No!* Isabella screamed to herself. *The salt will blind you!* How much longer could she do this? Thirty seconds? Twenty seconds? *Just ten seconds more,* she pleaded.

A few more seconds. That's all she needed. She had to break through. Her muscles ached. Was this really the end? It would be a quick, even noble end. Better this than have Stiles—Stiles?—display her head on the yardarm of the *Marée Rouge*. Stiles. Mutiny. Anger overcame her panic as she sliced, scooped, and clutched at the water. Her lungs screamed louder as her arms and legs weakened and slowed. Perhaps, this was her fate. Jacob. Jean-Michel. Juan Carlos. She rested, letting her arms and legs float effortlessly in the cold bay waters. The prophecy.

I can't give up, she suddenly told herself. She couldn't let go, not as long as Stiles controlled the *Marée Rouge*. Not as long as one Spanish plantation existed in the West Indies. Jacob's memory deserved more than that. However, she was so weak. Her arms were lifeless. Her legs were tired and worn out. She was dizzy.

Something gripped her shoulder and pulled at her body forcefully. She wondered, *had a shark grabbed her?* They prowled the bay at dusk, scavenging for food or a careless sailor. Was she so weak she couldn't feel it ripping at her limbs? Water streaked past, wiping her face, like the rushing streams that cut through the plantations.

Fresh air cleansed Isabella's face as some bizarre force pushed her head above the water. She gasped and gulped. Her body fell below the surface again, her legs and arms too weak to keep her afloat. The force grabbed her again, pushing her to the surface. She gasped. This time the air recharged her muscles and senses.

She was tired, too tired to move. She waited, listening, as her face broke through the water again and she drew in more air. She wanted desperately to flop around, to keep the water from pulling her down again. Urgent voices skimmed across the water. She began to sink again. This time, she didn't go under. Something had wrapped itself under her chin. The force tugged at her. It came in fits of power and ripples. She felt the water break over her nose and lips as it pulled at her, legs dangling helplessly in her wake.

The force pulled and tugged, tugged and pulled. It seemed like hours. Each ripple refilled her muscles. She peered into what seemed like a dark fog. Images began to take shape. Were those mangrove trees? She thought she saw the distinctive wide trunk of a kapok tree, too. Isabella looked up. She saw the stars. They seemed like beacons, brightening the bay around her.

She stared into the sky. One star stood out from the others—bright, constant, and illuminating. Its light seemed to strengthen her, clear her mind. This wasn't the end after all. Was it a beginning? The force tugged her again, but Isabella stayed focused on the star. Her star.

The force stopped. Had the shark given up?

Isabella felt something firm underneath her. She lay on her back, her eyes consuming the night sky, breathing calmly and deeply, still too weak to move. She heard something lift itself, and water dripped down on her. The force grabbed her again. It was a hand. It pulled hard, and her body surged forward. A wave lifted her gently up, pushing her even further forward. Her body fell with the wave onto something hard. She stopped, and the water raced past her. Another wave picked her up. The force pulled her again, and her body surged forward. This time, she seemed to rest onto an even harder surface. The waves lapped her feet, but she didn't move. Her body had stopped. She turned toward the sky. She saw Juan Carlos, looking pleasantly from the cliffs of Saint John. Isabella relaxed, accepting the comforting illusion under the light of her star. Pain surged through her stomach and arm. Blackness covered her once again.

9

Isabella opened her eyes, startled. Green. Why was she seeing green? Then she saw tan—tan lines, tracing light and dark green waves. Leaves? Palm leaves. She was under trees.

The trunk of a palm tree arched gracefully over her, shading her from the sun. She followed its outline to a crisply framed blue triangle. She was lying on her back, looking up. Something hard, but pliable, was under her. Sand? White sand. She was near a beach. Panther Bay? How did she get here?

Isabella lay quietly, expectantly, letting her head clear as a light wind pushed and pulled at the leaves. She used a light turn of her head to look around. A thicket of mangrove trees and branches seemed to hem her in. The familiar shine of a gumbo-limbo tree's bark began to settle her nerves. Brightly colored flowers provided a delicate under brush, despite the sandy soil. She was home. She sighed with relief.

She tried to pull herself up, but flopped back onto the sand. What had happened to her left arm? She could barely feel it; her stomach ached. Her legs were tired. Her head throbbed. Humidity thickened the air around her. Why wasn't she in her *bohio,* protected by its thick palm roof and plank walls?

Gradually, pictures formed in her mind. A ship. A brig. A cabin. Sabers. Cutlasses. A pistol. A gun shot. Stiles. Blackness. Water. A shining light. A beacon. Was she dead?

"*Bon,*" came a familiar voice nearby. She smiled. She wasn't dead—unless Jean-Michel could follow her into an afterlife. "You're finally awake. We don't have much time."

Isabella turned her head, this time more slowly, and saw Jean-Michel's bulky back working feverishly with some leaves and branches. She gathered strength with a deep breath. "Where are we?"

Jean-Michel turned and looked at her. "We've got to move. I hoped you would be stronger."

"What happened?"

"Stiles led a mutiny," Jean-Michel reported. He picked up a thick branch with another stick roped to its end. A crutch.

"Are you hurt?"

"*Comment?*" Jean-Michel looked at her confused.

"The crutch," Isabella said, turning on her side. "Are you hurt?"

He looked at the crutch. He huffed a smile and shook his head. "*Non, mon cher.*" He pointed it at her. "*C'est pour toi.*"

Isabella tried to sit up again and flopped back on the sand. She looked at her left arm and chuckled when she saw the sling binding her arm to her side. A bandage tightly wrapped her upper arm. A maroon stain discolored the cloth. Another bandage around her belly did little to hide a wide blood, red streak, extending from the middle of her stomach to her side. The cuts hurt. She was suddenly very tired again. "How long have I... we... been here?"

"Too long and not long enough," Jean-Michel said. "But, you can't sleep any longer. We have to go."

"Why?" Isabella winced as pain pierced her forehead.

Jean-Michel hurried over with a bowl cut from a palm tree branch. "Here," he said, pushing it to her lips.

"Ugh!" Isabella sputtered, instinctively pulling her head back, ignoring the pain. "Jean-Michel!"

Jean-Michel grabbed her head tenderly and steadied it. He pushed the bowl up again close to her lips. "Come on," he coaxed. "*Boit.*"

"Mick," Isabella sputtered again, "you know I don't drink *mauhi.*"

"*Oui,* but you don't have much choice now."

"Don't you have a mango?" she pleaded.

"Maybe later," he replied in a fatherly tone, shoving the bowl up to her mouth again. She scowled at him.

"Stiles' men are just around the islet," he continued. "They've been searching Panther Bay and White Cliff. Thirty minutes and they'll find us. It'll take us that long to get to the hills. They've guns this time; they know now that they will need more than cutlasses to kill us." He pushed the bowl up against her lips. Isabella turned, jostling the bowl, and spilled a few drops on her chin.

"No!"

"Drink it," he insisted. Jean-Michel's eyes softened as he saw her struggle to avoid the medicine. Isabella sat back, even though she felt embarrassingly childish for resisting him.

"Come on, *mon cher,*" Jean-Michel said. "You're not on the plantation anymore."

"It's too sweet," she objected.

Jean-Michel smiled. "*Mon Dieu,*" he chided, "sometimes I feel like your father."

Isabella scowled again, but swallowed the *maubi* in one gulp, holding her breath.

"The sweetness will give you strength," Jean-Michel pointed out. "Where do you think your mamma got all that strength for the fields? Faith can only take you so far."

Jean-Michel lifted himself off the sand and looked through a clump of tree leaves. "Quickly," he said. "We've been lucky so far, but our luck is running out faster than the rum from the vault."

"Rum from the vault?"

"Don't worry about it," Jean-Michel said, shoving the bowl up and pouring more *maubi* down her throat. For a second, he thought she was going to gag, but she kept it down. He reached behind him and pulled two mangos and a clump of finger-long plantains from underneath a log.

Isabella eyed the fruit greedily. "Now, that's more like it!"

"Thank your crew for those," Jean-Michel said.

"I will," she quipped, "just after I strap Stiles' head to a yardarm of the *Marée Rouge*." Jean-Michel stifled a protest. He continued to peel the skin off the mangos, letting her suck on the juicy pulp. He sat patiently, enjoying the sight of a reinvigorated Isabella finishing off the small bananas.

"Where are we going?" she asked, her voice stronger.

"Charlotte Amalie."

Isabella pushed herself upward, resting on her right elbow. She paused to let the dizziness fade. "Why Charlotte Amalie? It's three miles to St. Thomas from Cruz Bay, more than six miles to Charlotte Amalie."

"Stiles controls the camp," Jean-Michel said, stuffing food into a satchel. "His patrols have been searching for us since the mutiny. The camp is to the east. If we go to Cruz Bay, I can get a boat and we can be in Charlotte Amalie in half a day's sail with prevailing winds. Carl is there. He can get word to the crew."

"How many men does Stiles have?"

"Twenty-five who'll die for him. Another fifty will check the prevailing winds. We can count on a hundred, maybe a hundred and a quarter, to line up with us when its time."

"Let him find us!" Isabella said, twisting to find her sword.

"You may be ready to die," Jean-Michel said, grabbing her arm and forcing her to lay still. "But, I'm not."

"You're afraid," she said.

Jean-Michel looked at her disgusted. "You know better than that."

Isabella's face flushed. "Of course," she said. "I'm sorry Mick."

Jean-Michel stood and looked through the bushes. "Stiles got the stores. He's got the vault. He's got the *Marée Rouge*. I've heard he's been talking to Smith."

"Smith?"

"Aye," Jean-Michel confirmed. "Even with half our crew and a plan—if we have a plan—Stiles still has Smith."

"Smith put Stiles up to this?"

"Smith didn't get him to do anything that wasn't already in his heart," Jean-Michel said. He turned from the mangrove trees. He shook his head and walked back to Isabella. Kneeling down, he cupped her chin affectionately in his hand and looked into her eyes. "I don't understand you *mon cher.* You fight with the sureness of a panther, but you're still a girl. You have so much to learn about men and the heart."

"I know more than you think," she snipped. "I've loved."

"Aye, and you hate. Jacob was a worthy love. But, he was just one man."

"There've been others."

Jean-Michel raised his eyebrows skeptically.

"The American privateer—" she began.

"Robert left you for a revolution—"

"A calling I won't quibble with...."

Jean-Michel looked at her earnestly. "You're an accidental revolutionary. Robert knew what he was doing."

Isabella sat pensively. "There was Gamba," Isabella said more distantly.

"A slave?" Jean-Michel asked in disbelief. "A child's crush. Nothing serious enough to hold a mug of rum to what you had with Jacob."

"Gamba died for me."

"Many died for many things that night," Jean-Michel said. "Not all of them noble."

"Gamba loved me."

"Perhaps. I wasn't there. However, a sixteen-year old boy dying for a fourteen-year old girl? It's hard to tell if it was chivalry or foolishness."

"You know about chivalry?"

"I know enough," Jean-Michel said, growing more irritated. "Robert, like Jacob, was dedicated to an idea. They were willing to sacrifice for that idea. Jacob was even willing to sacrifice his love for you."

"Gamba died for an idea."

"I didn't know him," Jean-Michel repeated, "but I know the night. That night is legend in the Islands. Gamba's life lives on only in you and your memories. He didn't qualify as a saint."

"Gamba died for something he believed in," Isabella insisted. "He didn't go to your Church, so by what right can you judge him?"

Jean-Michel hesitated. "I don't judge him. At least, I don't judge him, as God will. That judgment has already been made, and I wasn't called to sit in judgment of him. If Gamba led his life prudently, without malice, and with a true heart for others, I'm sure he is resting well and looking over us. From what you have told me, he did not live his life for that idea. He died, and his death was tragic. As were the deaths of so many others, including your mother. The fires burned late into the night. Nevertheless, Gamba's memory does not stir the Islands. His actions only live in you. Perhaps that is enough. I am not here to judge. All I really know is what I saw with you and Jacob. And that was a deep love, one that could not have come if you had felt something equally deep with Robert or Gamba."

"You make too many claims about right and wrong for a pirate," she said.

"Isabella," Jean-Michel said with a father's sternness. "I've sailed these waters for almost twenty years. I watch the shore as well as the current. These seas have carried a lot of life, and death. Don't discount my life's journey."

She knew what love was. She loved Jacob. Jean-Michel couldn't be right.

"Santa Ana?" she spouted semi-consciously.

Jean-Michel looked at her sharply. "Forget the Dago captain. He's not worth your thoughts—any thoughts." Isabella looked at Jean-Michel, trying to disguise a hurt. Jean-Michel turned away. "Besides, he's dead."

"Think or hope?" Isabella asked. She looked at him confused.

Hadn't he just lectured her on malice, prudence, and charity? Jean-Michel wasn't a God. He was a man. She knew love. She could feel it as well as anyone. She remembered the night of Gamba's first kiss, and how natural she felt in Jacob's embrace. Isabella's heart skipped. Was the splash from the *Marée Rouge* Juan Carlos's lifeless body? "We're still alive," she said. "Does French charity extend to Spaniards?"

Jean-Michel looked down into the sand. He slowly finished shoveling supplies into the satchel. "Even if the Dago made it to shore, he doesn't know the land. He could just as easily stumble into our camp as Stiles' camp. Stiles would have killed him on the spot. Our men would have killed him. He would've starved to death before he could have figured out how to get to Cruz Bay."

"You underestimate him." Santa Ana had a power she couldn't explain. If he got to the beach, he would be alive. She was sure of it. "Besides, I'm sure he knows a plantation when he sees one. He is from the Court."

"Perhaps," Jean-Michel acknowledged. "I'll put my gold on Stiles. I don't think Santa Ana got out of the bay."

Isabella's heart deadened. How could she feel this way? She hardly knew him. He was the enemy. Her life—her calling—drove her to rid the islands and West Indies of his kind. She closed her eyes and remembered the stars—the light. The bright light seemed to draw him from the blackness of the bay. She felt stronger, more focused.

"Come on," Jean-Michel urged. "We can make Cruz Bay in a couple of days; Charlotte Amalie in a few more. We'll be dining with Carl next week. Put the Dago captain out of your head. Let's save ourselves before we worry about saving him."

Jean-Michel pulled Isabella to her feet. She struggled to keep from releasing a loud groan, as pain shot from her shoulder down to her stomach. Jean-Michel paused, sensing her pain. "Okay," she reassured him, inhaling deeply. "Let's go. I can heal in Charlotte Amalie."

"Then," Jean-Michel prodded, "we can show Mr. Stiles our true metal."

Images of the mutiny flashed before her eyes, carried by the pain throbbing in her arm and stomach. Her body stiffened. How dare Stiles challenge her, trapping her on her own ship? How could she have ignored the signs? Jean-Michel had warned her. She should have realized the crew was a powder keg. Capturing and holding Juan Carlos lit the fuse. How could she have been so stupid? Anger sparked another surge of energy, and she struggled to her feet. She swayed to one side, and Jean-Michel thrust the crutch under her arm to steady her.

"Our best bet is to go north to the Bordeaux Mountains, up the mountains, and then due west along the ridges just south of Camelberg Peak to Cruz Bay."

"I don't like walking so close to the plantations."

"Don't worry," he said. "The island's got a thousand slaves who want you alive. Only 100 or so whites work the plantations, and they're Dutch. Besides, we have friends in the villages. They aren't like the Carib. We'll find someone to dress and bandage those wounds."

***

The trail was much more difficult than Isabella had expected. She had walked Saint John's south ridges before, even spied on the steps of the sugar cane plantations, but these trails seemed brutal. They weren't the normal ones. Stiles' men would patrol the main trails. Worse, the plantation overseers would find them. Isabella would be quite the catch.

With a crutch under one arm and a hand on Jean-Michel, the trail seemed to sap every ounce of energy. She knew she was holding Jean-Michel back, but what could she do? She closed her eyes and remembered her star, her beacon from her escape from the *Marée Rouge*. As long as she could see that light, she would be okay. They would be okay. She knew it.

Cruz Bay would be risky, too many Spanish sympathizers, even among the Dutch. Charlotte Amalie would be their haven—the port was a free-for-all.

"How long do you think we should go today," she asked with labored breath.

Jean-Michel looked at her, worried. "A couple more hours at least."

That's not what she wanted to hear.

"Can we stop?" she asked. "I need something to drink."

Jean-Michel looked around impatiently. "Okay. Quickly. We'll stop if you'll have some *maubi.*"

She looked at him sharply, the first spark in her eyes since they had left the beach.

"It works," he said. "We won't make it unless you drink it."

She looked at the canteen Jean-Michel had fashioned out of a gourd. She lifted her hand as if to reach for it, but let it drop, shaking her head. "Come on," insisted Jean-Michel, grabbing the gourd and lifting it to her face.

Isabella closed her eyes, as if refusing it. The light. The beacon.

Jean-Michel looked at her again, almost pleading. "I'm not going to die out here because you're being stupid. I don't care what this stuff meant to you when you were working the fields on Hispaniola. But, we're here, on Saint John, and we're waging a war against those rats." He lowered his voice to a whisper. "Isabella, *mon cher,* I can't get justice from Stiles without your help."

Isabella grabbed the gourd and lifted it to her lips. The juice flowed into her throat. She gulped, surprised at how smooth it tasted. She didn't remember it tasting this good. In fact, she didn't remember it having any taste at all. She looked at Jean-Michel puzzled.

Jean-Michel looked at her strangely. "You look like you tasted this stuff for the first time."

"I think I have," Isabella admitted. "It's good."

"Well, then," Jean-Michel said, unsure of what to make of Isabella's transformation. Nonetheless, he was ready to go. *"Allons y."*

"Oui, mon ami," she agreed. "I feel like I can walk all the way to Cruz Bay tonight!"

Jean-Michel chuckled and picked Isabella up off the ground. They moved onward, sidestepping washed out gullies and winding their way through the lush island forest. Several times, Jean-Michel stopped to help her over fallen logs or cut through thick bushes. All Isabella could see was jungle, a vast sea of green. A heavy warm mist hung over the leaves, weaving its way through the jungle like a slowly moving river. Isabella thought she was going to pass out.

10

Isabella woke and her instincts told her—commanded her—to lie still. She looked for her star, but she could only see gray above her. A pale glow was rising from the east, but the shadows of the ridge and Bordeaux Mountains hid details around her. She felt like eyes were watching her.

Isabella pulled a thin gauze blanket and fresh palm leaves over herself, timing the movements with the breeze in the trees. She tried moving her left arm, but a sharp pain reminded her of the gash fighting to mend itself. She tried her right arm, but a slight rustle from the palm leaves convinced her to lie still and listen.

Isabella turned her head, scanning the shadows for something familiar. Jean-Michel should be close by. She couldn't see anything. Surely, he didn't go hunting for food, not before daylight. Why did she have a dark feeling that something was watching her, noting every movement, even her thoughts? She closed her eyes again. Where was her star?

There. A rustle in the bushes. Was it just the morning breeze? Isabella's eyes began to focus. She fought every muscle to keep herself still. Another rustle. Something was coming.

A long man-like figure emerged from the bushes, its frame a thin silhouette against the bleaching sky. It was too thin to be Jean-Michel. It didn't appear to be carrying a weapon. It couldn't be one of Stiles' men either. She waited.

The figure crossed into the trail. Seemingly satisfied that no one else was near; the figure turned back branches and poked through clumps of leaves. Her arm and stomach ached.

Isabella watched as the figure continued its search. It must be looking for her. How did it know she was here? What would she do when it found her?

The figure disappeared into the bushes. It came back, and searched the other side of the camp. The figure slowly made its way toward her hiding place. If she waited, maybe, just maybe, it would miss her.

Enough! She thought, disgusted with herself. What was she doing, hiding from this thing? How could she cower under these leaves? If she were going to die, she told herself, at least it should be on her terms. She wasn't going to let this thing have the satisfaction of seeing her paralyzed by fear. Where was Jean-Michel, anyway?

Isabella bolted through the leaves, lifting herself to her knees. She didn't even wince at the pain from her wounds this time. What did it matter? She stared at the figure.

"Who are you?" she demanded. "What do you want?"

The figure stood steadfast, unphased by the sudden appearance of the Creole buccaneer from the jungle floor. The sun broke over the mountain, lighting the clearing. The figure was a man. An African. He looked at her with unsurprised eyes, as if he were expecting her, almost as if he had invited her into the jungle and camp.

"Who are you?" she demanded again. "What do you want?"

The man pointed his finger at Isabella and shook his head, covering his mouth with his other hand. Why did he want her to be quiet? She grabbed a branch from the ground and held it threateningly. The man looked at her, amused. She blushed, thankful for the semi-darkness. She held onto the stick anyway.

The man said something, but his words seemed like gibberish. His long vowels vaguely reminded her of the conversations she heard when the elders talked at the plantation on Hispaniola. That seemed like another world, another life altogether.

Isabella looked at the man again. He was thin, muscular, and tall. His face was round, almost like a melon, but he had a long forehead. His arms were thick for a man of his stature, hardened by heavy lifting. His fingers moved colorfully and forcefully. A cutlass would find a nice home in those hands, she thought. The man said something else, this time more dismissively. Whatever he was saying, she couldn't fathom his meaning. Her face warmed with the frustration. She had to do something. Where was Jean-Michel? She couldn't wait here much longer. She glanced back along the trail, suddenly fearful that Stiles and his men were close.

The man walked toward her, almost as if he sensed her fear. Isabella lifted the branch and braced herself, using the same defensive position that she had used countless times before after she had boarded one of the *Marée Rouge*'s hapless targets. The strange man stopped, surprised by her defensiveness. He said something again. This time, his tone was more urgent.

The African looked at the sun, motioning frantically for her to follow him. She looked around the small clearing again. It felt like home in an odd way. If the African wanted to capture her, surely more of his friends would have arrived by now. Did Jean-Michel send him for her? How could she trust him?

Frustrated, the man waved at her with his hands and began to move down the trail alone. His clothes were easy to see now in the dawn light. His worn breeches and soiled shirt looked as if he hadn't washed them in weeks, if ever. He was a slave. Had he escaped from the plantation, a maroon, or was he leading her to it? She thought back to the night her plantation burned. She couldn't trust anyone.

"Wait!" she called to him. He stopped and turned, looking back hopefully.

"Do you know Jean-Michel?" she asked. His expression turned tentative. "He's tall," she said, gesturing to show his height, "and big," moving her hands apart to outline his broad shoulders. The African's expression turned pleasant. "He has a beard," she said, running her hands from ear to ear and over her chin. The African nodded. Isabella smiled. "I'll come."

The African smiled and turned back toward the trail. Isabella followed him cautiously, clutching the branch. Isabella smiled to herself. What would Juan Carlos have done? Would he have been the brash army captain, trudging onward on his own? Would he have used the diplomacy of the Court to accept the African's offer? Those questions would set off another round of lively sparring. She relished their little match on board the *Marée Rouge* after sending Smith packing back to the *Wasp*. Isabella's smile disappeared as she realized she would never be able to ask him.

Isabella's strength surprised her. The sleep left her refreshed. The sun energized her. The African's arrival seemed to push the blood through her veins. She almost felt normal. Isabella's feet stepped steadily along the trail. Perhaps she had just needed more time on land after three weeks at sea and so little rest. She felt confident she could walk to Cruz Bay, even without Jean-Michel's help now. A pain pierced through her, reminding her that the wounds were still fresh. She yelped softly despite a mighty effort to stay quiet.

The African stopped and looked back, his eyes betraying his concern. She clutched her side with her left hand, but this simply aggravated the cut in her arm. The African extended his hand as if to catch her.

"I'm okay," she insisted, pushing his hand away. Jacob had taught her never to show weakness, and she knew instinctively now was not the time to forget that lesson. She needed something to help her walk. Where was her crutch? She looked desperately around and swore. How could she have left it? Her heart sank. Stiles. The crutch would tell him everything. She was wounded; they were on her trail. He would be able to smell her blood. Isabella clutched her head and shook it violently. How stupid! If Jean-Michel had just been there.... Where was her head? She closed her eyes, hoping to see her star, but it had faded. Her heart began to race.

The African stared at her, his face a confused mix of concern and alarm. "It's nothing," she said, waving him on. How stupid. Anger boiled inside her as she cursed herself over and over. Juan Carlos. What would he think about such mental weakness? The crutch would give him a point up in their match. Surely, he didn't make these kinds of errors, at least not on the battlefield. They would have killed him long ago. However, Isabella reminded herself, he was likely dead, forced into Panther Bay, mortally wounded. Her heart sank again at the thought of Juan Carlos, struggling in the water. What was his last thought as death became the only path? Did he accept his fate and suffer the sting of salt water pouring into his lungs to end it quickly? Did he struggle, fighting for life, until he knew there was no hope? What would his God say about his death?

Stiles would pay for his disloyalty and cruelty, Isabella vowed. She had to get to Cruz Bay, and then to Charlotte Amalie. There, she would plot her revenge. She would hunt down Stiles and destroy him.

***

Hours passed as Isabella trudged behind the African, ignoring the arresting beauty of the jungle. They wound their way along increasingly unfamiliar trails. She struggled to keep up, pushing leaves and bushes aside, stomping flowers of all colors and kinds, skipping over gullies. Dead branches became major obstacles. At least, Isabella reminded herself, the trail's poor condition meant no one had used it for a while. She pulled a red finger-sized banana from a tree, popped it through its skin, and felt its mushy meat give her a quick boost. Once, in a rare moment, the African gave her a fresh mango. The juice recharged her, just as Jean-Michel had said it would do. The African didn't break step.

The trail eventually turned southwest, toward the plantations. Was the African luring her into a trap?

Isabella's uneasiness seemed to grow with each step. Perhaps he was just toying with her. No, she told herself. The African was about to leave the camp without her. Someone must have sent him. Could Jean-Michel have traveled this far at night? How long had she been sleeping? Had she really slept only one night in the clearing? What really happened to Juan Carlos? She tried to beat down her yearning to know, a secret hope he was still alive.

The African strode quickly and confidently along the trail, seemingly forgetting that she still had a foot long gash in her stomach and a hobbled left arm. He knew the jungle well. At times, he helped her cross small streams and down into the ravines. The humidity seemed to entrap them in palm trees and brush with an odor that curled her lip. The plantations were close. Jean-Michel surely would not bring her to a plantation. They would hang her in minutes. Who had sent the African?

"*¿Habla espanol?*" Isabella rasped, after what now seemed like days of hiking. Her stomach ached more than ever, and her arm throbbed. She was tired; she needed to rest. The African didn't slow or turn back. He simply walked on, ignoring her. Isabella fumed. Why didn't he talk to her?

Her nervousness heightened as the trail leveled off. They crossed a ridge and began a slow decent. Sugarcane. The smell seemed to steal her breath. She shuddered. The smooth slice of the machetes seemed to chase her through the jungle. She must be losing her mind!

"Wait!" she called. The African stopped, surprising Isabella. "How much longer?"

The African said something again but she couldn't understand. He motioned as if their destination was just around the corner.

A few minutes later, the trail flattened. The ground hardened. Rocks seemed to form a crude roadbed. The palm trees pulled back, letting bright sunlight in. Two people could now walk side-by-side comfortably. Soon Isabella could see the hoof prints of a horse or donkey.

They rounded a tight curve. The trees fell away dramatically. Isabella stopped, startled by what appeared to be a village. Wood frame buildings with palm roofs, similar to her *bohio*, walled in the trail. Children, tattered pants and shirts barely hanging to their little bodies, darted in and out. African women seemed to move deliberately about. It seemed like a normal slave village, but Isabella's instincts made her stop. She couldn't see any sign of an overseer or plantation foreman.

The African's steps slowed. Isabella's heart quickened and her breathing deepened. What did he see? Were they in the right village? A woman looked up as they rounded the corner. She turned and disappeared into one of the buildings. The African turned to Isabella and grabbed her arm. Isabella pulled her arm away. It was the first time he had touched her. The African's eyes were wide, even fearful.

"What?" she asked. He started to nudge her backward. Isabella resisted. "I'm not going back," she insisted.

The African said something again, this time more forcefully, although his voice was low. Isabella looked at him and shook her head. "I'm not going back into the jungle," she repeated. She looked at the *bohios*. "You brought me here for a reason," she said, mostly to convince herself. "Let's find out what it is." The African looked at her again and relented.

The village had six or eight rectangular houses from what she could see. They seemed like bunkhouses with doors, opening onto a main path separating the rows. The wood frames rested on a stone foundation, unusually sturdy for slave quarters. Well maintained buildings had fresh wood patched in the holes of the walls. The village was much better than the hellhole she had grown up in on Hispaniola. The plantation's owner must be vested. The slaves probably bunked in these buildings; most were obviously still in the fields. Why didn't she see any white men?

She looked down the path again. Her heart jumped from her chest.

"Jean-Michel!" she yelled, waving her hand. She started to walk toward him. Why didn't he wave back?

Jean-Michel stood like a statue outside the last building. He weakly raised his hand. Something was wrong.

"Jean-Michel," she called again. "*Comment ca-va?*"

Jean-Michel stood without responding. Isabella turned back toward the African. His expression was... angry? A trap!

SLAP!

"Don't move!" screamed a voice beside her in Spanish. Doors clapped open as boots shuffled across wooden floors. Isabella twirled, first right, then left. Bodies thudded onto the thick grass around her. A cloud of dust rose amid the buildings. All she could see were the muzzles of flintlock muskets. She knew instantly the fuzzy blobs behind her were Spanish soldiers—garrison troops.

Jean-Michel was walking toward her now, flanked by soldiers. One had a sword drawn, its tip obviously resting close to Jean-Michel's back. Isabella stood still. Any twitch could set off a flint. She would be dead before the lead balls left her body.

Anger overwhelmed her. How could Jean-Michel have done this? Why didn't he warn her? What did they promise him? How could he forsake his vow to Jacob?

Isabella's anger ebbed as Jean-Michel drew close. He had a noticeable gimp; his face swollen, blood dripped from his mouth. His eyes were white islands amid a sea of blue bruises. His beard was matted and stiff.

"Chain her hands and feet," said a jovial saber-wielding Spaniard. "We'll have a fine time in San Juan once we deliver her and the frog to the viceroy."

Isabella's heart fell into her stomach as she realized the gallows were no longer a fear, but a certainty.

11

"Good news, *Capitano!*" said a plump man behind an expansive mahogany desk. He used his thick fingers to push himself up from his chair. He skirted around the tabletop, wobbling like a carnival clown, rolling forward with each step. His fluffed up, tightly woven wool shirt, pants, and pastel blue coat would have been comical if it weren't for the place he worked and the territory he commanded. "We've achieved an important victory." He extended his hand excitedly.

Juan Carlos Lopez de Santa Ana dutifully approached the viceroy and respectfully took his hand, bowing deeply. Santa Ana kissed a bulbous gold ring, trying to hide his confusion about why Rodriquez had summoned him. Had he captured the mutinous Stiles? Had he recovered Isabella's body? Santa Ana's heart fell at the thought of her lifeless, cut body, drifting in the ocean currents.

Rodriquez's runner had been useless. A native, he could barely speak Spanish; all Juan Carlos could understand was the urgent tone. His only clue was the note with the official seal of the Colonial Office of the Viceroy of the West Indies. Now, he had to be patient. He couldn't let the viceroy know any more than possible about the sinking of the *Ana Maria*, or his embarrassing capture by his prey, the notorious Pirate of Panther Bay.

Juan Carlos could not help but think about them as he recovered. The escape from the *Marée Rouge* completely drained him. Another day in the jungle and he would have died. Thank God for Dutch neutrality.

"We caught them!" Rodriguez chortled, unable to contain himself. He thumped his palm down on the desk. "Our soldiers surrounded them. They resisted, but they're in chains."

Rodriguez walked between Juan Carlos and the desk. Oil landscapes, imported from Iberia, disguised the stone fortress's interior with a civil decor. Juan Carlos preferred the fortress. San Juan's plaster walls and military architecture comforted him. The viceroy's awkward attempt at making the fort a palace unsettled him.

"Excellent," Juan Carlos said, still unsure of what he meant. If they had captured Stiles, how could they have surrounded him? The viceroy had dispatched three schooners, but they couldn't have moved well enough in the bay to surround the *Marée Rouge*. Was the fight on land? "Did we lose any men in the fight?"

"Not a soldier or sailor," Rodriguez said.

Juan Carlos distrusted Rodriguez, and his suspicion nagged at his gut. He had hoped the feeling was simple fatigue. The trip from Cruz Bay on the small merchant bark had drained him even more than thrashing through the jungles of Saint John. The sail to San Juan seemed even longer. The feeling persisted. It gnawed at his insides.

"Two days ago," Rodriguez continued, waving Juan Carlos into an overstuffed chair. "A detail of soldiers searching Saint John found them, hiding like cowards in a plantation."

"A plantation?" Juan Carlos said, still standing. Why would Stiles be on a plantation? "The Dutch don't like to meddle let alone pick sides. Why would they help us?"

"Ahhh, you've done your homework," Rodriguez said, as if his son had passed his first exam. "They must teach our young leaders well at the academy. You've made the most of your recovery."

Juan Carlos closed his eyes, trying to squelch embarrassment. He now felt like the schoolboy when scolded by the headmaster. "I've learned much on the battlefield."

"Of course, of course," Rodriguez said. "You have learned much in the field… as your record shows." He looked at Juan Carlos more studiously. "Even the Dutch don't care for these high-seas criminals," he continued. "They need to sell their crops. They can't do that if traders are pillaged by rogues."

Rodriguez made a quick gesture with his hand and Juan Carlos sat down in an overstuffed, overly regal chair. Stiles, he thought, would certainly be a target. The Dutch wouldn't put Isabella or Jean-Michel in the same company as Stiles. Besides, her wrath seemed directed at Spain, not the Dutch. She seemed angry with him, too. Why? They had fought; she had won. Juan Carlos cursed himself for caring. He had his orders. They were all rogues. They were all little more than savages, only slightly better than the Africans hauled over to work the plantations. The West Indies needed purging of all pirates. How could he have any sympathy for them?

Rodriguez smiled at Juan Carlos. "I trust Rosa has made you comfortable?"

"Yes, Your Excellency," he responded. Rosa. Yes, she had helped his recovery. She was beautiful and smart. She seemed out of place in this New World frontier, a refined beauty among grizzled warriors. He couldn't help but be drawn to her. She reminded him of the women in the Royal Court. He watched them longingly, a stylish symbol of his King's empire. How could he resist?

"She's been very kind," Juan Carlos said, "and attentive. I feel fully recovered." He prayed Rodriguez wouldn't pry further. She was strong, but even he could see the bitterness eating away at her. The islands were suffocating her. She envied those far away—those at home—tending to the needs of the Court. "Once the pirates have been purged from the seas...," she had confessed to him just yesterday.

"Good." Rodriguez said, noticing Juan Carlos's smile. "Rosa was feeling quite alone on this God-forsaken island. I think she was excited to see a fresh face. Especially one with such an important assignment, one with news of the King and his Court."

"*Muchas gracias, Senor Rodriguez,*" Juan Carlos said. "I simply do the bidding of my King."

"So you do," said Rodriguez, a bit too dismissively for Juan Carlos's taste.

Rosa was much like Isabella, Juan Carlos thought, and wildly different. Isabella was comfortable and natural, standing on the deck of an armed brigantine. She could even command a ship of the line if asked—50 cannons or more, at least twice stacked. She said she was a slave, but he couldn't imagine her under an overseer's whip. Her reaction to Smith's quartermaster's whip seemed to come deep from within her soul, not a commitment to saving her prisoner.

Rosa would likely fall overboard. Her skill was men and ambition. Rosa could navigate the mud-covered mule paths of the Court's politics with ease and grace. Isabella would likely blow it up. He smiled at the thought of the two of them in a room together.

"Where are the prisoners?" he asked.

"Ahh," the viceroy nodded. "Of course. Business. Your reputation precedes you Senior Santa Ana. Even without your papers, you have a reputation for focus and determination. Admirable qualities. Qualities far beyond your years, for sure. You'll need these qualities in the West Indies if we are to succeed. That, of course, is why His Most Catholic Majesty has sent you to me."

"Thank you, Your Excellency," Juan Carlos replied formally. "I will do all God permits me."

"Still," Rodriguez said, "I am not sure you are ready."

"I don't understand."

"Your youth. I have never had anyone so young in such an important position. It's not a job for boys."

"I am up to the task," Juan Carlos said confidently. "My field experience against the French and rebellion surely puts to rest any concerns about courage."

"Indeed, it does," Rodriguez said. "But these are not the fields of Europe. Judgment is far more important than courage, or even battlefield tactics."

Juan Carlos grew frustrated. "I escaped pirates, navigated my way through the jungles of Saint John, and hired a sloop of natives to bring me to Puerto Rico."

"Impressive feats," Rodriguez acknowledged. "But the *Ana Maria* was lost."

"All the details are in my report," Juan Carlos responded tersely.

Rodriguez looked at him studiously.

"My intelligence on the pirates was accurate?" Juan Carlos said.

Rodriguez nodded. "To be sure, you've had more tests than all the other counselors dispatched from the Court combined. You've handled them admirably. Nevertheless, this is a difficult part of the world. It's the New World." He leaned forward and looked directly into Juan Carlos's eyes. "Most don't survive."

"Don't survive?"

"Oh," Rodriguez said, as if correcting a child's math error. "I don't mean dying. At least not physically. The island fruits give life we can only dream about at home, and a spot of rum here and there will do wonders. Most simply lose their spirit; they lose heart." He lifted his forefinger to his temple. "They lose focus and commitment." He looked directly into Juan Carlos's eyes again. "Their loyalties become confused." Rodriguez turned toward the window. "To me, that's death."

Juan Carlos looked at Rodriguez forthrightly. "I will survive."

The viceroy looked back. "I suspect you will. I'll be watching with a keen eye. It's a bit of a game I've developed—how long will the next one last? Will the West Indies make you stronger? Or, will it destroy you?"

"I will do more than survive," Juan Carlos said. "I will learn. I will grow. I will thrive."

Rodriguez gave a polite nod. He walked around his desk to an open window that stretched across the wall. The sky was unusually clear—not a cloud visible. The ocean glittered, giving it a soothing calm. The seagulls seemed to be flying in place against the stiff sea breeze.

Juan Carlos suddenly found himself on the *Marée Rouge*, the wind sweeping through his hair; her bow cutting cleanly through the surf. Isabella stood confidently at the ship's wheel, reveling in the freedom of an open ocean. Isabella. Isabella? How could he think of her? Now, of all times. Juan Carlos blinked himself out of his daydream.

Rodriguez was still looking out the window, his back turned to Juan Carlos. Juan Carlos let out a slow, deep breath to settle his nerves. The viceroy's office and quarters were odd places, he mused. What kind of colonial viceroy would govern from a prison? He suspected he would soon find out.

"I don't see how these islands could destroy me," Juan Carlos said.

"Don't be a fool," Rodriguez warned. "Your first worry will not be the Islands. First, survive the Carib. Then worry about the vile pests and diseases carried by these filthy natives. You'll find your easiest problem will be the high-seas criminals like those that sank the *Ana Maria*." Bitterness laced his words.

"I can protect myself from the Carib," Juan Carlos pointed out. "Disease is in God's hand; Spain's armies have—"

"Above all," Rodriguez interrupted, turning back toward him. "Stay loyal to your King." That seemed more like an order. Why would he worry about Juan Carlos's loyalty?

"I've risked my life for my King more than once," Juan Carlos said.

"Si," the Viceroy acknowledged. "I suppose I won't have to worry about you *going native* on me, eh?" He paused. "As long as your reports are complete and your heart remains loyal."

"Of course," Juan Carlos said. What did he mean by that? Juan Carlos didn't remember anything in his briefing in the Royal Court about mutiny or rebellion. "My information about the whereabouts of the *Marée Rouge* was accurate?"

"Very precise," Rodriguez acknowledged. "Unusually precise, as was your report on the sinking of the *Ana Maria*. The murder of her captain was a stunning act of cruelty. Too bad, you couldn't give me more details about the surviving crew. A truly barbaric act by those pirates. No food or water. How could they possibly expect them to survive? I'm impressed with your ability to remember such detail without any prior experience or knowledge of the West Indies. Unfortunately, the *Marée Rouge* was nowhere to be found."

"What?" Juan Carlos stammered. If Stiles was not the prisoner, who was? Smith? Only one other person would be found hiding in a plantation like a fugitive—Isabella! Juan Carlos began to feel warm under the cotton shirt and breeches. Thank goodness, he wasn't wearing his uniform yet.

"Don't worry about it, my young counselor," Rodriguez said lightly, almost playfully. "Surely you couldn't expect the ship to be there after a week? These pirates are not stupid. They would have moved on, assuming you would have survived."

"Of course," Juan Carlos said, embarrassed at his naiveté. "But, how did you find the Pirate of Panther Bay?"

"We searched the island with patrols," Rodriguez explained. "We heard that the pirates had been visiting the plantations and aiding the slaves. We simply followed the leads. The slaves are not stupid, either. They know harboring fugitives and criminals is punishable by death."

Juan Carlos sat, his head spinning. This wasn't making sense. He just couldn't see Isabella living with slaves, but she was alive. That was good news, he thought. Stiles was still free. What would they do to Isabella and Jean-Michel? A trial? Why was he even thinking of them? He cursed himself for caring.

The door to the room opened swiftly behind them.

"Ahh, Rosa," Rodriguez said with a pleasant coo. Juan Carlos scrambled up from his chair, turning to welcome her.

Rosa strode into the room, carrying the air of nobility. A breeze bubbled through her dress, giving her movements a flamboyance usually beat down by the humid air. She was older than Isabella, about

Juan Carlos' age. Her stride seemed to give her a grace that overcame the colorful simplicity of her clothing. Her dress was plain and didn't carry the ornate accessories of women in the King's Court. No silk or lace. Juan Carlos found this refreshing. Pulling her hair back and tight gave her a regal beauty unmatched among the women he had seen in the West Indies, despite the plain clothes necessitated by the sticky heat of the Caribbean. He couldn't help but follow her as she embraced Rodriguez and kissed him delicately on the cheek. She smiled at Juan Carlos. "What are you boring our hero from the Court with now, *padre*?" she teased.

"Nothing you haven't heard before," Rodriguez said with slight irritation.

"Now Father," she chastised. "You don't think he will go native, do you?"

Rodriguez looked at her, even more annoyed. "You were too young."

"I was fourteen; old enough."

"Your Excellency," interrupted Juan Carlos.

"Haven't you told him about Jacob?" Rosa said, with surprising intuition.

"Jacob is neither here nor there," Rodriguez said. "Let's move on; we've got business."

"Excellent idea," Juan Carlos said. He felt uncomfortable in the middle of the father-daughter sparring, but he found himself sucked into the intrigue.

"I was just telling our young captain that we've caught the Pirate of Panther Bay," Rodriguez spouted. Juan Carlos's heart skipped. "She and her rat of a lieutenant were hiding with slaves at a plantation on Saint John. They'll be in El Morro tomorrow night. She'll hang in San Cristóbal by the end of the fortnight."

"*Magnifico, padre,*" Rosa said, turning so that her dress lifted lightly, giving it a festive rustle.

Juan Carlos's heart seemed to stop. "Your Excellency?"

"Surely you don't have sympathy for these sea rats?" Rosa asked, eyeing him suspiciously.

"No," Juan Carlos said quickly. "I do not."

"Of course not. Deal with these vermin for what they are," Rodriguez instructed him.

"Deal with them quickly. Let everyone in the West Indies know we intend to enforce the laws of Spain throughout the New World. Stiff and swift punishment for those willing to break those laws is the only recourse."

"Of course, Your Excellency," Juan Carlos said, trying to hide a growing feeling of emptiness. Isabella, dead? Her body hanging lifeless on a scaffolding for all San Juan to see? Why not? She was a criminal. That was the punishment for challenging the Empire. Wasn't it?

"Good," Rodriguez said. "I need you to get whatever information you can from her and her lieutenant. You have two days to find out where the other ships are. We will organize a squadron and rid these waters of their filth. Our trading routes should be free of these vermin by the end of the year."

Juan Carlos's heart quickened. Isabella's interrogation on the *Marée Rouge* seemed like yesterday. She had smoothly seized the high ground. Would she be as clever and resourceful in El Morro? A veil darkened his thoughts. Isabella seemed to sense, but not know, his secret. Could she have guessed why the *Ana Maria* sank? Did any of the survivors overhear his argument with the *Ana Maria*'s captain? What would Rodriguez do if he found out? What would Isabella think if… when… she discovered the truth? Doubt began to eat into his confidence. *"Si, Senor."*

"Father." Rosa had been watching near the window. "Do you think Senor Santa Ana is the right person for this job?"

"Of course," Rodriguez said, turning his portly body from Juan Carlos. "His job is to counsel me on the pirate menace." Juan Carlos remained silent, pondering Rosa's warning.

"I was concerned," she said after a pause, "that someone more neutral should interview her."

Juan Carlos started to object. Rodriguez silenced him with a raised palm. "What do you mean?"

"He was her prisoner!" Rosa said with apparent disbelief. "Don't you think it would be a bit embarrassing for him to be interviewing her after she had so brutally chained him on her ship?"

"All the more reason for him to use whatever means necessary to get the information we want," the viceroy said with finality. "I'm sure the embarrassment will ensure Senor Santa Ana will get everything we need."

"Yes, Your Excellency," Juan Carlos said confidently. He wasn't sure, nor, apparently, was Rosa.

12

"How stupid," Isabella chanted repeatedly, resting her head against the cold stone of the prison walls. She was exhausted. Pulling at the shackles again sent an awful racket bouncing off the walls and into her ears.

"I'm sorry, *mon cher,*" Jean-Michel said dimly. They were the first words they had spoken to each other for days.

"How could you do this to me?" she questioned.

Jean-Michel lifted his head. "What do you mean?"

"Don't play with me Jean-Michel," Isabella snipped. *"Ne fait pas les jeux."*

"Stupid girl," Jean-Michel growled.

Isabella glared at him through the fading light. She was tired, hungry, and angry. How could she let them catch her like this?

Jean-Michel was barely visible across the room. "They wouldn't have caught me if you hadn't sent that African after me," she said.

No! She didn't really believe it, but she said it anyway. Her eyes began to glisten. A tear fell down her cheek, washing through the dirt and sweat caked on her face.

"What would you have done?" he asked, as if confessing. "A few more minutes passed and Jean-Michel whispered, "I didn't send the Dagos after you. I didn't even know they were on the island."

A low hollow whistle wound through the cell, sending up a funnel of red dust. They held their breath, hoping the wind would die down and let them breathe again. Where were they? The fortress was on a hill. She knew that from her perch on the aft crow's nest. She had seen it dozens of times. However, the halls and stairways had confused her. They went up at first, then down, down, down. At least they could tell day from night from the small windows lining the top of the cell.

"Did I betray you on the *Marée Rouge* when Stiles was hunting you like a wild pig?" Jean-Michel asked.

"No," she admitted, feeling very young and immature.

"That didn't change in the jungle. Perhaps you missed my bruises when you were captured."

Isabella sniffed, trying to hold back her tears. But she was too weak, and she began to cry softly. Isabella was thankful for the dim light now. She wanted to pull her hands from the shackles and wipe her face, but the shackles kept them too far away. Only her legs were free.

"Take heart, *mon cher,*" Jean-Michel said. "We're not dead yet." She knew he was trying to comfort her, but his voice was weak and timid.

The Spanish lieutenant at the plantation was the first to beat her. The lieutenant on the schooner bound for San Juan beat her again.

The beatings were nothing compared to her entrapment in the lieutenant's cramped cabin. Her shirt ripped open, her ribs were badly bruised. He was excited; she was weak. He pulled down her breeches. That's when she decided she would rather die in a pool of blood of her own making than submit to him. It should have been her last act of rebellion. *It had started in a run down slave cabin on Hispaniola when she was just fourteen.* As the lieutenant started to climb on top of her, it was going to end in a rundown slave cabin on Saint John. Was that such a bad run for a pirate? Isabella scraped the scab forming across her stomach, unleashing a torrent of blood onto the floor. Juan Carlos would probably laugh at the irony when he heard the news. The pagan pirate, sacrificing herself for a noble sense of self-worth. Perhaps he would visit her in the afterlife she mused, as blood gushed onto the cabin floor.

Isabella had shaken her head violently as blood poured from her body. She swore at herself for thinking of the Dago captain, as she lay sprawled on the floor dying. The only one she wanted to see rising from the dead was Jacob. What use was that? What counsel could he possibly provide now? He died at the tip of a sword. All those thoughts and more rushed through Isabella's mind as the loss of blood weakened her body.

Nevertheless, her time hadn't arrived yet. For some reason she could not understand, the officer sent for the ship's surgeon. Perhaps she would live to rebel yet another day.

That was more than a week ago. She now longed for the sway of the ship. Isabella closed her eyes as she sat in her cell and strained to think of something prettier and happier. She hadn't seen her star for days. She seemed to be falling slowly into a crevice, leading deep into a hole of nothingness, an endless black hole. She didn't mind; it seemed a better place; better than where she sat now, bound and helpless, imprisoned on a fortress island. She didn't even mind the stench anymore. She wasn't even sure she cared.

When Isabella woke up, a faint glow from the moon lit up a small box on the opposite wall. Was the light coming from her star? She was tired, so tired.

"Jean-Michel?" she whispered. Nothing. Her heart raced. Was Jean-Michel gone? What would she do without Jean-Michel? She was barely letting go of Jacob. She couldn't stand to lose Jean-Michel too. Her head felt heavy and large. She lifted it from her chest, and rolled over to where she thought Jean-Michel had been in chains earlier. She peered into the darkness.

"Jean-Michel?" she whispered more frantically. She thought she could make out the outline of a body. Panic seemed to overtake her arms; she yanked at the chains fiercely. "Jean-Michel!" she yelled. "*Mon ami! Mon père!* Are you there?" She rattled the chains again.

"I'm here *mon cher*," he said weakly. "Stop making so much noise."

"Jean-Michel, why didn't you answer?"

"Did you really think I would send the Dagos after you," he asked quietly. "What happened to your faith?"

Isabella didn't answer. "I was angry. I was blaming you because I could only blame someone I loved."

"That, my girl, is something we need to work on."

Isabella chuckled. "We have time to work on it now."

Jean-Michel laughed. "*Oui, mon cher.* Now is probably the best time."

They sat in the darkness, enjoying the brief, light-hearted exchange.

"Jean-Michel?" Isabella asked after a few more minutes. "Do you really think Senor Santa Ana is like the others?"

"Isabella. He's dead. Let him go."

"I know," she said softly. "I can't." It seemed like the thought of seeing him again was the only thing keeping her alive.

"Why are you even thinking of him? I don't understand it. Especially after Jacob."

"I don't understand it myself. He confuses me."

"Santa Ana is not Jacob."

"I know that." Isabella sat back again. Juan Carlos was definitely not Jacob. Nevertheless, he gave her something Jacob did not—could not. She wasn't sure what it could be. With Jacob, she felt young and inexperienced. With Juan Carlos, she felt weak and insecure. Jacob fed her confidence through strength. Juan Carlos fed her passion. He met her on her terms.

"Don't give Santa Ana another thought," Jean-Michel told her in the dark. "He will consume your thoughts and passions. He cannot share your destiny."

Her destiny. The prophecy. She hadn't thought of it since the mutiny.

"Why not?" asked Isabella. She was feeling tired again. Jean-Michel's voice carried a confidence she didn't share.

After a thoughtful pause, Isabella asked, "Do you remember Smith and his quartermaster?"

"Aye."

She could tell he was smiling, probably that proud fatherly smile he donned when she succeeded at something unexpected. "That should have been enough to send every rogue pirate out of our waters."

"Every rogue but the one under our own covers," Isabella said thoughtfully. "Santa Ana understood. He seemed to understand what we were doing."

"A Dago can never understand what we do."

"Jacob did."

"Jacob was not a true Spaniard. His mother was Spanish. His father was English. Jacob was a Catholic, not a Jew."

"He served the King of Spain," Isabella reminded him.

"Yes," Jean-Michel admitted. "But he left. Santa Ana is loyal to his King. Remember? King, God, Country. That was not Jacob's creed. Jacob was loyal to himself. He was loyal to his purpose." She could feel Jean-Michel's eyes on her. "Like you."

"Juan Carlos reminds me of Jacob."

Jean-Michel was quiet. "I suppose it really doesn't matter now; Santa Ana is dead. We'll all be dead by the Sabbath."

A door opened outside the cell. Sharp clicks echoed in the hall, as boots carried someone toward their door. One, two, now three pairs.

They heard the cling of metal on metal. The bolt on the cell door moved. The door creaked open. Light flooded the room. The lanterns seemed to be as bright as the midday sun, forcing Jean-Michel and Isabella to turn their heads and squint.

Isabella's eyes adjusted to three dark shadows against the flickering torches in the hall. One shadow carried a lantern and lifted it to a hook on the wall above their heads. The lantern swayed, forcing their shadows to dance.

"Wake up!" said one of the figures. He walked over to Jean-Michel and kicked his boot. Jean-Michel rattled his arms in symbolic defiance. The figure walked over to Isabella and kicked her boots. She didn't move.

"Give me a light." A second lantern appeared. The first figure lifted the lantern up against Isabella's face. The flames seemed to burn a hole in her cheek. She turned her head.

"The girl," he ordered, almost spitting in her face.

Two men walked over to Isabella and pulled her to her feet. They unlatched the shackles from her wrists and pushed her up against the wall. She faced the man for the first time as she leaned against the stones.

"I think it's time for us to talk," the first man said. He began a pace in front of her.

She could see them more clearly now. She didn't recognize the men flanking her, but the one giving the orders was vaguely familiar. He wasn't a soldier. He was a sailor. He wore a Spanish navy uniform without an officer's rank. His face was long and thin. A beard connected his ears. His eyes glazed over with anger, even hatred.

"Do I know you?" Isabella asked, trying to brace herself for whatever he intended to do. The image of a forgotten run-down cabin on a plantation on Hispaniola flicked through her mind. An image of the cabin on the schooner flickered before her eyes. Isabella felt her arms tense.

The man glared at her. They had met. She couldn't remember from where, but they had met. The man lifted his hand and pulled it across her face with a loud smack. She expected pain to shoot through her head, but she seemed barely to feel it.

"Remember me?" The voice seemed familiar now, too.

She turned toward him, a glint of defiance in her eyes. "No," she lied. She wasn't going to let him think his beating would work on her.

He slapped her again. Blood trickled from her mouth.

"You murdered my captain!"

The *Ana Maria*! He was the chief boatswain. Isabella had interrogated him just before she had killed his captain. What did she tell Juan Carlos as they watched Smith sail back to his ship? Letting the quartermaster live worked on the hearts and minds of Smith's crew. Perhaps Juan Carlos was right after all.

"Leave her alone," Jean-Michel called from the darkness. His tone was defiant, but it lacked the confidence of just moments earlier. "Your captain could have surrendered and spared his life. He chose to fight. He challenged us when the battle was lost. His fate and that of his crew—you—was his, not ours."

He had to know the Creed, Isabella thought. It was a just outcome by the laws of the sea.

The boatswain ignored Jean-Michel's plea and stood glaring at Isabella. "You sent us out to sea with no food or water." The boatswain was eerily calm, cool like an executioner. He turned back to the wall and picked up a cotton bag. She hadn't noticed it earlier, but it was long and thin. She began to breathe more quickly. The bag was long enough for a saber, or even a musket. Was he going to kill her now? The boatswain took off his jacket and rolled up his sleeves.

"Now," he said somberly, "you'll pay."

"Leave her alone," growled Jean-Michel more loudly. This time, the tone was a warning, but Isabella couldn't fathom how he could make good on his threat.

The boatswain leaned over and pulled a black leather whip from the satchel. Sweat broke over Isabella's face as her heart raced. He let the tail unfurl on the floor. The handle, decorated with an exquisite bird, had wings extended and wrapped in tight circles. He took the whip in his hand, brought the handle up, then pulled it down sharply. The tip cracked the air. Isabella began breathing deeper. Her knees weakened.

"Don't lay a hand on me," she barked. Her hands began to shake.

"Tell me," the boatswain said, his voice more sinister, "what do you think you can do about it?" He whirled toward Jean-Michel, snapping the whip toward his head. Jean-Michel yelped. The tip lashed into his cheek, creating a thin streak of blood from his right eye down to his mouth.

Isabella lunged, fists raised. Her captors stumbled forward as they tried grabbing at her arms and legs. She kicked wildly, pushing forward toward the stunned boatswain. She thrust her hand toward the whip, clutching it for a moment before the boatswain swung his left hand down on her head. She rolled dizzily to the ground as the two guards grabbed her arms and pinned her to the ground. Isabella lurched and pushed, kicked and scraped, trying to get free again.

"You idiots!" the boatswain screamed. "Get her up and chain her to the wall."

The two men pulled Isabella up on her feet and pushed her face into the wall. They pinned her hands into the shackles, her back toward the boatswain.

"It's a pity," the boatswain said darkly, "a young beauty like you would be of far better service in my cabin. Nevertheless, you've chosen your fate. Spain's got a punishment for runaway slaves like you."

The boatswain tore her shirt, letting the cloth fall to the floor in mangled ribbons. She clutched the chains, pulling herself up against the stones, feeling vulnerable and exposed. The stones felt cool against her breasts and stomach. She closed her eyes, waiting, trying desperately to keep panic from creeping into her thoughts.

"What?" the boatswain said startled. He took his finger and ran it across her back, letting it rise and fall with the ridges of old scars. "The stories." His tone was slightly mystical. "They aren't legends. They're true."

The boatswain waited a few more moments, as if to gather his thoughts. Somehow, this revelation changed his thinking, or his punishment. "I'll put you back where you belong!"

The whip cracked and a brain-numbing pain shot through her back. Isabella pushed herself up against the stones in a futile, instinctive attempt to keep away from the whip. She closed her eyes tightly and held her breath. She tried to fight back tears.

"Now," he said, his hot breath burning her ear, "you will experience my pain and humiliation."

CRACK. A dagger seemed to pierce her back, leaving a long thin aching streak. Isabella tried to muster her anger. Resist. She must resist. The pain seemed to swamp her fatigue.

"Hah," the boatswain said gleefully. "You deserve more than what you'll get tonight. It should be familiar enough to you. This'll teach you to go against your masters."

CRACK. CRACK. CRACK. Pain overwhelmed her. Isabella's legs buckled.

Get up, she pleaded to herself weakly. *Don't go down like this. Stand up like the captain you are.* CRACK. *Remember the rebellion.* CRACK. *Remember Jacob.* CRACK. *Jacob would want me to be strong.* CRACK.

It was no use. Jacob was not here. CRACK. She was alone. She was helpless. CRACK. She was tired, too tired. CRACK. What was the use? CRACK. All she felt was pain now. CRACK. Her skin seemed to melt from her back. CRACK. *What was that?* CRACK. "Jean-Michel?" she moaned.

"Shut up, wench!" the boatswain yelled. CRACK.

Isabella strained to talk, to shout, but her head drooped onto her shoulder. CRACK. The whip's snap was all she could hear. Her head was heavy; her body slumped from its weight, its muscles useless. CRACK. CRACK. A deep, dull ache consumed every limb, every inch of her body. She was beginning to feel numb. She wanted, she prayed, to see her star for one last time. CRACK. Blackness.

***

The sun was bright. The air was drenched in its warmth. Isabella drifted, from side to side, the hammock rolling with the ship. She looked lazily out to the sea, and smiled. How could she be so lucky? She couldn't see their faces, but she recognized Jacob's strong back. His figure was distinctive, carrying resolute commitment and loyalty in every stance. She loved every thing about him. Most of all, she loved his sense of purpose and duty. They had a common energy; it bound them together—forever. He had given so much to her. How could she continue without him? How long had it been? Was it just last night when they had slept, cradled in each other's arms, on the deck of the *Marée Rouge*? It seemed so much longer. Yet, it felt like yesterday. She could never forget that feeling: Security, submission, contentment.

Another man stood with Jacob. He seemed familiar, but she couldn't place him. His face was blurred. Odd. The mid-afternoon sun seemed to give everyone—especially Jacob—a crisp outline. Everyone but him. Was it Jean-Michel? No. This man had a leaner build. Carl? No. This man stood upright with military-like discipline. Carl was anything but military. Jean-Michel didn't carry himself that way either. This man's face was as lean as his body. He had dark hair. At least that's what she thought. He talked with an intelligent manner. Jacob seemed to be enjoying his company. *Good*, she thought. Why couldn't she see his face?

Jacob and the man talked on and on, as if telling stories over a mug of rum in Charlotte Amalie. No one was on deck; no warnings had sounded. The cannons were secure. The rifles locked away in their cabinets. It was just Isabella, laying comfortably in the hammock, Jacob, and this stranger. *It must be alright*, she thought.

Isabella turned her head toward the sky. The blue was brilliant, far brighter than any other sky she could remember seeing. The masts seemed to stretch all the way to the highest blue, the sails furled with care. There must be no wind, she concluded. Why hadn't she noticed that before? That explained the gentle roll. Were they near Panther Bay? Isabella turned her head to the left. She couldn't see anything but the horizon—a crisp line separating the deep blues and greens of the sea from the pastels of the sky. No clouds. No one was on deck either. Where was the crew?

She curled her eyebrow, puzzled. She looked upward again. What were those specks? They circled high above. Three? No, four. They seemed to be getting closer, falling as if through a waterspout. She trained her gaze, straining to see them. She wanted to get up from the hammock, but couldn't. Specks. Swirling specks. Birds? Big, black birds. Huge wings. They were circling, no, spiraling, downward faster and faster. They were coming toward her. Isabella's heart quickened. She began to sweat. They seemed to be at the top of the mast. Good God. They were albatrosses.

She opened her mouth to call for Jacob, but nothing came out. The birds were coming closer, faster. She couldn't move. Couldn't Jacob see them? She turned her head, mouthing HELP. Jacob continued talking to the stranger. Isabella turned toward the birds again. They were circling so fast, descending so quickly. Why couldn't she move? She tried to yell, vainly. She looked again at Jacob and the stranger. Why couldn't she see his face? *Help!* She screamed silently. Jacob stayed at the railing, looking out over the horizon. She turned toward the albatrosses.

"Help!" she screamed at the top of her lungs. "Can't anyone hear me? Help!"

Arms swooped around her as the birds came closer. She turned her head again, looking through the arms. Jacob was still at the railing, but the other man had disappeared.

"Help!" she screamed at Jacob. "The birds! Can't you see the birds? They're coming!"

"Ssshhh," said a man's soothing voice. "Easy. It's okay."

She knew that voice. The arms held her head, strongly but delicately. They rocked her calmly. They felt secure and comforting.

A sharp pain shot through her back, forcing her to moan. She began to weep. She couldn't stop. She wanted desperately to stop, but she couldn't. Then, everything went black. The sun was gone. The ship was gone. The sea was gone. Jacob was...

"Easy," said the soothing voice as she rocked gently. "You're safe Isabella." He was speaking Spanish.

Isabella opened her eyes. All she could see was the dark gray wall, flickering under torchlight. A man's hand gently stroked her arms. Her arms. They were bare. Where was her shirt? She tried to turn her head, but her neck was stiff and heavy. Her mind slowly began to clear. Her thoughts were fragments, pictures, and ideas, darting in and out.

She searched the room, her eyes blurred by tears. Stones peeked out of broken plaster. The room was cold and damp. She couldn't see any sign of a window. She was in a cell; a prison. She was lying on her belly, her arms stretched outward like wings. Her hands rested limply over the sides. She felt cool air tingle her toes. She felt her legs. She tried to move her legs, but a strong arm stopped her.

"Easy," the familiar voice told her. "You need rest."

"Where am I," she said without thinking.

The man seemed to hesitate, unsure of what to say. "You are in El Morro." The voice. It was warm and comfortable. It was familiar; she had heard it somewhere.

"Who are you?" she asked. "Have we met before?"

"Si, senorita," he said, his voice gentle and soothing.

"Who are you?"

Pain swept up her legs through her back and into her head, drowning out anything he might have said. She moaned as she fought to control her pain. She felt tears bubble into her eyes. *No*, she pleaded to herself. *Don't cry. Hold yourself together.* Why couldn't she feel her back? The pain overwhelmed any sense that her body connected her head and feet. The pain turned to an ache so thick she couldn't stand it. She began crying again. Sleep. Perhaps that would be the best—just go to sleep. Anything would be better than suffering like this. Everything went dark.

13

"Isabella?" The voice seemed hollow. Was she in a cave? "Isabella," the voice said again. "Wake up." It was a man's voice again. She couldn't tell if it was the same voice; it seemed so familiar. Once it was sharp, crisp in its intelligence. Now, it was soothing and comforting. It was trying to get her to do something.

"She's still too weak," said another voice, a woman's. The tone was very precise and refined, absent of the emotion it claimed to represent. Isabella had never heard it before.

"She can't lie here any longer," the man's voice said again. "Time is running out."

"Why do you care?" the woman's voice said spitefully. They were speaking very formal Spanish. Where was she? The Royal Court?

"Ahhhh," Isabella moaned. Something had come off her back, unleashing a horrendous wave of pain.

"Easy," said the man's voice again. His tone was not the rough street Spanish of Charlotte Amalie, Cruz Bay, or the alleys of San Juan.

"Be patient," the woman ordered. "It's going to hurt. I can't do anything about that."

"Then stop," Isabella rasped.

"Then you'll die," the woman said. "Is that what you want?"

"A little empathy would do you wonders, Rosa," the man said. "She was whipped into unconsciousness."

"She's a criminal," the woman said.

"She's human." Isabella knew that man's voice.

"She's a slave. A Creole one at that."

"We are all children of God."

"God bestows his blessing on those who deserve it. This girl is a criminal. She is godless."

"God judges on the purity of the heart and the nobility of our actions. Her judgment will come, but not in this life, or by you."

"She should be dead. We should kill her. I can't believe I am helping you. My father would hang you."

"Your father would understand. God decided to keep her in this world. She lay on the floor of her cell for almost twelve hours. No one tended to her wounds. She still lived."

"Another hour and she would have died."

"And your father would have been angry. Without her, your father's plans would drown more quickly than a slave on the high seas would. We must keep her alive."

Isabella's mind was clearing. The pain had receded to a dull ache, and she could feel her back. She wasn't sure if that was a good thing. The man's voice was now very familiar. Was that why he was keeping her alive? To get information? Had his voice fooled her so completely? Isabella could feel a different kind of hurt building inside her. Her arms were gaining strength. Her feet were gaining strength. She tried to pull her arms up.

"Argghhh," she yelled as the ache mushroomed into another paralyzing pain.

"Don't move!" the man insisted.

The woman placed something warm and wet over Isabella's back. The pain sharpened for a moment, then receded into a steady ache. She could think again.

"She's strong," the woman admitted.

"Isabella," the man said after a few more minutes, "can you hear me?"

"Don't call her by that name," Rosa objected. "She's a criminal. A rogue."

"I'm not sure you would say that if you had witnessed what I did."

"Witness? What could you witness? You sound like you saw the Christ himself."

"Not a prophet," the man said, his irritation growing with the level of his voice. "Leadership and strength. Not that much different from yourself."

"I am nothing like her," Rosa said.

"What name would you have me use?"

"Pest. Vermin. Don't give her a proper name that gives her more than she deserves."

Isabella wanted to sit up—protest, defend herself. This woman could not go on like this. Isabella had to say something, anything; but she couldn't. She lay there, as if grapeshot riddled her body, unable even to move her hands. She had never felt so helpless. Isabella held her breath in a final attempt to keep tears from streaming down her face. She couldn't let this woman see how weak she felt.

"She deserves to die," Rosa spat. "That's her place—in hell at the side of Satan."

"I'm not sure she believes in Satan." The man's voice was clearer. Isabella was feeling more and more alive. Satan? She didn't even believe in God. Did this man know that he was angering Rosa? Was that his plan?

Isabella could now see the outlines of his head as he spoke, even though he was speaking above her. The face was blurry, but it was emerging, slowly, through a mist. Her pulse increased with each recognizable feature. *It can't be*, she thought. The face came through her cleared vision. *No. You're dead. You can't be alive.*

"Isabella," Juan Carlos said, "you have to wake up. You have to talk to me."

The woman, Rosa, stayed quiet.

Isabella opened her eyes. "I'm alive," she said quietly.

"*Si.*" Juan Carlos smiled. "You are alive. You are very lucky."

"If I survive this to die at the gallows, I'm not so lucky." Isabella thought she could hear Rosa smile. Juan Carlos didn't say anything.

"Where is Jean-Michel?"

"Alive," Juan Carlos answered.

"Can he talk?"

"He can even walk. He's weak, but he'll make it."

"You sound like you belong with them." Rosa said suddenly.

"Don't be foolish." Frustration edged Juan Carlos's voice. "You need to leave."

"Sure," Isabella quipped, "just help me up. I'll be more than happy to leave this place."

Juan Carlos chuckled.

The pain seemed to double. How could she joke with him? A Spaniard and a Royal. "Damn you," Isabella said. "Damn you all."

"An interesting choice of words," Juan Carlos observed pleasantly. "Given your hatred for my God. Who do you think will damn me?"

"Don't play games with her," Rosa scolded. "We shouldn't even be talking to her. I'm sure she can't even understand you. What can a slave know? Only what they're told. That's why they're slaves. No need to put thoughts of things she could never understand in her simple brain."

Isabella wished the magical stories of her mother were true—she could will her saber into her hand and cut Rosa's wicked head in one movement. Now, she barely felt able to lift her hand. She was so helpless.

Juan Carlos turned to Rosa. "Leave," he ordered. "You are of no help here." Rosa was silent, but Isabella imagined the venomous look she must have given him.

"Get out!" Juan Carlos said, raising his voice. "Your place is not here."

"Let me do my job."

Spaniards were all the same. The overseer on Hispaniola. The lieutenant sailing to San Juan. The boatswain. Rosa. They were all the same. Their evil had left her here, little more than a bloody mess. They didn't even bother to chain her to the table. She was useless. She couldn't lift her hand to Rosa, no matter how angry she became.

Countless times she and Jacob had cheated death. For what? She lay exposed and helpless on a wooden slab, waiting for the gallows. She couldn't think of a death less noble. Was this her purpose in life? It would be so much easier if she believed in his God. Maybe she could become a martyr.

A heavy wooden door opened, and then shut. A deep, sharp clang echoed through the halls and room as the latch closed. Isabella waited.

Isabella became aware of her body. Someone had taken her boots. She still wore her breeches. Her arms were bare. Her shoulders were bare. She could feel her breasts against a hard surface. "Where is my shirt?"

"By the time the boatswain was finished, you didn't have a shirt."

He was still here. She let out a deep sigh. "I want a shirt."

"In due time. You're not ready for a shirt."

"I want a shirt."

"A shirt would open your wounds again."

He was right. "How long have I been here?"

"Six days."

"Almost a week. I didn't think I would last two."

"The plan gave you four."

So, she was going to die. Jean-Michel's faith must be giving him confidence. Faith counts for little inside El Morro. Rodriguez must want her strong enough to walk up to the gallows. She would be a public spectacle. "What happened to the plan?"

"You," Juan Carlos said simply. "The viceroy thinks you are more valuable alive than dead."

"Am I?"

"I don't know. Dead you become a martyr."

"A martyr? To whom?"

"I don't think you quite understand your influence over the pirates of the Spanish Main. Your exploits inspire a small navy."

She would rather inspire the maroons and slaves, Isabella thought. She wanted them to rise up, like three years ago, but in something bigger and more sweeping. If her death would bring that, she would die now. But, pirates?

Isabella heard Juan Carlos step closer to her. She felt the nudge of his hands tug at something covering her back. A bandage of some sort, she figured. His hand worked its way up her back. His fingers caressed her shoulders, moving up to her neck. She felt her anger ebb slowly and steadily. She had to resist. She couldn't let him do this. His hands were soothing, relaxing. Even the ache in her back seemed to lessen as they worked her muscles and neck.

"I think you're worth more alive," he whispered into her ear.

"What does Rodriguez want?" Isabella relaxed. She began remembering the comfort of her mother's hutch. The elders would sit around the fireplace at night, telling stories. They would teach Isabella and the other children of courage and strength. Juan Carlos's hands were helping her get back to that place. Now, she remembered Jacob's embrace. His protection. His conviction.

They contained a clarity she envied and longed for. It was a safe place, too; a place she wanted now. It was a simple place, a place where rules were clear and roles known. Her life was too complicated. Couldn't she make it simpler? Couldn't she go back to those safe days on the plantation? Why did life become so complicated after Jacob died?

"Rodriguez wants information," Juan Carlos said.

"What kind of information?"

"Information about pirates. When they strike. Where they hide. How to protect the Empire's trading routes."

"And if I don't have that information?"

"You do."

"If I don't give him that information?"

"Then your life means nothing."

Her life *means nothing.* Her life was already meaningless. She could do nothing for the things, or people, she cared about. Her captors did not even bother to bind her hands. Was her life that meaningless? What was her life worth on the plantation? One ton of sugarcane? Was that all that kept her alive? Yes—to the overseer and the noble living an ocean away in Madrid.

She thought back to the fireplace. Her mother spun stories for hours. Did she think her life meant nothing? Isabella felt a tingle of anger build in her legs and feet. Did Jacob think her life was nothing? How could anyone think her life was nothing? She couldn't. That's what led her into Santo Domingo at fourteen. That's why she teased the sailors and captains in the bars. She was something to them on those nights. That led to the revolt that destroyed the plantation. That's what led her, finally, to Jacob, to Carl, and to Jean-Michel. She was worth more than one ton of sugar. She knew she couldn't let herself die here. Not now. Not before she had completed her mission. Not until she had rid the West Indies of the Spanish plague.

She closed her eyes, fighting to keep back tears. "I die two weeks after arriving in El Morro rather than four days."

The fingers stopped. Isabella's muscles began tightening.

"Information keeps you alive," Juan Carlos said. "The more information you give, the longer you stay alive."

"I'm not interested in buying a few days." Isabella missed his fingers. The pain was coming back. Maybe she could give him a little information.

"What do you want?" Juan Carlos asked.

"I want what you can't give." She felt strength return to her muscles as her confidence increased with a renewed focus.

"How do you know?"

"You've never been a slave."

"You are not a slave."

"I am free only on the sea. On my ship. Under my command."

"I can't let you go."

"No," Isabella said. "You can't." She sighed. "No," she repeated. "Your first loyalty is to your King and Country."

"My first loyalty is to God."

"What if they don't agree?"

"They agree on the important things."

"Like me?" Isabella asked. "Tell me, what would your prophet, Jesus, say about slavery?"

"Slaves existed in his time. Slavery is a fact of life. Jesus never preached for slaves to rebel. Freedom is a privilege of Christianity; the freedom to serve God."

"Really?" Isabella turned her head, even though the motion sent a pain, shooting through her shoulder. "What about that woman they stoned?"

"Mary?"

"Maybe," Isabella said. "The prostitute. Not the mother of the Christ."

"What about her?"

"Didn't your prophet stop the stoning?"

"Yes."

"Why?"

"He said: 'Let he who has not sinned cast the first stone.' They stopped."

"She was a free woman, even though she was a prostitute."

"But she wasn't a Christian."

"No."

"Wasn't he saying that all people deserved the respect of God? That everyone was equal before God's eyes?"

Juan Carlos didn't say anything, but Isabella heard his steps. He was pacing.

"Where did you learn so much about Christianity?"

"I listen," she said, smiling to herself.

"Jean-Michel."

Isabella smiled more broadly. Yes, Jean-Michel. "Where is he?"

"He is safe. Nothing will happen to him unless something happens to you."

"How do you know? Is it your decision?"

"Yes," Juan Carlos said with certainty. "I can keep Jean-Michel alive, as long as you are alive. I cannot keep you alive. Only you can do that."

Isabella's heart grew heavy. She had to keep Jean-Michel alive. How could she forsake the one man that loved her without condition? She couldn't go on without him.

"So," Juan Carlos continued, letting his fingers lightly touch her skin as he walked to the head of the bed. He knelt to face her squarely, holding her hands gently. "Jean-Michel's life is in your hands. If you die, Jean-Michel dies. I can protect him, but I can't protect you."

Isabella looked at Juan Carlos. Could he see her fear? Her struggle? She couldn't forsake her crew, her mission. As a commander, he could understand that, couldn't he? "You want me to forsake my crew?"

"Your command was lost the night I escaped," Juan Carlos said with in a cool tone. "You have no crew. Would your crew have chased you into the jungle?"

Hot anger swept through Isabella's arms. She tried to pull her legs up, to move her along the table, and pull her hands from his. She could barely move her foot. She felt her face flush.

"Isabella." Juan Carlos's voice seemed older this time, almost like a big brother. "Face the truth. Your most loyal friend sits in this prison, waiting for the gallows. He is the only one that did not forsake you when you needed the support of your crew. Where were they? They were helping your quartermaster take over your ship. Steal your wealth. Steal your command."

"What do you know about Stiles?" she asked.

"I know he almost killed you. He almost killed me. He would have killed Jean-Michel as quickly as he would have killed me. He would have made you suffer."

"I am suffering now," Isabella, lamented. "What can be worse than this? I'm sitting in a prison. I'm waiting to hang. It would have been far less cruel to kill me, fighting for my command, on the *Marée Rouge*." But, giving herself for Jean-Michel?

Juan Carlos watched her. His eyes seemed to pity her, as if saying, *Some captain you are, pouting, and feeling sorry for yourself like a little girl angry because no one liked her.* Isabella turned her head. She couldn't stand the way he looked at her now. Was she fulfilling his expectations of a woman? Was this his proof that women should adorn the halls of the Royal Court, keep children clothed and fed, and raise sons so they can grow up to fight for God, King, and Empire? Could he see her purpose? Couldn't he see what Jacob saw? What her mother foretold?

Isabella closed her eyes to keep the tears from seeping down her cheeks. This is all she had, after four years of rebellion.

She felt Juan Carlos's hand touch her shoulder. His fingers softly rubbed the back of her head, stroking her hair. He lifted a ladle to her lips, and she sipped. It was sweet. Mango juice. The juice seemed to strengthen her.

"No one should suffer the way you have behind these walls," Juan Carlos whispered in her ear. He kissed her lightly on the cheek.

"Even a criminal?" she asked, in a barely audible rasp.

"Are you a criminal?"

"No. I fight for my freedom. I will gladly suffer for it. That's no crime, is it?" Isabella's mind was turning more quickly.

"It's a crime under the laws of Spain," Juan Carlos said.

"I follow a higher law than that of Charles III."

"The King's laws are our laws. His laws bind us all. His laws are the laws of the Empire."

"His laws are not my laws," Isabella insisted. "Doesn't he answer to a higher law?"

"No."

"Not even God's?"

"Yes, the King answers to God."

"I am not bound by Charles's laws."

"Everyone in the Empire is bound by the laws of the Court," Juan Carlos insisted.

"I cannot be bound by laws that do not respect me," Isabella snapped. Why couldn't Juan Carlos see this? His touch was easy and soothing, but his mind was hard and stubborn. "I won't be bound by laws that deny me. I won't submit to laws that ignore my will, my ambition, my future, or my dedication to my purpose."

She turned toward Juan Carlos. He sat close to her, peering into her eyes. "I am bound by a higher law," she said more forthrightly. "This law considers everyone the same. This law requires us to consider each other separately, as one and the same."

Juan Carlos sat back on his stool. He seemed sincerely provoked.

"Would you be a criminal if you followed God's Law and God's Law challenged a law of the Empire?" she asked, keeping her eyes trained on Juan Carlos.

"They do not conflict."

"Your prophet… Jesus…? He seemed to be quite clear about the equality of all people. Doesn't slavery contradict the laws of your God?"

Juan Carlos hesitated. "No. Christians can be slaves. I already told you Christians and slavery existed together. A Christian's first duty is to God and to obey his commandments."

"Christianity serves the purpose of your King, not men," Isabella said. She turned away and stared at the wall. "I think you understand only what is easy to understand."

"Christianity teaches life," Juan Carlos said, but his voice was less confident. "It teaches us how to live and forgive. It teaches that we are all equal before God…."

"Even if we are not equal among men?" Isabella was growing frustrated. At least on the sea, she felt equal among men.

"Isabella," Juan Carlos said, as if running from her. She felt his gentle touch on her arms. "We don't have time to talk about this. I need to report to Rodriguez. If I can't tell him where your crew is, he will hang you and Jean-Michel."

She couldn't hold back a faint smile, knowing she had trapped him in his hypocrisy. His God! Her smiled faded. What did it matter? She was going to the gallows. How could he ask her to give up her crew? Stiles was a liar, thief, and rogue. He did not deserve her protection. The others—didn't they help Jean-Michel on the beach? They gave him bandages and food. They pledged their loyalty to Jean-Michel. She couldn't give them up. That's all she had left. That's all she had left to give.

"You know about Stiles," Isabella said. She took his hand and gave it a light squeeze. "That's all I can tell you." She hoped—prayed—he would understand. It was her only chance.

14

"What do you mean," Rodriguez protested. "Why should I spare the life of that wench?"

"Killing her doesn't further the interest of the Empire," Juan Carlos said.

"That's my decision!" snapped the viceroy, standing up from his desk. The windows were open behind him. The horizon seemed to slice his head as he walked back and forth, hands clasped behind him. "Explain. Again."

"Pardon, Your Excellency. The wench has information. So does her lieutenant. Keeping her alive gives us time. It only benefits us."

"What about the lieutenant?"

Juan Carlos paused uncomfortably. "He's our tool. The rogue has a strange bond with him. She's immature. Impulsive. Emotional. He's more like a father than a colleague. I've seen it. She can't live without him. For us, he's expendable."

"How do you know?" demanded Rosa, sitting formally in an overstuffed chair. Her fan flitted in a futile effort to push the humidity from her face. The chair seemed to inhale the breeze winding through the room from the open windows.

Juan Carlos's throat seemed tight, constricted by the unusually hot day. He longed for the dry air of the plains over Grenada. He didn't like Rosa's tone. Sweat beaded on his forehead as he sat dutifully in a chair in front of the viceroy.

"Battlefields teach many things," Juan Carlos. He swung around to face her squarely. "To those who are there!"

Rosa's face reddened with anger. "Including how to get a woman to obey your every request? Is that God's command?"

"Rosa!" scolded Rodriguez. She turned, looking angrily down into her lap. "Excuse her, *Capitano*," Rodriguez said quickly.

"Apologies are not necessary," Juan Carlos responded, tipping his head. "Senorita Rodriguez knows my rank but little about my expertise."

"I'm not in the habit of divulging the Court's secrets," Rodriguez said, sitting back in his large chair. Rosa shot a hurt glance toward her father. His portly body seemed to weigh the chair down to the wooden slats on the floor.

"I never considered the possibility," Juan Carlos assured Rodriguez. He turned back toward the viceroy. "She should probably know more," Juan Carlos said. Perhaps a bone would calm Rosa's temper. "With the Viceroy's permission?"

Rodriguez waved his hand in agreement, but gave Rosa another scolding look.

"I interview prisoners," Juan Carlos told Rosa coolly. "I get the information I need to win."

"Against whom?" Rosa seemed hurt. Vulnerable. "Women? Children?" Rosa turned back toward the window, nervously fanning herself. Rodriguez looked at her, puzzled, and then looked searchingly at Juan Carlos.

Juan Carlos straightened his back and pushed himself into the cushion of his chair. He should have expected this.

"I interview everyone," Juan Carlos said, "from the lowest soldier to the highest general; anyone who carries a gun, dagger, or saber. Women do not fight in the Old World. Not even for the Basques."

"I guess these despicable islands are different from the Continent in more than one way," Rosa said. Juan Carlos opened his mouth to say something, but decided to stay quiet. He turned toward Rodriquez.

"The Panther gave us important information," Juan Carlos said, ignoring Rosa for the moment. Rosa's eyes slid over toward Juan Carlos at the sound of Isabella's nickname. "Yellow Jacket has three vessels. A frigate and a brigantine, armed with twelve and eighteen-pound cannon, and a small schooner for scouting. It carries eight nine-pounders plus a twelve-pounder in the bow. They sail from the southeastern beaches of Saint John."

"Three ships?" Rodriquez said, surprised. "Where did he get the third one?"

"The *Marée Rouge*," Juan Carlos said quickly. "The quartermaster mutinied. He allied himself with Yellow Jacket."

"Are you sure he joined with Yellow Jacket?" Rodriquez asked. "Yes," Juan Carlos said. "But, I think the wench can tell us more."

"Such as?"

Juan Carlos hesitated. "She can tell us where the key bases are on Antigua and Saint Croix. She has contacts in the Leeward Islands—Trinidad, Tobago. She knows enough to rid the West Indies of all these pirates."

"She's a rogue," Rosa snipped. "She won't tell you anything."

"She's a rogue," Juan Carlos admitted, "but she is loyal. We have her lieutenant. She knows he'll hang without her cooperation."

Rosa looked at him. She didn't trust him, Juan Carlos thought. He was sure of it. What would she tell her father?

"You don't believe me?" Juan Carlos asked. Rosa looked startled, almost panicked, by the question. She broke her stare and looked down at her lap again. "I don't know what to believe." That was a lie. Rosa knew exactly what to believe. "Sometimes a person's character is more important than their words," Juan Carlos said.

"She's a criminal; a rogue; a slave, a Creole slave," Rosa spat. "Who can put stock in her words or character?"

More than you will ever admit, Juan Carlos thought. Isabella had a purity in her passion he had never seen. He couldn't help but be drawn to it, even inspired by it.

"I'm only asking for more time," he said, turning back to Rodriguez. "Let's dispatch a squadron to search for Yellow Jacket. The mutinous pirates will be with him. We can trap them in the coves and destroy them."

"I don't see the need to keep the slave alive," Rosa said.

"It's not your decision," Juan Carlos said, keeping his eyes trained on Rodriguez.

"Her crew mutinied," Rosa said. "What use is she? We can scout the islands with our sloops and schooners. We have spies in Charlotte Amalie and Cruz Bay. Surely they can give us the same information as a slave girl."

Juan Carlos felt the blood move swiftly through his head. He thought he could hear his heart beat louder, more quickly.

"Rosa makes a good point," Rodriguez said.

"Your Excellency," Juan Carlos said, straining to keep his voice level and authoritative, "I don't think that would be wise."

"She hasn't told you anything we didn't already know," Rodriguez said.

"You knew about Yellow Jacket's fleet?" Juan Carlos asked, baffled. "Why didn't you tell me?"

"I wanted to see what you could get from that water rat," Rodriguez said scornfully. Rosa smiled, unconcerned that such obvious gloating might affect her father's decision.

He had been duped. First by Rodriguez, and then by his own sympathies. Now, Rodriguez and Rosa knew the truth. They would be convinced he could not glean any important information from Isabella or Jean-Michel. He mind reeled as he struggled to find a way, any way, to salvage his integrity and reputation.

"It looks like your skills are best used on the battlefield," Rodriguez said. "I'll assign you to the squadron that will hunt down Yellow Jacket. You can *advise* the captain and the soldiers. You will be in charge of the marines. Go to Panther Bay. Find their camps. Burn them. Execute them all."

Juan Carlos tried to absorb everything Rodriguez had just said. His mind whirled with plans and fears. "The plantations?" he said, almost without thinking.

"If they harbor these pirates," Rodriguez said, "burn them."

"They are Dutch," Juan Carlos protested.

"They are harboring criminals," insisted Rodriquez. "The treaties do not protect an attack on the Empire, or those that harbor the rogues that do."

"Surely the Dutch will not accept that," Juan Carlos said.

Rodriguez's face reddened as he rose from his chair and leaned over the broad tabletop, palms bracing his bulk above an ink blotter. His face seemed to loom in front of Juan Carlos as he sat expressionless in front of him. "They will have no choice. These are my orders. They come from His Most Catholic Majesty King Charles III. Are you questioning these orders?"

Juan Carlos sat straight and upright. "No… Your Excellency," he said, although the hesitation in his voice risked revealing a moment of questioning his superior. "I am a servant of my King. Your orders are clear."

"*Bueno,*" he said, sitting back down. "Have the slave and her companion executed tomorrow at dawn."

Juan Carlos sat stunned. "What?"

"I want their heads on the gates of San Cristóbal by breakfast. They will be an adequate warning for all those that dare question the laws of Spain."

"Do you disagree?" Rosa asked, the eyes shifting toward Juan Carlos in an obvious challenge.

Too late, Juan Carlos realized her plan; she wanted Isabella and Jean-Michel dead. But why?

"No, Your Excellency," Juan Carlos responded. "Your plan is the only real choice we have. That's my advice as your chief counselor on war and strategy."

"You're young," Rodriguez nodded. "Scarcely more than a boy. But your experience on the battlefield gives you the maturity of a man."

Juan Carlos felt a deep pit, burrowing into his belly. What had he done? Rosa continued to sit, fan weaving through the air in front of her, smiling broadly.

15

Rodriguez was wrong. Dead wrong. Juan Carlos was sure of it. What could he do? He began to pace.

His room seemed much smaller than usual. Each step seemed to bring him to a wall. Step, turn, step, turn, step, turn—why couldn't he stop? The open window provided little solace.

Options. He needed options. He paused once and marveled at how he walked so quickly without upending his bed or turning over his washbasin. Why was the room so small? He looked at the window, its fine lace curtains pulled aside to reveal the rooftops of San Juan. The clean rectangular lines of the buildings comforted him. The ragtag *bohios* on the outskirts of town and in the villages seemed unsettled and dangerous. The buildings near the forts would withstand an attack. At least he felt secure.

Tomorrow, at dawn, the streets would be empty as San Juan's citizens gathered in front of San Cristóbal to witness an execution. Juan Carlos looked at the back walls of the prison fort. The fading sun whitewashed the limestone into a deep, foreboding gray. The gallows were ready, he thought, imagining the public square as the sun rose. He wasn't.

Juan Carlos pulled his shoulders straight and lifted his hands to his face. He pushed his fingers through the sweat and into his hair. He looked at the ceiling. Is this right? Is this what his King really ordered? Surely, punishment was due the most heinous criminals. Was Isabella such a criminal? She saved him on the *Marée Rouge*. She fought the cruelty of Yellow Jacket. She had courage. She embraced justice. Granted, hers was a pagan justice, but she seemed to imbue an innate sense of right and wrong—and compassion. God, what he would give for ten like her on the fields of Avila or Segovia. What was her crime? She was a slave. She rebelled. She fought for her status as a person. She was willing to die for her crew. She was willing to fight—to die—for others like her. Was her fight so unjust?

Juan Carlos crossed the room to a mirror hanging idly over the washbasin. His eyes were deep and dark, his hair wildly disheveled. His white coat glistened with gold lace. Did he deserve his rank? Was he running? What was his responsibility to God and King? He marveled at how Isabella—a simple slave girl—had forced him to these questions. Less than a month ago, his life seemed so simple. Loyalty. To God, King, and Country. What other principles did he need? Now, this woman—this girl—had forced him to question everything he valued most.

Juan Carlos leaned over the ceramic bowl. It rested comfortably on its post, waiting for his next desire. The basin was far more elegant than anything he had seen in the West Indies. It was foreign to the battlefields he knew, save the political ones in the King's Court. Now, it seemed small and unimportant.

A small pool of clean water sat patiently at the bottom. He rested the palms of his hands on the edge, sending a ripple through the water. What would he do? What could he do? He watched the ripples become smaller and smaller, eventually vanishing altogether. All he could see was his face. The same disheveled hair and sleep deprived eyes. He had to shake himself from these thoughts—from her.

Juan Carlos cupped his hands. He dipped them in the water. He had to do something. He brought the water up onto his face, dissolving the sweat, caked from ear to chin. He pulled the water up into his neck. Then up into his hair. He looked up again, letting the water drip over his eyes and nose and into the collar of his shirt and coat.

"No," he said with quite resolve. "This is wrong. Isabella and Jean-Michel stand by God, even if not my King. This injustice cannot serve Spain, or the Empire."

***

"Papers?"

Juan Carlos unbuttoned his coat and pulled several letters into the pale moonlight. He handed them to the guard who lifted them up to a torch.

"Bueno, Capitano Santa Ana." The guard saluted. He propped his musket against a nook in the wall and handed the papers back. Juan Carlos directed a firm nod to another guard standing near the door.

Together, they lifted the large iron latch and pulled. The thick wooden door rumbled open.

Santa Ana felt relaxed, even comfortable. The confusion over Isabella's impending death had gone as soon as he had settled on his plan. It would be over soon. He felt good about it. All his anxiety disappeared into the cooling night air.

Juan Carlos followed two new guards inside the fortress walls through a maze of hallways and stairs. They seemed to walk and climb for more than an hour, but he knew it had only been a few minutes. He relaxed, even as they came closer to the cell, her cell. He tapped his saber lightly. He checked for the hidden dagger in his boot. He wished he could have brought his pistol, but the guards would never have let it inside.

All Juan Carlos could hear were footsteps—thick leather soles, clacking against the damp stone. It was an oddly pleasant sound. He shivered as he remembered his first trip inside El Morro. The crack of the whip had seemed frighteningly normal as they approached the same cell three days earlier. His curiosity turned to horror, when he realized what was happening inside. This was a different day. No whip. He hoped she was still alive.

The trio finally arrived at the cell door. Inside, the dark stone hovel was just as it was the day before. This time, only one person, conscious and alert, was shackled to the wall.

"Come back for more fun and games?" Jean-Michel grumbled. Shadows hid his expression, making it difficult for Juan Carlos to see his expression. A single torch cast a flickering glow across the room.

"I have my orders," Juan Carlos said.

He signaled to one of the guards. The guard walked over to Jean-Michel and released his chains. Jean-Michel sat motionless on the floor.

"Get up," Juan Carlos ordered.

Jean-Michel sat, stretching his hands and massaging his wrists. Juan Carlos watched patiently. "Get up," he ordered again.

"When I please."

"Defiance is futile." Juan Carlos gripped the handle on his saber. "You know your fate. Why resist?"

"Je suis francais. What else do you need to know?"

Juan Carlos smiled. "*Rien.* Nothing"

Juan Carlos walked over to Jean-Michel. He leaned down, close to his face. "You have a choice. You can stay and die. All I have to do is tell the guards to cut your throat." Jean-Michel looked at him, expression absent from his glare. "Or…," Juan Carlos continued, "you can come with me and see your captain."

Jean-Michel looked at Santa Ana hopefully, then angrily. He looked at the guards. They stood ready, sabers pulled. Juan Carlos kept his blade in its sheath. Jean-Michel turned back to Juan Carlos. "What are you going to do to her?"

"Does it matter?"

Jean-Michel remained silent; his eyes now sparkled with hatred. "Where are you taking me?"

"San Cristóbal."

"Prisoners go to San Cristóbal for one reason."

"Then you know the choice before you." Juan Carlos shook his head. Why was he doing this? He was smarter than this. Jean-Michel must know that this resistance was pointless. Disobeying an order from him was a death sentence. Juan Carlos wondered for a brief minute if it were his age. Jean-Michel was not quite old enough to be his father, but he was close. Yet, Isabella was younger. Perhaps his hatred of Spain was too great for him to think rationally.

Juan Carlos walked over to the door, signaling the guards to stay. "I'm giving you an opportunity. A once in a lifetime opportunity."

Jean-Michel massaged his wrists again and looked at the floor. He brought his knees to his chest, and then stretched his legs. "I've been in this cell for almost two weeks. How do I know if my legs will hold me?"

"That is something for you to determine."

Jean-Michel rocked himself onto a knee. He swayed for a moment, but then steadied himself. He stretched his legs again, gingerly bringing himself up on his feet. He braced himself against the wall.

"Jean-Michel," Juan Carlos said. *"Defendez votre coeur."*

Jean-Michel stared at him. He opened his mouth, but Juan Carlos glanced over to the guards before he could say anything. The guards were looking at Juan Carlos suspiciously. Jean-Michel remained silent.

"You are a despicable river rat," Jean-Michel said. "You belong in the sewers of Paris." Juan Carlos smirked, and the guards relaxed, smiling broadly. They walked over, grabbed Jean-Michel's arms, and began tugging him toward the door.

"Preparez," Juan Carlos whispered in Jean-Michel's ear as they clattered out the door. Jean-Michel resisted an overwhelming urge to look at Santa Ana. Why was he talking to him in French? What was he telling him to prepare for?

***

Juan Carlos Lopez de Santa Ana stood before the cell, waiting for something. He just didn't know what.

"Well," Jean-Michel urged impatiently.

The two guards flanked Jean-Michel, sabers pulled.

"Don't worry!" Jean-Michel said to the guards. "I'm not going to commit suicide." At least not until he knew what was behind the door.

"Open the door," Santa Ana ordered.

One of the guards pulled on the latch with a loud crack. The door swung open on heavy, iron hinges. The stench of dried blood and mending flesh seemed to keep them in the hallway. Several seconds passed before their eyes adjusted to the dank light. The fuzzy outline of a wood table and body were barely visible in the center of the room.

Juan Carlos crossed to the bed. He slapped the shoulder of the figure. "Wake up," he barked. The body lay motionless. Jean-Michel strained to adjust his eyes. Who was it? It wore pants, but the back was bare. Was it a crewman from the *Marée Rouge*?

Juan Carlos pulled a pail from a shadow and dumped water on the figure, drawing a moan. Jean-Michel gasped as he realized the voice was Isabella's.

"Cochon!" Jean-Michel yelled. He lunged at Juan Carlos, but the guards instantly beat him to the floor. "Pigs!" Jean-Michel repeated shaking his fists. The guards raised their sabers.

"Alto!" Juan Carlos ordered, just as their tips reached the peak of their arc. "Hold him!"

"Who's there?" Isabella's voice was weak and distant.

"It's time to go," Juan Carlos ordered, pulling at the body's arm.

"Leave her alone," Jean-Michel growled.

"Quiet!" Juan Carlos motioned to the guards to restrain Jean-Michel even more.

"You lay a hand on her—"

Santa Ana swung back toward Jean-Michel, pushing his hand across his jaw with a resounding crack. "Silence! Bind him. We need to move these criminals."

Jean-Michel resisted, but soon found his hands bound behind his back. Juan Carlos walked back over to the table. They could recognize Isabella now. Strips of dirty cloth draped her upper body.

"Mon Dieu!" Jean-Michel said. "What have you done to her?"

Santa Ana motioned to the guards. They threw a woolen blanket over her and wrapped it snuggly. She sat, not fully understanding what was happening. "Where are you taking me?"

"San Cristóbal," Juan Carlos said.

The guards pulled her up on her feet. They couldn't tell if Isabella understood, or simply resigned herself to her fate. "She's too weak to walk," one of them said.

Another guard pulled a wooden pole from a corner of the cell. "She's strong enough to walk with this." The guard bound her arms over the pole, letting her hang limply, feet scraping the floor.

"You're treating her like a dog," Jean-Michel protested.

One of the guards cast a broad smile toward him. "I think you had it right the first time. Roast pig."

Jean-Michel tried to lunge, again, but fell hard onto the floor. The guards kicked him furiously.

"Stop!" Juan Carlos said, walking over to the guards. "Any more and we'll have to carry him, too."

The guards hoisted the pole holding Isabella onto their shoulders. As the guards walked out, struggling to keep Isabella upright, Juan Carlos leaned down to Jean-Michel. "I told you to be prepared," he said in a low voice, putting his hand firmly on Jean-Michel's shoulder. "Come on, quickly, if you want to help your captain."

Jean-Michel looked up at Juan Carlos, bewildered, but he had already moved into the hallway. Jean-Michel stumbled to his feet and followed him.

They walked for several minutes, down stairs and back through corridors. They were strange to Jean-Michel, but Juan Carlos seemed to have the plans firmly engraved in his brain now. Soon, they stood in front of the main entrance. Two more guards were inside the door.

"These prisoners have been ordered to San Cristóbal," Juan Carlos told the guards. "I have to return to my quarters to write tomorrow's execution papers. Escort the prisoners, and I'll meet you at the gate."

The guards looked at each other.

"You've seen my papers. Was something out of order?"

"*No, Capitano.*"

"Go on, then. You have two guards on the outside and one still on the inside. You won't be gone more than an hour."

The guards opened the door, and the group moved into the crisp night air. The humidity had evaporated. The salt air invigorated them under the shadows of the buildings. Isabella's legs seemed to gain strength; her feet supported every other step, although her head still rolled from side to side. A full moon lit their way, a late night beacon, as Juan Carlos watched the two pirate prisoners and the four Spanish army guards descend into the alleys of San Juan.

***

Isabella opened her eyes. Why were they outside? The air was refreshing. Her muscles were recharging. She was feeling strong again. She pulled her feet under her as they bounced down the narrow road between plaster walls, rising three and four floors on each side. Someone had told her they were going somewhere, but who was it? She vaguely remembered yelling. Then, something jerked her shoulders. She pulled her head up to look at her arms. They were bound to a pole. She looked at the man pulling her. A Dago soldier.

"Where are you taking me?" she asked. The soldier ignored her.

"San Cristóbal," said a familiar voice.

"Jean-Michel?"

"Aye, I'm here, with you, *mon amie.*"

"It's good to hear your voice. I was worried."

"Your voice is soothing as well."

"San Cristóbal?"

"*Oui.*"

Isabella stumbled forward. San Cristóbal only meant one thing. She struggled to walk upright. Her dignity bristled at the mere thought of them strapping her to a pole, as a hog, tied to the spit over a fire.

"I think I can walk on my own now," she said, forcing her voice to project strength that still wasn't there. "Can't you release my arms?"

The guard in front of her stopped and turned. He looked at the guard behind her. "Surely you would rather guard me than carry me."

Both guards looked at Isabella standing under the pole. They were walking downhill now, but they would soon be walking up toward San Cristóbal. The one guarding Jean-Michel had his saber pulled, ready to cut him at any hint of a fight. The guards nodded to each other and the one in front pulled a dagger from his belt and cut the binding.

"*Gracias,*" Isabella said. Dizziness forced a stumble at the first step, but she steadied herself against Jean-Michel. She was so tired; could she really make it to San Cristóbal? She would rather collapse in an alley, skewered by the blades of Spanish swords, than be dragged to the gallows, strapped like a pig to a pole.

The guard threw the pole against the side of a building. "One move," he warned, "and we'll slit your throat." He grabbed Isabella's arm and pulled her roughly forward.

"Okay, okay," she pleaded, rising anger feeding strength. "Leave me alone. I'm coming."

Isabella wished she could see Jean-Michel's eyes: All she could make out was his shadow. She did, see however, the long sliver that could only be the saber of one of the guards. That was enough.

Isabella summoned all her remaining strength and stopped. "I'm not going any farther." The guard in back pushed her forward. Her knees buckled, but she held her ground.

"Isabella," Jean-Michel said in French. "We have several hours before the sun rises."

"What do we have to look forward to? I don't think I have the strength to face the gallows."

The guards pulled their sabers.

"We have a choice now," she said, her voice steady with resolve. "Why wait until we have none?" She had hoped Juan Carlos understood her in El Morro. Perhaps he did. He knew that moving her now would give her a choice. By making that choice, she could die with dignity. She was tired.

"You die either way," the lead guard said, nudging her with the tip of his blade. "I've seen the orders."

Isabella looked at the guard. She edged closer to Jean-Michel.

If this was her destiny, so be it. At least it would be on her terms and by her choice. "We can die as cowards, or with dignity."

She swung her fist around, boxing the first guard on the side of the head. His head bounced to the side. Jean-Michel surged forward, hands still bound, pulling his guard into the one behind Isabella, throwing them both off balance. The punch had taken everything Isabella had, and she fell to the ground. The first guard lifted his blade against the moonlight. Jean-Michel rushed forward, forcing himself between the blade and Isabella.

"No!" Isabella sputtered. She pulled Jean-Michel down, across her body and away from the blade's arc. They rolled to the side as the blade clattered against the cobblestones. Isabella pulled herself to her knees. Jean-Michel knelt beside her, fists clenched but useless while still tied together. The three guards, sabers pulled, moved closer.

"I could really use a window now," muttered Isabella, struggling for breath and strength.

Jean-Michel chuckled. "A pistol wouldn't hurt either."

Jean-Michel stood up, shielding Isabella, as she gasped for air. She struggled to pull herself up. She couldn't let them slaughter Jean-Michel. She backed up to a wall, ignoring the pain, using her legs to push her upward. She was too tired to struggle any longer.

"On my count," Isabella said. "On three. We'll do this together. For my mother and for Jacob."

"Aye," Jean-Michel agreed. "And, perhaps for us."

"A trois. Un, deux...."

It was over before they had a chance to blink. The glint was barely visible but unmistakable. The Spanish guards lay lifeless on the stone roadbed. Jean-Michel and Isabella stood dazed, but alive.

"Come," said a heavily accented voice. Three figures approached them, but their movements were inviting, not hostile. Jean-Michel raised his voice. "No time," said the man's voice again. "Any more minutes and soldiers come." Whose voice was that? He was the leader. The shadow seemed to sketch a thin African, but the dim light relegated his face and features to little more than a silhouette. It wasn't a crewman. She knew them by how they moved. This voice was familiar, but different.

"It's okay," Isabella said, pulling gently at Jean-Michel's arm. She could feel Jean-Michel's curious look, but he relented. One of the men sliced the ropes binding Jean-Michel

The small band lifted Isabella up and surrounded her, as if protecting her, and hustled down an alley descending toward the bay. They turned and went down another alley. They turned again. The salt smell was becoming stronger.

"Where are you taking us?" Isabella asked, too weak to do anything but let the group of men pull her along.

"No time," the leader said. What accent was that? "Come, come... fast." He was waving frantically as they tumbled recklessly downward.

The group rounded a corner, and the bay spread thick and dark before them. The hulls of fishing boats dotted the pier. The waters were calm, but the soles of their boots disrupted the tranquility of the early morning.

Two more men suddenly appeared from the shadows and pulled Isabella and Jean-Michel toward the water. Their bodies smacked against the gunwale of a long boat. Strong arms and hands pushed them over the side and onto the boat's bottom with a summersault. Pain shot through her back, arm, and stomach as Isabella landed with a thud and clatter among buckets and oars. Her legs straddled a sack of something hard, but the pain in her back forced her to gasp. She heard other bodies clamber over the gunwales, and the boat slid with a gentle sway into the bay. Oars dipped into the water, and the boat pulled away from the shore, faster and faster.

***

Above the bay, a single figure watched the small boat pull into the water and to safety. He felt good, but anxious. Had he forsaken his King? This surely was God's will, he told himself. God told him to spare this woman—the girl slave who commanded pirates. Would his King agree? If not, would he forgive? He took a deep breath, releasing the air slowly to ease his muscles. Isabella would live for at least one more day. That was God's will. Still, he couldn't help but feel heaviness in his heart beyond the fear. The boat, now just a pinpoint, disappeared into the night. He turned to see what this new day would bring.

16

"How could they have escaped?"

Rodriguez's booming voice forced the two soldiers back several paces. The viceroy pounded across the floor in a violent march, his arms waving. His face puffed outward like a jellyfish. He swung around at the guards, dramatically drawing his sword. He thrust the tip at them. "Who was in charge?"

"The guards are dead," one of the soldiers said quickly. "Who was in charge?" Rodriguez bellowed again.

"We don't know."

"Who gave the order to move them?"

"Capitano Santa Ana."

"Santa Ana! Who authorized him to move the prisoners? Didn't you look at his papers? Get Santa Ana in this office. Now!"

The guards turned to leave and almost ran over Juan Carlos as he barged into the room. "Your Excellency, I just heard the news. What has been done to find the criminals? The guards who let this happen should be punished quickly and directly."

Rodriguez looked at Juan Carlos with a mix of suspicion and pleasure. "You should know that answer."

Juan Carlos looked at the viceroy. "What are you saying?"

"You ordered them moved from El Morro. They were your charge. What are you doing to find them?"

Juan Carlos stood still. "But, I found out about the escape perhaps an hour ago."

"How can that be?" Rodriguez said. "You're a field officer. Do you run your battlefield this sloppily?"

"Of course not." Juan Carlos's voice verged on panic. "I told the guards I needed to prepare their execution papers. There were four guards. She couldn't even walk because of her wounds. They tied her to a pole to carry her to the gallows. We bound her lieutenant's hands, too. I saw to that personally. No one reported their escape until this morning. They must have had help from outside the garrison."

"Filthy natives," Rodriguez muttered. "You can't trust any of these pagans. They probably attacked them for sport." He looked at Juan Carlos again, this time more relaxed. He nodded. "Where are the rogues?"

Juan Carlos walked over to the window. "We don't know, but they couldn't have gotten far."

Rodriguez waddled back to his desk and started fidgeting with papers scattered on the tabletop. "They are most likely halfway to Saint John or Saint Croix by now."

"Their boat was too small," Juan Carlos observed.

Rodriquez shot another suspicious look toward Santa Ana. "How do you know what kind of boat they had?"

"The harbor master tracks and inventories all large boats and ships each night," Juan Carlos said with military precision. "The same boats were moored this morning as last night. They must have commandeered a long boat or small fishing vessel."

Rodriguez circled his desk, tapping his fingers against the wood. He looked at the papers and maps. "What do you recommend, counselor?" he asked without looking at him. "What wisdom can the boy emissary of His Most Catholic Majesty King Charles III bestow upon me this morning?"

"We have three choices," Juan Carlos reported, mustering his most authoritative tone and ignoring the sarcasm in Rodriguez's voice. "We can let them go and hunt them down later—"

"And let them mock me across the West Indies? That's not a choice. We need to move swiftly and forcefully."

"Then we have no options."

Rodriguez picked up a navigational map and a ship's manifest from the table. "We have a brigantine, a schooner, and two sloops ready to sail. Your squadron will be the albatrosses that dog the Pirate of Panther Bay's every move. You are my envoy, *Capitano Santa Ana*. *Capitano Hernandez* will be in charge of the squadron."

"Are you sure?" The viceroy's call to action mystified Juan Carlos. "Two brigs are scheduled to arrive next week. We can send out a full squadron then. The sloops will be useless against these pirates."

"Such inexperience." Rodriguez was stern, impatient, and direct. "Every day these rogues run free, they are a living challenge to my authority. San Juan is already brimming with dissent. Pirates stalk the bars and alleys of Charlotte Amalie and Cruz Bay. We need to act decisively and quickly. For the sake of the Empire."

Juan Carlos hesitated, knowing further argument was useless. "Yellow Jacket is also sailing with a frigate and a brig."

"You don't have confidence in well trained Spanish sailors and marines to take on a mish mash of water rats?" It was a clear challenge, but Juan Carlos paused again. Wisely.

"Don't worry," Rodriguez said, dismissively. "You'll have help."

Juan Carlos felt small and insignificant. Rodriguez seemed to have a plan in place, before he even entered the room. He felt like a schoolboy again as Rodriguez tutored him in the art of military strategy.

"I don't need help," Juan Carlos said, growing irritated. "Hernandez should be under my command."

"You betray your youth again." Rodriguez seemed gleeful. Juan Carlos now was sure he was back at the academy. "You're too impulsive," Rodriguez continued, barely containing his enthusiasm. "I would have thought the battlefields would have hardened you better. Frankly, I'm disappointed in the Court for sending someone so inexperienced."

Juan Carlos's anger flushed his cheeks. He clutched the handle on his saber, trying desperately to contain his frustration. Rodriguez must know something. Rosa. "Your Excellency."

"Enough!" Rodriguez boomed. "The criminals were your responsibility. Letting them escape simply demonstrated my own foolishness. I should never have trusted the Royal Court's orders." Rodriquez signaled to a guard at the door.

The door opened. Juan Carlos heard footsteps from behind him, but he kept his eyes trained on Rodriguez.

"You have one chance." Rodriguez said as if reading his mind. "Bring the girl scoundrel back—alive."

Juan Carlos let out a sudden sigh. He could do that. They captured Isabella and Jean-Michel once. They could capture them again. Juan Carlos straightened his shoulders with new confidence, forgetting, for the moment, the man standing behind him.

"I've assigned an experienced sailor as your personal aid," Rodriguez said after another minute of silence. Juan Carlos's muscles suddenly began to tighten. "He has experience with pirates. He's met this pirate they call the panther. He's eager to bring her back to justice. *Capitano Santa Ana*, meet your new aide. I think you've met before, on the decks of the *Ana Maria*."

Juan Carlos pivoted, trying mightily to contain a growing sense of fear. Boatswain Perez!

"*Si, Capitano,*" the boatswain sneered. "At your service."

"I thought you could use each other's company," Rodriguez said. "Between Senor Perez's knowledge of these seas and your knowledge of ground tactics, you might be able to stumble across and even re-capture these eels."

Juan Carlos glared at Perez, angry with suspicion and disgust. Had Perez told Rodriguez it was he, Juan Carlos, who had stopped his merciless flogging? Had he told Rodriguez the real reason for the defeat of the *Ana Maria*? Perez seemed gleeful at the thought of standing by Juan Carlos's side in the heat of battle. What was Perez planning? Whose idea was this, anyway? It seemed far too subtle and wicked for Rodriguez's style.

"This time," Perez promised, almost as if warning Juan Carlos, "they won't get away."

"Viceroy Rodriguez wants them alive," Juan Carlos said, keeping his eyes trained on Perez.

"That's right Señor Perez," Rodriguez confirmed. "I want to see them hang from the gates of San Cristóbal. This is not a revenge mission. I know you both want them dead. After all, the loss of the *Ana Maria* was embarrassing to yourselves as well as your King. I think this must have been the first ship in King Charles's fleet to be defeated by a girl slave. Needless to say, I'll be expecting your complete loyalty to the Empire on this mission." Perez shifted his weight anxiously as Rodriguez talked.

"Si, Your Excellency," Juan Carlos said, now more fearful than ever that he couldn't keep Isabella, or even himself, alive.

17

The sun lit the small room with an unusually comforting warmth, given the balmy day. It gave Isabella a false comfort, as she lay in the bed above the pub she knew all too well. For the next few hours, at least she was willing to accept it.

She still didn't quite understand her rescue from San Juan, how it happened, or why. She barely seemed to care. Everything seemed uncertain and vague, and she seemed to be floating rudderless ever since she had awakened in this bed.

The windows were open. The worn cotton curtains filled with a breeze breaking away from the busy market below. Isabella rested easily on the wood frame, her body folding neatly into the lumpy feathered mattress. She wished, at this moment, she was the young girl on the plantation, coming in from the fields to help her mother and the elders prepare for dinner. She had so few worries then. Get up, work in the fields, help in the kitchen, and go to bed. Her life was so much more complicated now. It seemed unbearable; a feeling made worse by the fact the only man she wanted to be with was her sworn enemy. It seemed to overshadow everything except one overriding desire: Revenge.

Isabella's back didn't hurt nearly as much as when they had carried her to this room. The crusted scabs across her belly were thin and almost gone. The scars would be ugly. At least she was still alive. Each minute in bed seemed to strengthen her. Two more days. That's all it would take. She was sure of it. Stiles will never know a fury like the one she was about to unleash.

"That's it," she muttered, mostly to herself. "Focus on Stiles. Juan Carlos isn't worth another second of your thoughts." Stiles was a treacherous pirate. No ship was safe on the sea with Stiles loose. At least she knew Juan Carlos and his loyalties, or so she thought.

"It won't be long," said a thick masculine voice from across the room. "You're getting stronger. I don't know why I'm surprised. Most men would have died weeks ago."

"I'm a nasty old woman," Isabella quipped.

"Old?" the man chortled. "I've seen children younger than yourself take the cat. More than one of us was surprised when you joined our merry band of buccaneers two years ago. You had scars then, too. Those scars were ordinary. Now, you have the scars of the Empire. Those marks are your diary. They will be your destiny."

Isabella turned toward the man. *"Mon ami,"* Isabella said, "if not for some strange destiny which I still don't understand...."

The man looked at Isabella admiringly. He had propped his chair back against the wall on its hind legs. He clasped his hands behind his head, his ear cocked toward the closed door. He was handsome. She had always seen that. In his twenties now, the stubble of his beard kept everyone but his closest friends from knowing his age. His gentleness was a mystery to Isabella. The rum never seemed to change it. His voice was smooth and familiar. His voice took her back momentarily to that summer of her sixteenth year in Charlotte Amalie....

"Jacob was a lucky man," he said, a smile breaking through the scruff.

"Carl," Isabella said, looking down at her bed sheets. They were his best sheets—Chinese silk. "Jacob is gone." She looked back toward the window.

"Not in your heart," Carl said, walking over to the bed. He dipped a rag in a pail of water and lifted it over her head. He gave the rag a delicate squeeze, releasing a thin waterfall. The beads bounced coolly on her forehead as they turned into a small stream. "Ahhh," Isabella cooed. She closed her eyes, letting the water soak into her shirt and bedding. She relaxed. She smiled. She saw her mother stitching together her dress….

"I have a few tricks here and there," Carl said. "Owning a pub and boarding house in a port has its advantages."

"Aye," Isabella said. "I've used those advantages more than once."

Carl nodded. "You've grown a lot."

"I still feel like a girl. Especially now."

"Perhaps you feel what you still dream."

"Aye, but those days are gone."

"They never existed."

Isabella opened her eyes. She looked at Carl sharply.

"You were a slave," Carl pointed out, as if reading from a history book. "You worked the fields with your mother; you never knew your grandmother. You can only guess about your father. You were fourteen when you ran to the bars in Santo Domingo. You were fifteen when the plantation burned and your mother died. Surely you can't think of the machetes of the sugarcane fields so idly."

Isabella looked down at her hands. The palms and fingers were still hard. "These calluses are nurtured by a new life. One that I choose."

Carl took her hands gently and turned them over, palms exposed to the light and ceiling. "I still see the grip of a machete. I still see the hands of a small girl carrying water into the fields. You have not grown that far from the fields." Carl dipped the rag in the water bucket again and washed her forehead and neck.

"You don't need to wait on me like this." Isabella's face reddened with embarrassment.

"The shop can wait," Carl said. "It's my privilege to service the Pirate of Panther Bay."

"Only Jacob has touched me in this way," she said. Was that true? Her heart pounded as she remembered the hands of another man, in the cell in El Morro.

"Tell me about the Spaniard captain," Carl said.

"What?" Isabella blurted, bolting upright from the bed.

Carl put his hands on her shoulders, pushing her down gently and calmly to the mattress. "Tell me about the Dago captain."

"There's nothing to tell," she said quickly.

"Jean-Michel doesn't seem to think so."

"Can Jean-Michel read my mind?"

"Jean-Michel has known you as long as I have."

"Can you read my mind?"

"We read your actions."

"You haven't seen me with him," she protested.

Carl looked at her. He brought his hand up to her cheek, gently pushing her hair to the side. "I don't have to."

"What does that mean?

"It means whatever you want it to mean." A hint of indignation was building in Carl's voice. "Isabella, tell me the truth. You owe it to me. You owe it to Jean-Michel. You owe it to Jacob's memory and your love for him. What do you know about this Spanish army captain?"

Isabella brought her hand up to his, holding it in place. It felt warm and soothing, healing. "I can't."

"You have to."

Isabella lay silently, listening to the street below her room. Someone was haggling over a lamb and mangos. "I don't know," she said honestly, tears welling in her eyes. "I'm so alone."

Carl brought her hands down to her waist. He leaned toward her. He kissed her lightly on the lips. "You are not alone."

"Carl," Isabella whispered. He leaned over to kiss her again, but she turned toward the wall. "I can't. Not yet."

Carl pulled his face away. "You have me. Why don't you let me be part of you?" A tear fell from his eyes.

"Jacob has been dead just six months," she objected.

"Eight."

Eight? Had it been that long since the *Ana Maria* had sunk? Since Juan Carlos had escaped? Since her imprisonment in El Morro and sentence to hang? Since Juan Carlos—

Isabella sat up, propping herself up on her elbows. "Juan Carlos," she muttered, as if forgetting Carl was in the room.

"Who?"

"The Spanish captain," Isabella answered.

Carl stood up and turned toward the wall. He swung back toward the bed, anger flushing his cheeks and forehead. "Jean-Michel was right."

Isabella looked at him, confused. "What do you mean?"

Carl began a quick pace across the room. "He said you had fallen for the Dago. I didn't believe him." He looked at her again, his eyes wild with frustration. "I can't believe you've fallen for a Dago. An army captain of all things!"

Isabella swung her feet around the side of the bed. Her feet were bare. The floor seemed cool and refreshing. She stood up, hesitating for a moment to make sure she wouldn't lose her balance.

Carl grabbed her arm. She pulled it away, and stood. She wavered in a rush of dizziness, but steadied herself against the wall.

"Isabella," pleaded Carl, "let me help you."

"No," she insisted. "I'll not sit here and let you treat me like a child."

"You are a child."

"No more than you. I've killed dozens of men. I've led a ship of drunken pirates into battle. I've suffered in El Morro. I've endured the overseer's cane working a plantation. Men have forced themselves on me. I have survived! How many children suffer like this? How many men can make these claims?"

"You're still a girl."

"A girl, but not a child." Isabella walked, stumbled really, across the room. Energy pumped through her veins. She had suffered. Her suffering strengthened her. It didn't beat her down. She could feel her purpose now more than ever. "Where is my blade?"

Carl, surprised by Isabella's strength, motioned to a chair on the other side of the door. A saber and sash hung over the arm on one side. A shirt and breeches hung over the back.

"What are you doing?" he asked, regaining his courage.

"I'm getting dressed." Carl still didn't understand. Could she expect him to? "I have business to attend to."

"What?" Carl said sarcastically. "Are you going back to your Dago man in El Morro?"

Isabella swung around, throwing a vicious slap across his face. Carl stood, too stunned to react. He looked at her. His face immediately softened. "Isabella," he said, his voice hollow with shame, "I'm sorry. I... I...."

"How dare you question my love!" Isabella raised her hand again, but stopped.

"Carl," she said, shaking her head. "I'm sorry. You're right to question me. My own self-doubt has caused enough trouble. It probably lost the *Marée Rouge*."

The two stood next to each other, struggling to find words. Finally, Isabella looked directly into Carl's eyes. She walked up to him and lifted her hand to his wounded cheek. "I'm sorry." She lifted her lips to his cheek.

"Forgive me," Carl pleaded softly, accepting the kiss.

"There is nothing for me to forgive," Isabella said. "I love you like a brother, Carl. That's all I can offer. Is that enough?"

"Aye." A sheepish smile broke through the shock of the last few minutes. "That kind of love can fill my heart long enough."

Isabella slipped her arms under his and pulled him close. She rested her head on his shoulder, the palm of her hand resting comfortably on the hilt of her saber.

"What is it about this Spanish captain," Carl asked.

Isabella leaned back against the post at the foot of her bed. She looked at Carl again. "Jean-Michel is wrong," she said after a moment, lifting her hand again gently to his cheek. "He freed us from El Morro."

"What?" Carl cried. "How do you know that? His loyalty is to his King and Country. He would never disobey the Court's order. His Creed would not allow it. The Court would not have sent him to serve Rodriguez if he would."

Isabella nodded in agreement. "But he is loyal to more than King and Country," she said. "He is beholden to a higher power than his King. He owes his allegiance to his God. His God cares most about justice and goodness."

"Many men claim allegiance to God," Carl said. "The Church is full of men every morning claiming allegiance to God—a Christian God. Then, in his name, they hunt down and kill women and children; they enslave them to serve their own purposes."

She grabbed Carl's arm gently, pulling him closer, and looked into his eyes. "Juan Carlos set us free from El Morro."

Carl's eyes grew wide with suspicion and disbelief. "How do you know? He's a Spanish officer. How could you know?"

"I know," Isabella insisted. She didn't dare tell him about the private conversations in her quarters, or on the deck of the *Marée Rouge*, or in the cell deep in El Morro. "How else could we have escaped? How would the buccaneers who freed us know our captors were moving us to San Cristóbal on that night? At that time?"

Carl looked at her, confusion still marking his face. "They had a note—"

"From whom? Who would know they would take us from El Morro that night? Only three people would have known. Rodriguez, his executioner, and his chief aide."

Carl was perplexed. "I don't understand."

"Neither do I," Isabella admitted. "But I'm sure we were freed by Captain Santa Ana."

"Why?" Carl asked again. "What purpose does your freedom serve?"

"It frees his conscience," she said with a knowing smile.

"What does he think you'll do?"

Isabella stopped at the chair, looking at her clothes. What would she do? She was still tired and drained. She wasn't even sure she could face the bar below let alone command a ship. She felt small.

"I didn't ask him," she said lightly. "And I don't care. I am grateful for the freedom he has given me. I don't feel beholden to him. I have a score to settle."

***

Thick smoke filled the bar. Sailors created a dull roar as Isabella and Carl descended from the second floor. Tired men, fresh off the boats drove these conversations, voices loud and fingers wagging, fed by rum. Lots of rum.

Isabella felt stronger, at least physically. Her hands made their way down the intricately carved railing. Her scarlet shirt was crisp and clean, forming smooth and clean lines around her body and breasts. Her saber swung securely from her sash. Somewhere, Carl had even scrounged up a pair of deck boots, recently resoled with new leather. As she placed her feet on the last step of the staircase, she practically dared the sailors in the room to challenge her.

"Look what we got here!" yelled one large man. His shirt, matted with grease and sweat, was fouled further by a pint spilled on himself. His hands were huge, well seasoned by a life at sea running yardarms in stiff and rolling waves. He listed slightly as he straightened up from the table and lumbered over to the pair. He towered over Isabella by at least two heads.

"What's a pretty little lady doin' in this hellhole?" the man said as he stumbled into them. He looked at the saber hanging from her waist. "What's this? The little lady's got some protection?"

Isabella ignored the drunkard and began to walk past him. Where was Jean-Michel?

"Hold on there, lassie," the sailor bellowed, grabbing Isabella by the shoulder. "Let me treat ya t'a drink, won' ya?"

"Let go," Isabella ordered. She was surprised at the crispness of her voice. For a split moment, she envied her role as captain. Perhaps she was ready.

"What's this," the man asked lazily, his rum-soaked breath streaming down on her face. "A little uppity ain't we?"

Isabella pushed at his chest.

"Let her go," Carl ordered.

"Ah, come on, I'm just having a little fun wi' da girl."

Isabella bristled at the word "girl" slurring off his lips.

"Let her go," Carl insisted.

Isabella's blood began to run; it seemed to bubble through her veins. She was embarrassed: How could she let Carl come to her aid? She didn't need his help! For the first time since the mutiny, she felt truly energized. She narrowed her brow and pushed against the man even harder. "I'll take care of him, Carl."

The man let out a thunderous, playful laugh. The other men in the bar broke into cackling laughter.

"Oh," the drunkard mocked, "the little girl's goin' ta take care o' the big sailor man."

Isabella's muscles tensed. She gripped the hilt of her saber.

"O', come on, Mr. Carl sir," the sailor taunted, "Ya had your way with her upstairs. Now it's our turn, eh? How much little lady?" He grabbed Isabella's arm and pulled her violently close.

Isabella pulled her knee up hard into the sailor's crotch. His arms released her as a piercing cry rang through the bar. The sailor stumbled backward. He looked at Isabella, arched at his waist, surprised at the fury of the blow. Another chorus of laughter filled the bar. The sailor's face reddened with embarrassment.

"Whore!" he rumbled. Isabella smiled. She was in control again. She relaxed and fixed her eyes on her prey.

The sailor straightened himself. His drunkenness evaporated. His eyes now had a rare focus. Isabella was in for a real fight.

"Ya want a fight, do ye?" he said again in a low steady voice. He pulled a long dagger from his deck boot. He waved the tip menacingly. "This one's got the blood of five Algerian corsairs on it. I'll give ya a fight you ain't never bargained for."

"I doubt it," Isabella said, pulling her saber from its sheath. She let the tip fall deliberately to the sailor's chest. The confidence of the move didn't make him falter. "You better have more than that toothpick before you take me on."

The bar fell silent. All eyes were riveted on the dueling sailors.

"I ain't worried about no girl," the sailor spat. "It ain't how long the knife is that counts. It's how you use it." The man charged, raising his dagger in a lunge.

Isabella parried, pushing the dagger to the side with the ease of experience, but remained in a defensive position.

"I couldn't agree with you more," she quipped. "But, you should know your enemy before you attack."

The sailor seemed unfazed by the failure of his lunge. "Ain't worried about no girl with a kitchen knife."

He approached her again, this time more deliberately. The sailor moved with more refinement, defying his own bulk. Isabella tried to calm her excitement. She couldn't resist the exhilaration pumping through her chest; she couldn't help but revel in the fight. She hadn't felt this much alive since she boarded the *Ana Maria*.

The sailor lunged. Isabella deflected the dagger, again, and retreated a step. She let her saber's tip drop slightly. The sailor took the bait. He brought his dagger up and began a forceful arc toward her throat. Isabella pulled back, letting the dagger swish harmlessly in front of her. She quickly pulled her blade up and over his arm, bringing it down on his shoulder. The sailor screamed with pain as the blade cut into his skin and muscle. The dagger clattered to the floor.

The sailor rolled on the floor, moaning. Isabella walked up to him, lifted her boot, and pinned his shoulders to the floor. He looked up at her, his eyes consumed with the pain from his shoulder. She brought the tip of her saber to his throat. The sailor's eyes turned to panic. She leaned closer to his face.

"Know your enemy," she repeated in a coarse voice. "Don't toy with the Pirate of Panther Bay."

Recognition swooned across the sailor's face. "You're supposed to be dead," he sputtered.

Isabella smiled. "I'll let you judge the truth of that rumor." She let her tip tick from point to point on the sailor's shirt. It finally rested on a leather button on his shirt. "You're lucky these buttons aren't brass."

She released him from under her boots and continued her stroll through the bar. Out of the corner of her eye, she caught the glimpse of a young lanky sailor—about the age of Juan Carlos—at a table in the back. His build was slight, almost feeble, but clearly English. He seemed familiar, but she couldn't place him. He tipped an English naval officer's hat respectfully and smiled. Isabella smiled, but Carl nudged her to another table.

Jean-Michel was sitting at a small round table at the end of the bar, well away from the main entrance. "It seems you've recovered."

"Well enough for a drunk," Isabella said with a chuckle.

She turned her head to look for the English officer, but he had disappeared, like an apparition in the night. Slovenly tars from an East India man now hosted the table, not the crowd this officer would associate with. Perhaps it was a ghost.

"Seriously," Jean-Michel said, concern clear in his tone. "How do you feel *mon cher?"*

"I've got a ship to claim."

Jean-Michel looked at her, sizing up her resolve.

"What are you looking at?" She asked.

"You've changed," Jean-Michel said, almost sadly.

"I'm the same girl who fought alongside you when Stiles betrayed us."

Jean-Michel shook his head. He looked at Carl. Carl was watching them both out of the corners of his eyes, hands clasped behind his head, leaning up against the wall. "No, you're different."

Isabella looked at Jean-Michel intently. "Perhaps I'm a woman?"

"Not quite a woman," Jean-Michel observed. "You're hard. El Morro did something to you. You're not quite a woman. You're not a girl. I don't know what beast you've become."

Isabella stared at Jean-Michel, unsure of what to say. Jean-Michel was right. She felt it. What was she? "I'll be a lot better after Stiles is dead."

"That will be harder than you think," Carl interjected finally.

"I'll sneak on board the *Marée Rouge* and slit his neck by myself if I have to."

"That's a nice fantasy."

"Buccaneer justice."

"Only one hitch," Jean-Michel warned. Isabella looked up at him from a cup of rum. "Stiles wasn't alone."

"He was too stupid to act by himself," Isabella said. "He had to have help. I counted six on deck with him when he came after us."

"If there were only six," Jean-Michel said staring at his tin cup, "it would be an easy task to take the *Marée Rouge* back."

"How many of our crew did he enlist?"

Carl sat his chair upright. "It's not the crew that is the problem. Most would still be loyal to you. They would have fought with you if they knew of Stiles' treachery. That's why Stiles didn't find you in the jungle after the fight on board the ship. He couldn't get enough of the crew to follow him. He didn't dare leave them to their own devices. They didn't mutiny against Stiles because they thought you were probably dead. Bounty is bounty, whether delivered by Stiles or by you."

"What is the problem then?" Isabella was growing impatient.

"Smith," Carl said, watching for her reaction.

Isabella threw her hands up in frustration.

"Stiles works for Smith," Jean-Michel said. "He's been working for Smith since before Jacob was killed."

"Arghhh," Isabella growled. She bolted from her chair, tipping the table and spilling the rum. She clenched her firsts, twirled, and punched them into the plaster. Pain shot up her arms as dust spewed from the dent. She pounded the wall again. "That dog! How dare he!" She kicked the wall with her boot, sending another veil of dust to the floor.

Carl watched, a faint smile edging up the corners of his mouth. "That's the easy part," he said after she had calmed down. "Smith is working with Rodriguez."

"What?" she sputtered. Isabella stood dumbfounded. Her hands relaxed, her fingers becoming listless.

"How could that be?" Isabella swung around again, fist raised, then turned back toward the table. She grabbed the back of a chair hard. White beads capped her knuckles as she squeezed the blood from her hands.

"They have a pact," Carl said matter-of-factly.

Isabella shook her head. "That can't be." She looked up at him. "How do you know?"

Carl looked at her as if she were crazy. He shook his head and stared into her eyes. "What is it about the Dago captain?"

"Nothing!" Isabella screamed, exasperated. "There is nothing about that pig you need to know." She pulled her saber from its sheath, brought it up to the ceiling, and pulled it down with all her might. A lengthy gouge split the tabletop.

The entire bar fell silent. "Adding a little character to my establishment?" Carl chortled.

Isabella looked around, embarrassed. Hundreds of eyes trained on her. She turned her eyes back to the table and the split. She wanted to run. She wanted to be alone. She lifted the saber off the table and put it back in its sheath.

It reminded her of a fierce young English lieutenant, sworn to run pirates out of Bermuda and Port Royal. An English naval officer who despised the Spanish as much as she did.

Isabella looked back at the table where the officer had sat, watching her duel with the drunk. She hadn't thought of him in two years—just before she had met Jacob—but it suddenly seemed like yesterday. She yearned for his company—an old friend who would appreciate her brush with death and mutiny. Was he her destiny?

"Still a girl," Carl whispered to Jean-Michel. Isabella shot a dark stare at him.

"Calm down," commanded Jean-Michel. Isabella wasn't sure who he was talking to, but she took a deep breath. "All is not lost," he continued. "Carl and I have a plan."

Isabella sat back down in the chair, eyes latched to the new groove in the table. "What does Smith get out of the bargain?"

"Guns, rum," Carl said. "What does any pirate want?"

She looked at him. "Justice?"

Carl looked at her, smiled broadly, and shook his head. "Smith?"

"What does Rodriguez get?" Isabella said before Carl could say anything else.

"A clean sea," Carl said. "Smith does the dirty work. Rodriguez gets the glory before the Court."

"Who else is working with him?"

"Can't know for sure," Carl admitted. "We have to assume all the senior officers know."

Perhaps Juan Carlos didn't know. Perhaps Rodriguez was playing him, just as he was playing Smith. Why else would he have let them escape? Perhaps he didn't. No, she thought dismally. The Spanish knew what they were doing. Juan Carlos wouldn't have organized the escape. He is loyal to his King. Isabella's heart sank. How could she have let Juan Carlos play her like this? Her head dropped into her folded arms on the table. Carl lifted his hand to touch her head, but pulled back at the last minute. She looked up. "You have a plan?"

"Smith has a frigate and a brig," Jean-Michel said, eyeing Carl. "We still have the loyalty of most of our crew. We can get word to the loyalists. Carl has two sloops outfitted with six cannons we can use. We can man them with about 60 men who left the *Marée Rouge* after Stiles took over.

They came ashore as soon as the *Marée Rouge* made port, here in Charlotte Amalie. They helped free you from San Juan. They're waiting for our orders."

Jean-Michel looked at Isabella. "They're waiting for their captain."

Isabella looked up at Jean-Michel. Her eyes began to water. Then they hardened. "How many can we get all together?"

"More than a hundred," Jean-Michel said. Isabella nodded approvingly.

"There's another wrinkle," Carl said, glancing over to Jean-Michel. "Rodriguez has dispatched a squadron of ships to hunt you down."

Isabella looked at the two. "So, we have to strike now, before the Dagos find us. Do we know where Stiles is moored?"

"He's off Privateer Pointe."

Isabella looked at them and nodded. "We have a plan." She looked at Jean-Michel hopefully. "This time, I'll have a real quartermaster."

18

Coves, caves, and canyons overlooked the beaches lining the southern shores of Saint John. Finding the *Marée Rouge* seemed like a miracle the day before, a good omen for a nasty mission. Isabella wondered now if it were really a curse. The sun would break the horizon in another hour. The *Marée Rouge* had to be hers before daylight or all would be lost. Huddled under the gunwale, squeezed together with more than fifty of her crew, she waited. She waited for the moment. The right moment.

The two sloops pushed quietly into the bay, pulled by steady oars of experienced pirates. No one moved; no one talked. The oarsmen seemed ghostlike and distant, almost mystical, in the fading moonlight. Isabella marveled at their skill.

Isabella felt vacant. *Can I really do this*, she whispered to herself, pushing her head between her forearms. She held onto a rope tightly as she crouched close to the deck. Isabella wanted to disappear into the jungles of Saint John. She cursed herself for letting revenge drive her this far. She wanted to stop everything. No. She had to push her fears and doubts aside.

A throw rug of clouds smothered the moon. Isabella turned toward Jean-Michel. "It's time."

Jean-Michel signaled the helmsmen to slow. He peered over the gunwales. The *Marée Rouge* was less than a hundred feet away. "Idiots," he mumbled. "They won't know what hit'm."

Isabella lost her balance and drifted into the gunwale. Jean-Michel dropped his hand to her shoulder reassuringly. She paused to collect herself.

"What would Jacob think?" she asked, using a low chuckle to mask her doubt. "I can't even keep my feet under me in a long boat in calm waters."

"Four years ago," Jean-Michel reminded her, "you had never stepped foot on anything bigger than a river raft. The sugarcane fields, the revolt, three years at sea, mutiny, El Morro... don't you feel stronger?"

Isabella felt tired, and worn, not stronger. "It was hard."

"Of course it was hard. How can you really know what you want without suffering? Suffering sharpens your direction; it helps you choose your path."

Isabella sat silently, letting Jean-Michel's words churn.

"This isn't Jacob's fight anymore," Jean-Michel said, sensing Isabella's self-doubt.

Jean-Michel's words rang in Isabella's ears. She closed her eyes and leaned her head against the plank siding. Of course. She should have seen it. The men pulling her toward the *Marée Rouge* were not Jacob's men. They were following her. They sought her revenge because it was their revenge. The mutiny was unjust. Stiles had used the methods of colonial tyranny. No pirate could stomach that for long. They knew she and Jean-Michel would return. They wanted revenge. Not for Jacob, but for themselves.

Revenge, Isabella thought. Was that what this was really about? Revenge or vindication? Was there something more important? Was this the prophecy her mother had seen?

Isabella felt stronger. She could do this. El Morro didn't take all of her; it channeled her. She felt the wall of the sloop's hull for support, hoarding the few remaining moments to gather her energy. She lodged her foot up against a small, nine-pound cannon. Everyone was ready to board the *Marée Rouge* on her order. Now, she knew she could give it. She had to give it. She closed her eyes again, trying to push away the last doubts. Jacob. He would not have hesitated. Jacob wasn't there in El Morro; he didn't give her strength. How did she get through those nights? She did it, not Jacob. Or, was it a touch from a stranger? A comforting touch. Whose? Not Jean-Michel's, his hand could never direct her, or nurture her. Maybe, her strength was coming from herself. This strength seemed bigger, more encompassing, more empowering, more directed.

Isabella sat, consumed by her thoughts, as the sloop sliced through the last yards of water. She remembered the dream. Jacob was at the rail of the *Marée Rouge*. He was talking to someone else, not her. He was talking to.... Juan Carlos. God, how could she still think of him that way? The albatrosses. What did they mean? She still didn't know. Was Juan Carlos directing the albatrosses? Her heart sank.

The prophecy. Was recapturing the *Marée Rouge* just a step toward fulfilling her destiny?

Isabella felt a strong hand squeeze her shoulder. She opened her eyes. Darkness surrounded her, but the sun was rising quickly. She could feel the crewmen nearby, sabers and cutlasses pulled. Pistols cocked. Hands worked their pants to keep the sweat from greasing their palms. She could barely make out Jean-Michel's face. She nodded to him. She looked up. A long, constant star seemed to beam down on her. She smiled.

She had to push Juan Carlos out of her mind. She had to focus on Stiles and recapturing the *Marée Rouge*. She had to vindicate herself. She had to enforce the Creed. Then, only then, after Stiles was dead, could she plot her revenge on Juan Carlos Lopez de Santa Ana. Perhaps then, she would understand her true purpose.

"Aye," Jean-Michel said, as if he had heard all of Isabella's silent debate. "That's the captain Jacob hoped would come." He jerked his arm up in the air and looked toward the bow.

The deck and hull shuddered as the forward cannon thundered through the sloop in rapid succession. A blue haze blanketed the boat. Isabella gripped a rope tightly. The oars pulled harder, bringing the brig closer. They must be within a few dozen feet by now. BOOM. BOOM. Scarcely two minutes had passed, but it already seemed like an hour. BOOM. BOOM. She couldn't see, but she knew the first shots must have shocked the mutineers awake. The second round of shots should have torn at the rigging, or even disabled some of the aft cannon. The mutineers would be on deck by the time the third round fired. The damage was done. She hoped.

Muskets flared from the aft deck of the *Marée Rouge*. Isabella's men held their fire—patience. Shouts drifted over the water; chaotic yells and orders drifted over the railing into her boat.

They're doomed, Isabella proclaimed to herself. The anticipation of victory began to calm her nerves. The familiar, acrid smell of burnt gunpowder overwhelmed her senses. Her focus was back.

Jean-Michel had crawled to the bow, scarcely thirty feet from her. She squinted to make out his shadow. Musket balls zipped through the air, but the *Marée Rouge* still didn't fire its cannon or deck guns.

"Jean-Michel," Isabella called.

"Oui," Jean-Michel called back. He was calm, just what she needed now. His voice strained over the pok-pok of increasingly steady musket fire. The oars pulled even harder. A poisonous mist hid everything now but a dull glow from the rising sun off the horizon.

"On your mark!" Isabella yelled. Blood streamed through her veins, recharging her. Her thoughts were sharp. The pulse of the battle wiped away her suffering—El Morro, the plantation, Jacob's death, the mutiny. Stiles was about to be hers.

Isabella climbed above the gunwales to survey the battle. Jean-Michel had positioned them brilliantly; the sloop angled just enough to let the forward cannon pick at the *Marée Rouge*'s rigging and scatter her crew. The *Marée Rouge* sat dead in the water, its guns unable to train on the attacking sloop.

Jean-Michel's saber lifted as the sun crested eastern ridges of the horizon and its tip rose high into the air. The ships crashed together. Swivel guns popped as grappling hooks soared through the air, thumping onto the railing above. Jean-Michel's sword sliced, sending two sloops of buccaneers onto the decks of the *Marée Rouge*. The dawn mist flashed with ignited flints. Pistols flared. Cutlasses clanged in hand-to-hand combat.

Isabella's fingers twitched as she gripped the handle of her saber. *Focus!* She screamed to herself. Move forward. Retreat will be death. Anger and defiance coursed through her body. She stood steady. Musket balls buzzed inches from her head.

Isabella hoisted herself up a rope as the sharp reports of pistols and muskets buffeted the air. She lifted herself over the railing and plopped on the aft deck. Bodies littered the wood around her as she ducked. A sailor stood startled just a few feet from her wearing a yellow sash—the mark of Yellow Jacket. Carl was right. The pirate pulled a gun, but Isabella's pistol dropped him first. She released the spent firearm and snatched up the unused pistol of the slain mutineer.

Isabella ducked and rolled as a musket ball zipped into the railing behind her. Scampering to one knee, she pivoted toward the sound of the shot. Two more yellow-sashed mutineers charged toward her. She fired into the chest of a deck hand, and he fell, mortally wounded. Isabella searched for the second man, bracing herself as her mind spun like a waterspout: *Skill, patience,* she chanted to herself. *Finesse, not strength; that's what Jacob taught you.*

A shadow lunged forward through the smoke, cutting a powerful swath with his cutlass toward her head. Isabella lifted her saber, deflecting the blade. The blade gouged a hardwood plank as the man tumbled into the ship's gunwales.

Isabella scrambled to her feet, turning just as the pirate began a second run: Parry left, parry right, metal clashed with metal. He attacked again, pushing Isabella into the ship's railing. She positioned her saber smoothly, efficiently, precisely, intuitively: thrust, parry, slice, and parry.

A tinge of fatigue tempered her moves—he was wearing her down. Thoughts of her cell and the lash flickered before her eyes. *Curse El Morro! Damn Rodriquez! To hell with Juan Carlos Lopez de Santa Ana! Take control! Focus. The past means nothing. Focus on the now.*

Isabella parried again, training her gaze into her enemy's eyes. Smith's quartermaster. Of course. Smith needed him to get Stiles. Why didn't she understand that when they dueled on the deck of the *Marée Rouge*? The quartermaster was the key to the mutiny.

"We meet again!" Isabella shouted.

"Aye, but this time you're in my sites. You don't have your crew to protect you this time."

"I didn't need them before," Isabella said. They circled each other on the deck, ignoring the din of the battle around them. "I don't need them now." Isabella sliced at the quartermaster. The tip ticked his arm and a spot of blood appeared through his shirt. The quartermaster lunged, but Isabella deflected him again. Just a few more seconds of rest, Isabella thought, and she would have him. She felt her muscles relax as they recharged. A calm eased through her body as her resolve strengthened. "Quartermaster to Stiles? That's not much of a promotion."

"It gets me where I want." Revenge filled the man's eyes, as his gaze fixed on Isabella's every move.

"What did Smith promise you?" Isabella demanded.

The quartermaster's brows furrowed. His teeth clenched. "Stiles is not my concern."

"What can Smith give you?" Isabella asked, slicing a half-hearted arc over his head. The mate lifted his cutlass easily, foiling the cut. "Is your life worth the rank?"

"I'm not worried about my life. You should worry about yours." The quartermaster advanced, arcing, cutting, and slicing as anger energized his body. His anger was becoming her advantage. She sensed it. She knew it. Her focus was her advantage. Her control was her edge. Resolve. That was the key. The quartermaster was experienced but lacked instinct. His aggressiveness was desperate. His thrusts and parries ran against his groove.

Musket shots punctuated a momentary silence as the sound of hand-to-hand fighting subsided. Isabella rotated her saber around the quartermaster's wide blade, pushing it down and to the side. She pulled her blade up in a forceful arcing cut across his chest. He wavered, stunned by how quickly the bout had turned.

Isabella regrouped. Confidence began to move the tip of her saber. If she controlled the pace, she controlled the result. Perhaps she could persuade the quartermaster to question his allegiance to Smith. The quartermaster lunged, despite his wound, burying any thought of quarter. This was a fight to the death. Parry, thrust, parry, riposte.

Isabella pulled her saber up cleanly into his chest, piercing his uniform. The quartermaster blinked, then stood, dazed. His sword drooped to the deck, blood soaking through his jacket as he collapsed.

"Idiot," Isabella grimaced, looking at the dying body. Was revenge that important?

She looked around the aft deck, unwilling to savor a victory. The *Marée Rouge* was not hers. How could something so familiar feel so strange?

As suddenly as it had begun, the climate on deck shifted. The heave of battle subsided to a hum. The moans of the wounded lifted over the haze of the main deck as feet padded across the wood. No one, save Isabella, stood on the aft deck. Who was victor, avenger, or mutineer?

***

Isabella took a deep breath as the night gave way to morning. She felt the sting of salt in her eyes. She quickly lifted a sleeve and swiped away a channel of sweat. Rubbing her eyes, she refocused: More than a dozen men lay near her, mingled lifelessly among broken muskets, swords, and pistols. Almost all wore yellow sashes. Jean-Michel was right. Smith's crew was undisciplined and weak.

Smoke sifted up from a coiled rope near a destroyed cannon.

The heavy smell of burnt grease wafted through her nostrils, churning her stomach. This was a strange place. She could hardly believe it was the same deck, the same hard wood, from which she had ordered her own crew into battle. Some of them, the same men lying dead and wounded now. The planks seemed tired and worn. Who could inspire a will to fight from here?

She looked down at the corpse of the fallen quartermaster. His face was pale, his lips ashen. For the first time, she noticed his face: He was a handsome man. He couldn't have been much younger than Jacob. A mustache and beard gave him the appearance of experience well beyond his years. He looked like a man of the sea, not the rogue he had become. For that, Isabella felt sad. She fancied that they could have enjoyed exotic ports like Barcelona, Cadiz, or the jewels of the West Indies: San Juan, Kingston, Havana, Port Royal, or Charlotte Amalie. Was he really destined to die? Like this? What was his name? Was it worth loyalty to someone like Smith? Someone like her?

She cursed. *He is not a victim*, she reminded herself. He chose his course and its risks. She should have no sympathy for him or his fate. Nevertheless, she did. What had changed?

Jean-Michel burst onto the aft deck. He carried a bloodied sword, a spent flintlock pistol lodged in his pants. His eyes darted from corpse to corpse, visually checking faces and uniforms.

"Mon capitaine!" he said as he recognized Isabella. He looked at the collapsed bodies around her and smiled. "And I was worried about you?" he said in a hoarse whisper. Isabella glanced around to make sure no one heard him.

"S'il te plais, mon cher," he said, detecting her uneasiness. "Please, I understand the prudence of silence."

Isabella smiled. *"Oui, je te crois, mon ami."* Isabella was oblivious to how the tenderness of her voice contrasted with the death surrounding her. A rush of adrenaline lifted her spirits.

"The *Marée Rouge*?" she asked.

"Ours." A smile cut across Jean-Michel's face. "Your revenge is almost complete."

Isabella clutched his shoulders, but Jean-Michel's eyes didn't match her spark. She let her hands drop. Other crewmen emerged from the lower decks before she could say anything else. They marveled at the carnage.

"I can only claim three mutineers," she said, tossing her hair with youthful pride. She immediately regretted the comment. How could she take a life so easily, after what she had been through in El Morro?

Jean-Michel remained silent as he looked down at the body of the quartermaster. What was his name? Isabella hesitated before the tip of her saber dipped efficiently to his jacket, and a brass button flicked cleanly into her hand. "He fought well," she said, a hint of sadness lingering in her voice. "His loyalty should have been rewarded. Instead, his treachery cost him his life." She lodged the button securely in her belt.

"Another souvenir?" Jean-Michel said.

She looked at him. "Tombstone. Death seemed to weigh much more on her now. She wished she could understand it better. These were new feelings. She needed to understand them.

Isabella turned toward the *Marée Rouge*'s newest boatswain. "Is the ship secure?" she asked. Sweat dripped from a smoke-stained bandana of a thin African. Sarhaan had come a long way since he led her unknowingly into the trap at the plantation. His actions freeing her in San Juan told her all she needed to know about the power of freedom. Even the battle's ashes couldn't hide his serious face. His gangly body was unmistakable, even under the loose-fitting, striped pants and shirt.

"*Si, Capitano.*" His Spanish was barely understandable through his African accent. He lifted a shirtsleeve to wipe a band of sweat grudgingly attached to his eyebrows.

Jean-Michel sent a quick confirming glance to Isabella.

"*Gracias,* Sarhaan," she said, placing a comforting hand on his shoulder. "This is a bit more exciting than cutting sugarcane I suspect."

"Aye," Sarhaan said smiling. "Like San Juan."

Isabella smiled and clapped his shoulder. She strode toward the aft railing to take stock of the main gun deck.

"Clear the decks," she ordered. Sarhaan used a few gruff shouts and mumbled words, and deck hands scrambled to ready the ship. Isabella sheathed her sword and mentally scored their victory as Jean-Michel looked cautiously on.

"It's not over," Jean-Michel said.

19

Fatigue overcame Isabella. She grabbed the railing to steady herself. Jean-Michel stepped closer. The crew couldn't even sniff weakness, even though they knew she had been beaten and tortured in El Morro. Not now. Not so soon after they had retaken the *Marée Rouge*. She cursed to herself. Stay focused.

"Isabella, you need to eat."

"Fermez la bouche," Isabella retorted, irritation rising in her voice. "Be quiet. I'm fine."

"Relax. We won."

Isabella closed her eyes and inhaled deeply. The victory seemed hollow. Stiles was somewhere. She couldn't rest until she found him. The stench of decaying bodies had yet to fill the air, but the morning's breeze couldn't cool the smell of burnt flesh. Scarcely thirty minutes had passed since the first cannon shot. The sun was above the horizon now, flooding the ship with bright light. A quiet satisfaction invaded her body again. Isabella tried to relax, but her muscles remained taught. Stiles was a fool.

They had recaptured the *Marée Rouge*, but a darkness huddled in her chest; it should have been harder. Where was Stiles? Where was Smith? Where was the *Wasp?* Jean-Michel was right. It wasn't over.

"Congratulations," Jean-Michel said in her ear. "Rodriquez has just raised the price on your head another hundred gold doubloons. Smith will be livid. We've made more enemies today."

A sheepish smile cracked the veneer of the buccaneer captain. "No King's Pardon for me?"

"No, Captain. The King won't be happy when he finds out." Jean-Michel studied Isabella. "Of course, a true King would grant a pardon without another minute's hesitation."

"Come now. Doesn't your Bible say you shouldn't kill? A king couldn't ignore that commandment."

"Aye, but its real meaning is 'thou shalt not murder'. There's a difference. I've not seen much murder on this ship. Not on our side."

Isabella didn't have time to think about such a fine distinction among words. She smiled as if her expression could change the subject.

"It's good to have her back," she cooed, caressing the familiar railing as she looked over the main deck. What would Juan Carlos say? Would he be proud? Angry? After all, she had achieved yet another victory under his nose. As an officer, he wouldn't question her tactics or conduct. She wondered if this is what he thought might happen once they had escaped from San Juan. "Hoist the scarlet flag of the Pirate of Panther Bay!" she ordered.

Isabella closed her eyes. She lifted her face to the newborn sun and stretched her hands deep into the sky. The late night clouds had all disappeared. The day was fresh.

Pulling her saber from its sheath, Isabella circled the tip in a wide arc. She let the tip rest, for an instant, at its highest point and looked at her flag flapping in the morning breeze.

"Let all those who challenge the Pirate of Panther Bay beware," she proclaimed. "Judgment for those who betray the Creed!"

Cheers swooped up from the main deck as her loyal buccaneers celebrated their victory. Propped up against the rail, her black leather boots lodged in its wood frame, Isabella basked in her victory. Jean-Michel stood; calmed by the sober work that still lay ahead.

"Count?" Isabella asked, as the cheers died down.

"At least twenty of our men were wounded," said Jean-Michel. "Five are dead. Four more will be lucky to live another day or two. The mutinous dogs took a beating; they've got a handful left. They wouldn't give up. They knew they'd be dead even if they surrendered. Or, else, they just couldn't stand being captured by their former captain."

"You mean a woman?" she asked indignantly.

"Call it what you will," Jean-Michel said. "You killed three. You can judge for yourself."

Isabella's eyebrows narrowed as she remembered the quartermaster. "Their spirit disturbs me. They weren't fighting to stay alive. They were fighting for something. I can't figure it out. The quartermaster. His eyes were angry... hard... calculating."

"Smith?"

"Perhaps," Isabella said. She felt there was more. The alliance smelled of something larger than Smith or Stiles.

Isabella scanned the *Marée Rouge* for something that might piece the puzzle together. Broken cannons, scattered muskets and pistols, and smoldering fires still pockmarked the ship. Her crew skipped from place to place, checking, turning, inspecting, and sorting. Loyal sailors darted up and down rope ladders leading from the sloops, carrying armloads of supplies, as they lay tethered lazily to the *Marée Rouge*. Soon, they would be ready to embark for Panther Bay, restock, and set out for the shipping lanes. The *Marée Rouge*'s forward mast stood with a cannon ball lodged near its base. It would need repairs soon.

Jean-Michel was talking to her, but his words had faded, barely audible, as if he were deep in one of the caves on Saint John. A half dozen prisoners sat huddled in the center of the main deck. Isabella stood for a moment, trying to comprehend the sight. These men, just weeks earlier would go into battle under her orders. They were willing to die for her. Now, they were going to die for fighting against her. Wasn't that what they deserved? What would Juan Carlos's God say about their justice? These men were scoundrels.

Jean-Michel shifted his weight. Isabella pulled herself from her trance.

"*Allons y,*" Isabella said, vainly attempting to brush off the sudden lapse. Jean-Michel stepped aside as Isabella strode toward the midship, grabbing her elbow. She pulled her arm free. Her hands followed the railing as she walked, dodging the splinters sprouting from musket balls. Without hesitation, she began a journey along the gun deck that she was sure would put her one step closer to her destiny.

Isabella absorbed the scene before her. Wounded littered the decks: their moans softened as some eased into their last moments of life. Still others fell into shock. Tufts of black smoke twirled up in a half dozen spots where small grease fires smoldered. Soiled yellow sashes lstrewn across the hard wood. Isabella struggled to keep her emotions in check, now that the urgency of battle had gone. Was this really worth it? Her men had taken revenge in more than one way, as the bodies thrown violently across gun carriages gave testimony to the anger harbored by some. .

"Standard orders," Isabella barked.

"Aye, Captain," said Jean-Michel. "Sarhaan?"

"Aye, sir," the boatswain responded. He dispatched two crewmen, pistols, and cutlasses in hand, under the aft deck toward the captain's quarters.

"Sarhaan," reminded Isabella. "I want to see the ship's manifest. I want to know where she's been. I want an inventory of all her cargo, not just the powder, shot, and clothing." The quartermaster acknowledged the command with a quick, sloppy, salute. "Don't forget the ship's charts, either."

Sarhaan motioned to a lanky gunner's mate in soiled white breeches and a pin stripped shirt. They disappeared with two other men into a hole leading below deck.

"Their spirit disturbs me, Mick," she said again as they started toward the main deck.

Jean-Michel nodded. "They were better armed and manned than when we left her."

"Peut-etre," Isabella said. "Perhaps, but Stiles let them just sit, as if they were waiting for us. They didn't even have guards posted. Their cannon were not primed. Their rifles and pistols were stowed." She stopped and looked around. "Why risk… this?"

"Je n'suis pas certaine," Jean-Michel said. "A clue might be in the manifest or Stiles himself." Isabella's eyebrows rose. She felt her heart pound. Stiles is still alive and on this boat. Finally, she could seek her revenge.

Jean-Michel nodded to a dirty, crumpled figure, propped up against the far railing of the ship. Soot, blood, and makeshift bandages obscured the insignia, but Isabella recognized them. Even near death, she could see Stiles carried the entrapments of his command. Nothing could obscure the yellow sash.

Isabella walked to the prisoners and stopped near a young, bearded sailor. "Where's Smith?"

The sailor ignored her. His deeply tanned skin and severe, weathered lines suggested his age was close to Jean-Michel—about thirty-five—although his rank suggested a more junior position junior. *Just like Smith,* she thought to herself. The sailor still wore his deck boots, and his clothes were in good shape. His name was Jeffrey, she remembered. He was her boatswain before the mutiny. Isabella's anger flared; she fought to keep herself calm.

"I asked you a question," she insisted, but Jeffrey kept silent. Isabella unsheathed her saber and pressed it menacingly against his throat. A bead of sweat broke across his forehead.

"I answer to my captain," the sailor said, the bead becoming a flood.

"I am your captain." Isabella turned the blade and its edge snaked under his chin. The air thickened. Jean-Michel moved closer to Isabella, almost as if his presence were a warning. She lifted the blade into the sailor's jaw. He winced, but the blade failed to draw blood.

"Don't answer the wench," came a strained, angry voice from across the deck. Fury surged through Isabella's body. She pressed the edge of her sword tighter. Jeffrey didn't say anything but struggled to lift his head away from the blade.

"Boatswain," Isabella said again. "Answer my question."

How dare they still take orders from Stiles. Isabella's face flushed with frustration. Then, she relaxed. She eased the edge of her sword back from the sailor's throat.

"Is your life worth so little, Jeffrey?"

"I don't know where Smith is."

"The *Wasp?*"

"With Smith I would guess."

Even in defeat, these men remained loyal to Smith.

Isabella found herself abreast another crewman. She didn't recognize him. He still wore his yellow sash. His clothes were complete—shirt, breeches, and deck boots—with a bandana wrapped around his head. She didn't see any cuts or wounds. How had he survived the carnage? Her instincts hinted that he might not be a pirate. Was this Carl's proof?

She glared at the man. "And you," she said, nudging him with the point of her saber. "Who are you?"

The man sat silently. No strange authoritative voice came from behind to rescue him. "Boy!" she said, flicking his shirt collar with the point of her sword. "You don't carry the signs of a pirate. You don't need a captain's permission to talk. You're alone. Why are you here?"

The man remained silent.

"Perhaps you're just the cabin boy," she taunted, "doing a rogue pirate captain's bidding." His jaw tightened. She could see him struggling to control his emotions. "I'm sure Mr. Stiles had lots of things for his cabin boy to do." Isabella lifted the edge of her sword to the man's chin. "You're a tiny field mouse caught in the paws of an island panther. I can have your head now or you can answer my questions… and live." She lifted the blade into the crook of his neck. Jean-Michel watched, inching closer to her side.

"I will likely die, either way," he said, anger edging his voice. His voice. It was refined, like Juan Carlos's. His voice was too smooth to be a pirate.

"Senor," Isabella whispered in Spanish, bringing her face closer to his. "Tell me why you are here. I am a captain of my word."

The man said nothing.

"You are neither army nor navy," Isabella speculated. "But you fight. Why? A privateer? Perhaps you're a mercenary sent by *Señor Rodriguez* to die in his place."

The man's jaw locked.

"I fight for my God, my King, and my Country," the man said. His gaze remained steady and straight, his eyes disciplined and focused. Isabella practically swooned from her revelation; Carl was right. Smith and Rodriguez had a pact.

Admiration overcame Isabella, and her blade relaxed. This kind of single-minded loyalty and commitment was refreshing. It was honest. It was noble. It reminded her of Juan Carlos. Why would they ally with a rogue? What had convinced them to change their allegiance? Was it as simple as the fact she was a woman? She pulled her face back, sheathing her sword. "What's your name?" Isabella asked the man.

"I fight for my King," he repeated.

She looked at him. Juan Carlos said the same thing when they first met on board the *Ana Maria*. She wanted to see Juan Carlos. She wanted to ask him questions. She wanted to learn from him. "Perhaps you might one day realize that fighting for your God is more noble and just than fighting for King and Empire."

Jean-Michel looked at Isabella, her voice carried a maturity he had not found earlier. "Just like the Dago captain," Jean-Michel said bitterly. Isabella had forgotten Jean-Michel was standing right beside her.

"Just like *Capitano Santa Ana*," Isabella said, with a deliberate look cast toward the prisoner.

The prisoner's face changed. His eyes darted to the side, making contact with Isabella for a brief moment. He knew Juan Carlos. Carl was right about Juan Carlos. Her heart slumped as a lump lodged itself in her throat. Her stomach twirled. It couldn't be true!

The presence of another man pulled Isabella back to the main deck.

"We find gunpowder… shot… hard tack," Sarhaan reported. "Many muskets and pistols. Many ammunition. They plan something big."

"Excellent." Isabella tried to shake her thoughts of Juan Carlos. She couldn't spend any more time on him now. Smith and the *Wasp* were still missing. With the sloops tethered to the *Marée Rouge*, their position was precarious.

"Unpack all the arms and ammunition," instructed Jean-Michel. He motioned to the ropes threaded through pulleys, jury-rigged to one of the *Marée Rouge*'s main mast yardarms, guiding an iron cannon toward the deck. "Load those two nine-pounders from the sloop and mount them in the stern to replace the busted cannon. We should cut off the sloops in a half hour," he reckoned. A few other crewmen rearranged ropes and hooks to prepare for casting off.

Isabella nodded toward the prisoners. "Give them enough hard tack and rations for one week. Put them on one of the sloops after we've stripped it of guns and shot. That should be enough to get them to Tortola. Under normal sail, they should make port in a day, two at the most."

"Edward England would be proud," chided Jean-Michel.

"Edward England didn't have enemies as vile as ours," she spat. "England had the luxury of time and compassion. We live in different times. You disapprove?"

"I don't really care," Jean-Michel said, looking around to the deck. "As long as we stay on course."

"*Oui,*" Isabella nodded, confident they were working as a team again. "Where's Stiles?"

Jean-Michel motioned to the body leaning against the portside gunwale like a crumpled old man. He barely stood, propped up against a spent gun carriage, his left arm hanging at his side, soaked in his own blood. His head dipped low, even as he tracked Isabella's confident figure. The captain's sword laid at his feet, stained by the short battle.

"At least you didn't jump ship," Isabella said.

She looked at his wounds. He didn't have much time. Powder burns splotched his uniform, obscuring a mortal wound in his side. Blood oozed from a musket ball hole in his left shoulder. A cutlass had found its mark, tracing a thin red line across his shirt from his collar to his waist. Pale, he still managed to carry the defiance of a mutinous rogue, a wannabe more interested in demanding than offering. Isabella squared off against him. "You should have surrendered."

Stiles spit at her feet. "I would never surrender… to you. Not to you or any woman."

Isabella struggled to control herself. He had been plotting against her even when Jacob lived. Her fingers tapped the handle of her sheathed sword. She paced in front of him, studying his face. He glared back. She wanted to cut his head off. "You're a fool."

"It ain't over yet missy."

She looked at him again. "Why didn't you post watchmen last night?" She smiled. "Your plan didn't have the expected end."

"My hunts end with the carcass of my prey," Stiles said.

"You didn't count on the stealth and speed of a panther," Isabella said, a speck of pride sifting into her tone.

"More like a jackal." Stiles lifted his head. "A scavenger."

Isabella pulled her hand hard across his face. "You stand here near death. Your ship was lost in this battle, not mine, and your crew now feeds the scavengers of this sea."

Stiles tried to straighten himself, summoning his last drops of energy. His eyes burned with hatred, the same hatred that fueled his quartermaster. Jean-Michel nearby straightened his shoulders as his muscles tensed.

"Do you really think Smith would have let you keep this command?" Isabella asked. She struggled to keep her contempt for Stiles controlled. She didn't want to kill him. She wanted to torture him, to whip and beat him as she had been whipped and beaten in El Morro. "Why do you think he posted his quartermaster on your ship? Why didn't he let you—the captain—promote one of your own men?"

Stiles looked at her. Isabella couldn't tell if he was too angry to talk, or he was actually beginning to understand the depth of Smith's treachery.

"Why do you have an emissary from Rodriguez on your ship?"

Stiles' face softened. She was closing in on the truth. Isabella smiled at him. Stiles thought he was in on the plan, too. Now he wasn't so sure.

"Where is Smith?" Isabella asked. "Why isn't he here to rescue you?" Isabella brought herself so close she could smell the sweat from his body and the fresh blood on his jacket. "Was it worth it? What did he promise you?"

Stiles spit into her eye. Jean-Michel rushed forward, raising his pistol to Stiles' head. Isabella pulled him back before he could pull the trigger. She raised her sleeve to wipe her face. She was calm. No hint of anger twitched through her fingers, or flickered in her eyes. Jean-Michel pulled back, knowing the course was set. Isabella had no choice. It was the law. It was their Creed.

Isabella stepped back. She looked at Stiles. His eyes drooped from fatigue. He was barely alive. Stiles knew what he was doing. Why was he so stubborn? An execution was pointless. She looked at him, studying his expression. "Do it" his eyes seemed to plead. It was the Creed.

Isabella pushed the wounded captain into the gunwale, forcing him to his knees. She hated him even more now. The Creed. Damn Stiles. She felt helpless and weak. Stiles controlled her even in his last moments. Was the Creed that important? It was the Law—a pirate's code.

Isabella unsheathed her saber, turned the blade flat, and sliced a wide, dramatic arc through the air. She dropped its point as her hand shifted to a dagger grip. The tip hovered over Stiles. Standing over him, she brought the tip to his chest. She gripped the captain's tattered collar. Pulling his face close, she forced him to breathe her air. She looked deep into his eyes, blinding him to all other sounds and sights.

"I am the fruit sown by the ambition of our actions, a bloodied descendent of Ferdinand and Isabella, and the laws of Castile," she whispered. "My heart bleeds for those who do not understand; it grows stronger from those who do."

Stiles said nothing. He seemed content—even glad that Isabella had to kill him, forced by his actions to execute him. He even seemed amused. He sensed her empathy, her dilemma, her weakness. He reveled in her inner torture. "You're weak," he said in a low voice. "You can't do it."

His words rippled through Isabella's calm façade. Her cheeks flushed with anger. Damn Stiles! Damn Smith! She didn't have a choice. It was the Law.

Isabella pulled her sword vertical over Stiles and lifted her weight over the tip, ready to drive the blade deep into his chest. Stiles was too tired to smile, but his eyes sparkled. Isabella hesitated. He wanted her to kill him—on his terms—out of anger. Anger and revenge. Murder. That's what he wanted. Isabella pulled the tip to his chest. The sparkle faded.

"See my eyes," she implored with an icy clarity that rattled the mutineer. The point of her sword cut into the first layers of Stile's uniform. "You think your death emboldens Smith or your men?" Stiles winced as the tip cut into his skin. "But, it swells my ranks, and broadens my shadow over these seas." Stiles closed his eyes.

Isabella paused, ever so slightly, but long enough for Jean-Michel to see it. He stepped forward. She had to finish this. Backing down now risked everything. It was the Law. Jean-Michel knew it. Stiles knew it. Isabella's blade slipped further into his chest. Stiles must think this final act was his parting victory. He was wrong.

"May God have Mercy on your Soul," she counseled in low half-prayer. "In the name of your Father, the Virgin Mary, and the Holy Ghost, blessed be those that sin; let their redemption not keep them from the Gates of the Hereafter and the tender Mercy of the All Powerful." In one quick, almost effortless motion, the sword drove deep into Stiles' chest. His death was silent. Instant. Without a moan, gasp, or gurgle. A more merciful death than he deserved, but she would not judge him now. It was not her place. It was the Law.

Isabella pulled her saber from Stiles' chest. She wiped the blade on a discarded cannon swab. She ticked a brass button from the tattered uniform and tucked it discretely into her belt. She then bowed over the slain mutineer. With the delicacy of a midwife, she closed his eyes. Isabella hesitated over the body, almost in prayer, before turning her attention to the remaining prisoners and the Spanish emissary. Stunned, the prisoners had watched the ritual in silence.

"I've never heard you pray," Jean-Michel said in a puzzled, reverent voice.

"I never have. Is that what I just did?"

As the shock of Stiles' death wore off, the mood among the prisoners turned volatile. Isabella signaled a gunner's mate, and a stocky African pulled his pistol. He cocked the hammer and raised it in the air. The sight of an armed freedman seemed to quell any thought of rebellion—for now.

"You won't get away with this," snarled the Spaniard.

"I already have," Isabella replied.

"Sail!"

20

"Sail! Starboard, off the stern!"

Isabella's heart raced. Isabella and Jean-Michel jumped to the railing. The ship was close, much too close. The unmistakable colors of the *Wasp* flapped from the mizzenmast. Isabella's knees weakened. A trap!

The morning's first wind pushed the ship toward them at a surprising speed. Jean-Michel studied the ship's distance. They wouldn't have enough time; two battles in a matter of hours. The *Marée Rouge* was still recovering from the first fight.

Smith's plan. Stiles was the sacrificial lamb. Smith surely understood that the battle would weaken the *Marée Rouge*. They were sailing from the west, using the cover of darkness to hide their masts in the early minutes of the rising sun; the same strategy Isabella used to retake the *Marée Rouge*.

Isabella held the railing, leaning her body against it for more support. All the confidence of the last hour evaporated. Panic slipped under her skin. Her body seemed too slow, unwilling to keep pace with the speed of the battle.

"Give the sloops fifty yards," Jean-Michel ordered. "Run the prisoners into the hold and lock them up. Prime the guns and run the cannon. Don't fire until I give the signal!"

Sailors scattered. Isabella stood, hesitant to move. Smith had a full crew. They were experienced. Isabella looked at Jean-Michel. He seemed so confident and determined. She wanted that confidence. "What can we do with one hundred men?"

"With the *Marée Rouge*," Jean-Michel said with a wink, "more than Smith bargained for." He watched the crew pull the cannon back on their runners, jam powder cartridges and balls into their muzzles, and tamp them securely. Dispatching the men and watching the preparations for battle seemed to strengthen Jean-Michel. "Our men are more disciplined. And focused."

Boom and a whistle through the air sent Isabella to her knees, covering her head. A cannon ball splintered the railing on the port side, less than twenty feet from her.

"It's been that long since someone shot a cannon at you?" laughed Jean-Michel. Isabella scrambled up again.

"I'm no fool," she said embarrassed. "I'm not going to let Smith take me out this early."

"Don't worry. His rogues're no match for a dozen of our men. Besides, we've beaten more than one frigate in our day. The *Ana Maria* was better armed than the *Wasp*." Jean-Michel's enthusiasm was odd, even maddening. She wished for Jacob's steady head.

Isabella looked at the pirate frigate bearing down on them. She hoped Jean-Michel was right. She felt helpless; all her effort seemed sapped by the retaking of the *Marée Rouge*. The crew and ship seemed strange and unfamiliar. The scars on her back hurt again. The scab across her stomach throbbed. The prophecy. This was all part of the plan. She needed to remain strong and focused. Like her crew. She looked at Jean-Michel again.

Her eyes must have betrayed some of her panic, because Jean-Michel put his hand on her shoulder and gave it a reassuring squeeze. "Let me do my job," he said. Isabella relaxed.

Waiting. That was the worst part. Just like in the sloops as they approached the *Marée Rouge* less than two hours earlier. Isabella tried not to pace. Anxious thoughts—fears—churned through her head. More and more seemed to come, until her brain felt tight and clogged. Her head pulsed from all the emotions—anger, fear, anxiety—packed inside a skull five times too small. She pulled a scarlet bandana from her breeches and tied it around her head, settling the pain into a steady hurt. At least now she could think.

Cannon from the *Wasp* thudded more loudly as the ship drew closer. Five hundred yards. Why hadn't we returned fire? Surely, the rifled nine-pounders could pluck at the rigging by now. *Patience*, she told herself. *Don't act like the flit playing tag in the sugarcane fields on the plantation. Trust Jean-Michel. Believe in him.*

More than a score of buccaneer sailors moved as well-oiled machines, tapping the fuses on the cannons and running them out, ready to engage the *Wasp* at the right moment. Each crewman, three or four to a gun, stood ready to swab muzzles and reload. The cannons on the *Marée Rouge* that still worked were solid on their runners. Most of her men were healthy and alive, crouching below the railing. One crewman at each cannon watched Jean-Michel. They were ready—on his order.

Smoke bellowed from the *Wasp's* cannons as it closed on the *Marée Rouge*.

Boom. Boom. Boom.

Cannon balls whistled through the air, slicing through rigging on the *Marée Rouge*. Smith still hadn't scored a major hit. Isabella inspected the rigging: One fallen mast could destroy any chance of survival.

"You'd think this was Smith's first fight," sneered Jean-Michel. "Losing a little rigging won't turn a victory today." Isabella thought the *Wasp's* haphazard shots were uncharacteristic, too. Why wasn't Smith more strategic? More focused? A hazy mist now obscured everything from the horizon.

Isabella's stomach turned. She was scared. Victory had been hers. Now, Smith was about to snap it away again. Just like the *Ana Maria*.

She was so tired. Stiles. Stiles had delivered her to this point. Spain delivered her to Smith. Juan Carlos Lopez de Santa Ana, Counselor to the Viceroy of the West Indies, was responsible.

She closed her eyes, fighting back tears. She had to pull herself together—now. Her crew depended on her. Jean-Michel depended on her. Jacob depended on her. Jacob. He was dead. What salvation could he provide now? "Damn him," she muttered to herself. "How could he leave me like this?"

Eight months ago, she would have been on the forecastle with Jean-Michel, using her will to pull the ships together. For the sake of Jacob. What kept her whining on deck like a whipped dog? Stiles was dead. Juan Carlos had betrayed her. Something was missing. Why did this fight seem so strange? Something was missing from her. What? She couldn't understand it. The world seemed to be spinning out of control during the slave revolt, too. Jacob steadied it. Jacob was gone. She was alone. All she could think about, lying in bed the last two weeks, was a Dago captain named Juan Carlos Lopez de Santa Ana.

She didn't want to believe Carl or Jean-Michel. The same man whose gentle touch comforted her inside the cold walls of El Morro couldn't do this to her. Could he? Could someone be so deceitful they could steal her heart and scheme against her the way Carl said he did? How could she be so naïve? How could she be so stupid? How could she have let Jacob's death leave her so vulnerable?

Isabella wanted to be back at the plantation. She wanted to be sitting at the knee of her mother. She wanted to be listening to the stories about her grandmother, of Ghana, of the tribal elders who led the villages far across the ocean. She didn't want to be here, fighting for her life, and the lives of others. She couldn't command a ship. She couldn't lead these men. Jean-Michel could. That was his destiny, not hers. The scars on her back ached. Her arm throbbed. Her head hurt. Right now, all she wanted to do was curl up and wait for it to be over.

An invisible hand seemed to pick Isabella up and throw her against the port gunwale. She fell to the deck, her body numb and useless, her head ringing, the sounds of battle faint and distant. She lay dazed—seconds or minutes? She rolled over onto her knee. The crease along her stomach ached. Pain shot through her back in streaks. She grabbed the railing. A piercing pain in her hand forced her to pull back. She looked down as a sliver of blood trailed down her palm from a large wooden splinter.

Isabella shook herself. Focus! She grabbed the splinter and yanked it. More pain shot through her arm as she clamped the wound to her breeches. Black smoke swirled around her and among the splintered planks in the deck. She rocked to her feet, holding her hand tightly against the fabric. The masts were still up. No one else seemed hurt.

The near miss seemed to recharge her. *Smith will not get away with this*, she promised herself, as the noise of battle returned to her head. *Not on my life, or that of my crew. Damn Spain. Damn Rodriguez. Damn Juan Carlos Lopez de Santa Ana!* On Jacob's grave, she would not let the *Marée Rouge* slip through her fingers again.

Isabella looked down the deck. Each cannon's nose had disappeared through the gun ports. The crew, like marionettes, waited for the signal from their puppeteer.

Smoke continued to puff from the *Wasp*. Missiles whirled toward the *Marée Rouge*. Isabella closed her eyes, grasping at the rail again. She didn't dare duck. A wind flipped her hair with a loud whistle—CRASH, CRASH, Splash. Two hits, one near miss. The pain in her hand seemed to race through her shoulder again.

Isabella opened her eyes. A hole had appeared near an unmanned gun on the port side. Another cannon ball dented the deck, but had not fallen through to the lower deck—too much arc. The men stood at their stations, unfazed. She felt so useless, so vulnerable. How could they stay by their guns so resolutely? Let Jean-Michel do his job.

Isabella's heart accelerated to a fierce beat. She felt younger—and more scared—than ever before aboard a pirate ship. Beads of sweat broke out along her forehead. She had to do something, anything. *No,* she told herself. *Don't do anything foolish.* She was no longer a girl. She couldn't be that girl that met Jacob just two years ago. Follow Jean-Michel. He knows what he is doing. She had to be the captain. Jean-Michel depended on it. The crew depended on it. Let Jean-Michel do his job.

Isabella looked up at the masts. They stood as stick men, naked without their sails unfurled. Their fabric bound tightly to the yards. The *Marée Rouge* was dead in the water. God, they were sitting ducks! They needed speed to maneuver. One or two knots would be enough.

"Steady!" Jean-Michel ordered, pulling his sword. He lifted it toward the sky. "Steady," he repeated. "On my signal!"

Isabella scanned the deck. A clump of sailors crouched behind each gun, waiting to board the *Wasp.* Their cutlasses were drawn. Their pistols were ready. She didn't have much time.

"Quickly," she ordered two tars nearby with muskets, "to the forward mast. Set the fore mainsail and fore topsail." She ran toward the bow, ignoring Jean-Michel as his saber cut through the air. A thunderous boom consumed the *Marée Rouge* as its first broadside flared, lighting up the bay.

The *Marée Rouge* shuddered as the recoil pushed it up from the water. The ship rolled, sending Isabella tumbling to the deck again. A cannon ball from the *Wasp* whistled through the small band of crewmen, sending curdling screams across the deck in the shot's trail. Two men lay writhing on their backs, arms and legs bloodied stubs. Another sailor rushed over, grabbing nearby rags, and tore what was left of their shirts for makeshift bandages.

"Hurry!" Isabella shouted to the other men, pointing to the mast. "The sails. We need the wind!"

The two battling ships moved closer to each other. The *Marée Rouge* began to stagger her shots, sending balls into the *Wasp* every minute. The *Wasp* fired randomly. Neither ship seemed to damage the other as they lumbered through the bay, trading shots. The *Wasp* closed within two hundred feet of the *Marée Rouge*. Smoke enveloped the ships. Muskets fired from the masts. Dozens of sailors fell to the deck, wounded or dead.

Isabella scrambled up the mast with two crewmen. They sliced the ties with knives, letting the sails unfurl and clap in the wind. They shimmied down the ropes, fastening the ends. The *Marée Rouge* shuddered again as its second broadside crashed into the *Wasp*. A breeze filled the canvas, and the ship nudged forward.

Isabella descended to the quarterdeck, dodging musket balls as they frayed ropes and canvas. Another cannon ball crashed through the *Marée Rouge*, lodging itself near the base of the aft crow's nest. Isabella looked up at the crow's nest—her early morning sanctuary—just as a cannon ball tore into its thick pine. The topmast tilted, and then slowly fell, sending sails and yards spinning around the sailors on deck. Blue smoke enveloped the ship.

Isabella's head pounded. She slammed her fists into the railing. "I won't let it end this way!" she yelled into the din, shaking her fist at the *Wasp*.

Then, she added under her breath, "Please, God, don't let it end this way! Juan Carlos Lopez de Santa Ana, why have you forsaken me?"

Another broadside thundered from the *Marée Rouge*.

21

What had he done? Juan Carlos Lopez de Santa Ana massaged the side rail of the *Grenada* nervously. Capturing the Pirate of Panther Bay would confirm his loyalty to the Empire. He cursed himself for doubting the Empire, but he couldn't expel his worrying. The *Grenada* was not the *Ana Maria*, but it could take care of itself. It was the most heavily armed in the squadron, an equal match to the *Marée Rouge*. However, Isabella was a strong leader, and her crew was as disciplined as an English man-of-war. They were no ordinary pirates. Juan Carlos worried more about the schooner and sloops in their little flotilla. They were armed, but was that enough? They were fast and nimble. That should give them the edge, shouldn't it? He began tapping the toe of his boot on the deck as he watched the two ships in the distance.

"You better know what you're doing," said a gruff voice. Juan Carlos turned. A boyish looking Spanish lieutenant, not much older than himself, stood next to him. Juan Carlos breathed a sigh of relief—it wasn't Perez. The lieutenant was every bit as fit and confident as Juan Carlos. A worn sword hung from his belt, clinging against his leg and boots. A navy pistol nested in his belt. His coat was open at the neck, letting the breeze cool his chest. Sweat glistened from a bushy moustache. A thick passel of black hair, tucked beneath his officer's cap, gave it an awkward tilt. They would have been a good pair on the plains of Grenada.

"It's too late for bickering, Lieutenant Gonzalez."

"That's what Captain Hernandez thought too." Gonzalez said.

"We'll see who's left standing at the end of the day. I know I will be."

"That kind of arrogance might score with the King and his Court," Gonzalez warned, "but it will get you killed here." He grabbed Juan Carlos by the arm and thrust his index finger at the two ships several miles away. The sun had just crested the horizon, giving enough light to provide a clear view of the masts and hulls. One ship, a three-masted vessel, was under full sail, while the more distant one, a two-masted boat, seemed at anchor.

"Look at that flag. What does it say to you?"

Juan Carlos stood looking toward the ships. How dare this junior officer challenge him? He was the colonial viceroy's counselor and a royal emissary. "If you have an issue to discuss, take it up with Captain Hernandez. Perhaps you would rather deal with Perez. He can send it to the viceroy."

"Look at the flag," Gonzalez insisted. "What's the viceroy going to think when he asks you to read the flags of the pirate fleets? Your arrogance will sink what's left of Spain's colonies."

Indignation raged through Juan Carlos. How dare he question the authority of the Empire? Juan Carlos peered at the ships, too angry to focus. Their masts seemed to fade into thin lines against the palms of Saint John as they approached from the northeast, but their hulls were easily visible. In another hour, the *Grenada* could open fire.

Juan Carlos inhaled a deep breath. He lifted a telescope to his eye and studied the ship. His mouth opened to respond to Gonzalez when his eye caught the oddity. The pirate ships' cannons were through their gun ports, as if ready for battle.

"I see a brash lieutenant who underestimates the power of our Empire," Juan Carlos said after a few moments, now trying to cover his own doubts.

"Hah!" Gonzalez said, lifting his arms in disbelief. "You act like a school boy on his first crush!"

Juan Carlos spun toward Gonzalez, grabbing him by the collar. "How dare you?" The lieutenant looked at him, shocked. Juan Carlos let go of his collar. Was the lieutenant right? He had tried to fight it, but he couldn't ignore the flip in his chest every time he thought of Isabella.

"I can't tell if you're blinded by arrogance or ignorance," Gonzalez continued, using a more patronizing tone. Juan Carlos felt like a child, angry because his friends wouldn't play his game. He turned back toward the ships, embarrassed. What made him act this way? What made him feel so small? He looked at the pirate ships, closer than ever now. The scarlet flag of the *Marée Rouge* flew in the morning breeze. What would Isabella think of his indecision?

"Look at the yellow flag," Gonzalez said. "That's the *Wasp.* Its captain is the most bloodthirsty of the rogue pirates in these waters. He won't stop at anything to get what he wants. Look at the other ship. She flies the panther on a scarlet background. That's the flag of Jacob the Red. She's the *Marée Rouge*. No other ship has a captain more cunning. They've formed an alliance."

No! Juan Carlos told himself. Isabella couldn't have joined with the pirate that sent his own quartermaster into the jaws of death on the *Marée Rouge*. Could he have misjudged her so badly?

"We have seized ships of the Royal Navy," Juan Carlos said, trying to project an air of confidence. "Our sailors are trained and seasoned by the West Indies. I'm sure we can handle a pirate frigate and brig in broad daylight. A Spanish brig, schooner, and two sloops should be more than enough."

Gonzalez looked at Juan Carlos, lifting his eyebrows in disbelief. "I heard you were a prisoner on board the *Marée Rouge*. After the sinking of the *Ana Maria*, you should understand what I mean."

Juan Carlos did, but he had his orders. He was in service to his King, an emissary of the Court, under direct orders from the colonial viceroy. Isabella couldn't ally herself with Smith.

"Jacob the Red's dead," Juan Carlos said. "Killed by privateers. He's no threat."

"At least you can read dispatches. All that royal education wasn't wasted."

Juan Carlos blushed.

"Jacob the Red died, but his flag still flies," Gonzalez continued. "The Pirate of Panther Bay now stalks these waters. We've heard the rumors in San Juan and Charlotte Amalie. Four guards died just a few weeks ago when she escaped from El Morro. If those ships are manned by the crews of Jacob the Red and Yellow Jacket, we'll be lucky to survive two hours. Even with a full squadron of His Most Catholic Majesty's ships."

"Pirate crews don't survive the loss of their leader," Juan Carlos said, knowing he was wrong. He couldn't let Gonzalez know the truth. "They elect their captains. If they lose a strong leader, they disband. No one else sails the West Indies with the stature of Jacob the Red."

"You can't fight in these waters from a book, or from charts," said Gonzalez.

Jean-Michel and Isabella were strong, he tried to convince himself, but surely, they couldn't rival the loyalty of Jacob. After all, Stiles led a successful mutiny. Smith was too ruthless to command loyalty. He had seen troops break at the sound of cannon under Smith's kind of leadership. Sailors were no different from soldiers. Could Isabella really be back aboard the *Marée Rouge*? Juan Carlos's heart beat more quickly. Why did he feel he was back in school? Isabella couldn't have overtaken Stiles and the *Marée Rouge* since her escape. There wasn't enough time. Her wounds were too deep. It was too soon. Wasn't it?

"I have experience," Juan Carlos said, although he didn't dare divulge its depth.

"Not in the New World. These aren't the plains of Seville or Grenada. We're not fighting the corsairs off North Africa, or chasing them into an island fortress like Malta."

"They're pirates," Juan Carlos said. "They don't think beyond the next bounty. They forget their bounty in tins of rum."

"Fool. Jacob the Red was different. The crew on that ship is different. They did not elect Jacob. No one forced his crew into service. They joined willingly."

Like Isabella's crew, thought Juan Carlos. What about Smith? Would Isabella really ally herself with someone like that? Was his judgment that far from the mark? Had he really forsaken God and his King?

Juan Carlos peered across the water at the two ships, still dancing toward each other as if in another world, searching for a clue. A puff of smoke emerged from between the two ships. A dull thud followed several seconds later. A cannon. "Jacob hasn't risen from the dead, has he?" Maybe he was wrong, disastrously wrong.

Gonzalez looked at him. "No. It's captained by his woman."

"His woman?" Juan Carlos said, smothering a laugh. Isabella would be enraged by such a petty reference—his *woman*?

"Then, we'll make quick work of her," Juan Carlos said, still trying to hide his true worries.

"Old World prejudices will not help you here. She's cunning. Cat-like. Four years ago, villages on Hispaniola burned to the ground during a slave revolt. The locals say a slave girl led the uprising… as beautiful as she was clever. The same girl joined Jacob the Red.

Together, they've captured dozens of ships. I would think you would have known that after your time on the *Marée Rouge*."

Juan Carlos cast a quick glance at Gonzalez. He had a distant look in his eyes. "Lieutenant Gonzalez, I'm not sure I'm the one smitten by a school girl."

Gonzalez looked at him, alarm flashing through his eyes.

"Nonsense. I respect the sea. I respect what she's done."

Juan Carlos continued to look at him.

"I've never met her," Gonzalez said. His look now seemed accusing as he met Juan Carlos's eyes. "I can respect her. I can't love her."

"Slaves and drunken sailors," Juan Carlos mused, turning his back to the ships. Was Isabella on that ship? Even if she were, she couldn't have had time to put a crew together and ally herself with Smith. Impossible.

More reports from cannons drifted over the sea. The plantations of Hispaniola? A slave revolt? Isabella had the fire; it had drawn him from the first time they had met in her cabin. Juan Carlos wanted to see her now more than ever. He wanted to touch her, as he had in her cell. He wanted to run his hand over her shoulders and down her back. *No,* he told himself. *It couldn't be.* Isabella couldn't have returned to the *Marée Rouge* so quickly. *It was impossible,* he said repeatedly.

"It's time to add an army mind to your strategy, Lieutenant," Juan Carlos said as he tried to overcome his doubts.

Gonzalez looked at him. "Your skills on land are well known. However, you're untested on these waters. They're more perilous than anything I've sailed before. I would rather face a fleet of British sloops than these two pirate vessels."

"Then you need more courage."

"You, *Señor*, need common sense. You're sailing in a different world. Your charts are old and outdated."

"We'll manage," Juan Carlos said with more force than even he knew could be justified. "I'm looking forward to bringing our prize through the gates of San Cristóbal and to Viceroy Rodriguez. If we have Yellow Jacket's head on the yardarm, all the better."

Gonzalez shook his head at Juan Carlos's boast.

"Besides," Juan Carlos said, "if what you said is true, why did Captain Hernandez agree with me?"

The officer stood, seemingly caught off guard. How could anyone question the authority of the Court or the viceroy? The captain of the *Ana Maria* didn't. Now Hernandez had a squadron of Spanish warships.

"Patience," Juan Carlos counseled. The words seemed far more mature and experienced than he felt. Gonzalez surely must know that as well. "Patience wins on the battlefield. Patience will win on the sea, too."

The lieutenant turned toward the helmsman as Juan Carlos continued to look at the pirate ships. More smoke emerged between the two ships. Juan Carlos dared not risk letting the lieutenant know his worst fear. Isabella, he prayed, could not be on the *Marée Rouge*. He bowed his head as the four Spanish ships bore down on two pirate ships now engulfed in the haze of battle. A cloud hovered over the *Wasp*, obscuring any sight of the *Marée Rouge* and the two sloops drifting beside her. Then, he prayed that all the West Indies would know soon about the new era dawning over Spain's empire and the Court of His Most Catholic Majesty King Charles III.

22

Isabella was confused. She had never seen a ship maneuver the way Smith was directing the *Wasp*. What was he doing?

The two ships had drifted along a parallel course. The westerly wind had pushed them around to the north side of Privateer Pointe. Now, the *Wasp* sat between the *Marée Rouge* and the eastern horizon. In the haze of battle, Isabella and Jean-Michel could not have seen the fateful approach of the Spanish flotilla.

The *Marée Rouge*'s last broadside was solid. Rigging now burned and hung useless from the yards and masts of the *Wasp*. One shot silenced a cannon. These hits were good ones but not enough for Smith to turn the ship. He must be counting shots and scoring the damage to the *Marée Rouge*. Why was Smith turning the *Wasp* into the wind?

Impatience boiled inside her. The acrid smell of gunpowder burned her nostrils. She pulled a cloth up to her mouth and began to breathe through it. Why couldn't a strong wind sweep the haze into the hills and give her a clearer look?

She looked toward the bow. Jean-Michel was watching the *Wasp*, too. Isabella jumped over the railing and sprinted across the main deck. She hopped on the forward ladder, just clearing a gun carriage as the cannon recoiled from another shot.

"What's he doing?" Isabella shouted.

"Je ne sais pas," Jean-Michel said, perplexed, his telescope trained on the *Wasp*. *"C'est tres curieux."*

The ships were a few hundred feet from each other now. If the *Wasp* stayed on her new course, they would completely disengage. This was her chance.

"Sarhaan!" Isabella yelled. "Take the rest of the men and set them up as snipers. Start firing onto the deck of the *Wasp*."

Sarhaan quickly began directing sailors as the deck burst into a beehive of activity. Sailors took up stations with their muskets and began firing at the *Wasp*.

"She's firing her starboard cannon," Jean-Michel said, his voice hollow with disbelief. "It looks like they're being attacked!"

Cannon fired from both sides of the *Wasp*, thickening the cloud around it.

"What should we do?" Isabella asked, standing awkwardly as they looked at the ship.

"Stay the course. We can't do anything about the other ship until we can see it. It must be a privateer, or another pirate who just couldn't pass up the opportunity."

A blinding flash consumed the *Wasp*. A volcanic boom shook the *Marée Rouge* as a thick black cloud mushroomed over the *Wasp*. Bodies flew haphazardly into the air as debris shot high above the *Wasp's* hull and then began a meandering arc down to the water. All three masts fell into the cloud, pulling the sails with them. A sudden wind swept over the *Marée Rouge*, forcing the ship to list steeply. Isabella grabbed the railing to steady herself. Flames lashed at the thick black smoke as the crew of the *Marée Rouge* looked on in stunned silence.

Yet, even the shock of the *Wasp's* destruction couldn't prepare them for what was emerging through the smoke like ghosts in Saint John's deepest forest.

23

Isabella's heart drummed so hard she thought it would burst.

"Mon Dieu, Jean-Michel," she stammered in disbelief. All Jean-Michel could muster was a drifty *"oui"* as he surveyed the scene before them.

Just a few hundred yards beyond the flaming wreckage of the *Wasp* was a flotilla of warships—all flying Spain's colors.

"One brig, a schooner, two sloops," Jean-Michel said, as if recording items in the ship's manifest.

Isabella peered over the choppy waters. "It looks like Yellow Jacket had more luck with the Dagos than us. One of the sloops is on fire. The schooner looks like it lost its main sail; it's harmless for now. We can put skeleton crews on our sloops. They can engage the Spanish sloops while we go after the brig."

Jean-Michel surveyed the *Marée Rouge*. He guessed—hoped—they had lost fewer than a dozen men. The winds had stiffened. His plan could work, if everything went their way.

"Sarhaan!" Jean-Michel yelled down the main deck. "Set all sails! We need speed. Take two dozen men and send one of the sloops to engage the Dago sloop. Take another two dozen and have them engage the other sloop. Ignore the schooner unless it looks like it can re-engage."

Sarhaan looked at the Spanish ships, back to Jean-Michel doubtfully, and then to Isabella.

"We don't have time," Jean-Michel called. "They're set for full sail. They'll out run us with these winds. Make sure our ships keep their distance. Accuracy. Accuracy and patience. Don't let them get close enough to board, or we're all doomed."

Sarhaan looked at Isabella as if hoping for some sign he could ignore Jean-Michel's warning.

"Go!" Jean-Michel ordered without looking at Isabella. The force of the order sent Sarhaan down the deck, tagging men and directing them to the two pirate sloops dragging lazily behind the *Marée Rouge*.

"Can we do this?" Isabella asked Jean-Michel.

"We have no choice."

"How did they find us?"

Jean-Michel looked at her, his eyes glaring with anger. "How do you think?" he roared angrily.

Isabella looked at the Spanish brig, now visible through the haze of the *Wasp's* fading ghost. It didn't make sense. Carl said Rodriguez was conspiring with Smith. Why would he destroy Smith? Her heart leapt with sudden joy and paralyzing anxiety. Juan Carlos. He had not allied with Smith. He was commanding the brig. Could he really hunt her down like a dog and send her back to that hellhole in San Juan? She leaned into the railing, peering at the brig, hoping to catch a glimpse of Juan Carlos.

A deep foreboding gripped her insides. She sensed this was a critical part of the prophecy. Her destiny did not lay with Yellow Jacket. It lay with Spain.

"You're right," she said. "We have no choice. Our only salvation is to fight. I will not go back to El Morro."

Jean-Michel was already barking orders to the crew. The *Marée Rouge*'s guns seemed restless as their masters made preparations for what could be their final task. The deck seemed ghostlike. The only men left were those manning the guns. Any casualty risked rendering a cannon useless. A dozen casualties could end the fight altogether. Isabella mentally mapped the *Marée Rouge*, plotting each passageway to the powder room and magazine. She remembered the prisoners locked in the ship's hold.

"Jean-Michel," she said. "The prisoners. They are rogues, but can no longer have loyalty to Smith. Their lives depend on us now.

"Aye," Jean-Michel agreed. "Bring them on deck to man the guns!"

Isabella vowed she would not go back to El Morro. She would not disgrace herself before Juan Carlos, or the memory of Jacob. Juan Carlos must be on that ship, she told herself. Isabella closed her eyes and let the humid Caribbean air refresh her lungs.

The bow of the crippled *Marée Rouge* heaved over a swell as it rolled toward the two-masted Spanish brig. They could barely make out the *Grenada's* name through the telescope, but its lines were unmistakable. The Spanish ship was well armed and her captain patient, a combination that could spell the death of the *Marée Rouge* and her fragile sloops.

"Patience, mon capitain," coaxed Jean-Michel, the rural accent of southern France more evident than ever. Startled, Isabella looked at him. She forced her gaze back to the *Grenada.*

"At five knots," Jean-Michel said, moving closer, "we should engage in 15 minutes."

"We can't risk wasting shot."

"Aye. Every shot counts today." Jean-Michel looked at the former mutineers as they took up their positions at the cannon, desperate loyalty in their eyes and moves. "Every crewman counts. We'll see what the Dago ship will do. It will be a good test of her captain's experience."

Jean-Michel was now oppressively close. Isabella glanced down at his rope callused hands. Could he sense what caused her anxiety? Could he sense her desire for Juan Carlos? She gripped the railing, white knuckles spotting her dark hands.

"Nerves?" said Jean-Michel. "First on the sloop before we retook the *Marée Rouge*. Then when Smith fired his first volley. Now, when we are about to engage a Spanish squadron of pirate hunters." Jean-Michel chuckled. "Anxiety like this is good. It keeps your mind alert."

Isabella remained silent. "At times, this life still seems new to me," she confessed. "I live for the fight, but I feel poorly suited for the life that puts me here."

Jean-Michel's hand fell over hers. "Eight months have passed since Jacob's death." Isabella shook her head. Jacob's memory didn't haunt her as it did when they engaged the *Ana Maria.*

"Two years under the watchful eye of a master," Jean-Michel said. "El Morro. An escape from San Juan before the hangman's noose. That's enough to season the best. Take heart *mon amie.* Your experience will carry you through this day and many years to come."

"Four years ago I had never stepped foot on anything but a river raft."

"Courage. The crew will follow your actions, not your fear. As always. Unless that's where you lead them."

Jean-Michel looked up at the sails, now fully extended by the stiff breeze whisking them through the harbor. "The Dagos'll be picking at our rigging now."

"Aye," Isabella said nervously. She left her hand on the railing—it felt strangely normal for it to be so close to his. He seemed so safe. She wondered if Jean-Michel was what her father would have been like. The *Marée Rouge* heaved again as her bow sliced through another swell. Isabella drummed her fingers on the oak.

How many times had she gone into battle? Dozens. Why was this any different? She was captain, now, for sure. The crew was together again, bound by loyalty and purpose. Stiles was dead. Smith was dead. Only Juan Carlos stood between them and freedom. She was confused. Why did her heart fight against her mind? Why did she still want to see Juan Carlos?

The rising sun revealed a beautiful pale blue sky. The noses of Spanish cannon waited for the approaching pirate ship. The gun ports formed a clean line, tracing her gunwale. The artistic formality seemed fitting for the colonial squadron. Isabella wondered at the irony. Would this be the end or a new beginning?

Isabella peered through the telescope, mentally noting every detail, from stern to bow. The *Grenada* had twelve cannon portals, two masts, and a raised aft deck. She seemed slow, almost lumbering, in the water. Dozens of Spanish marines and sailors scrambled on board, preparing for their second battle of the day.

The captain stood in a cluster near the ship's wheel on the aft deck, surrounded by several men. That seemed odd. Isabella squinted, adjusting the telescope, to focus on the small group. Two Spanish naval officers, golden fleece sparkling in the sun, were waving their hands urgently. *It's too late to disengage,* she reasoned to herself. W*hat could they be arguing about?*

One of the men turned his back. A third man was now visible. He was clearly the center of the argument. He was much younger, but his presence dominated them all. His clothing was civilian, not naval, or even army. Juan Carlos! Isabella breathed deeply, fighting to calm her nerves. Anticipation tightened her chest again, as she turned back to the *Marée Rouge*.

Isabella looked down at the main deck of the *Marée Rouge*. She couldn't go back to El Morro. She couldn't submit herself to the Empire. She had only one choice.

Jean-Michel and Isabella stood at the railing, listening to waves count down their last moments before battle. They had closed within range.

"How many times have we done this?" she asked. Jean-Michel stood, watching the Spanish brig. "The Dago captain is patient."

"The captain is not the only one who is patient," Jean-Michel said. "Rodriguez's lap dog seems to be calling the shots."

Isabella felt her heart leap. "Don't underestimate him."

"I'm not," Jean-Michel said, turning toward her. "I don't have to like him to respect him. I'm not so worried about *Señor Santa Ana*. I know the devil when I see him."

Isabella turned to face him. "Don't doubt my loyalties."

She looked down at the deck, embarrassed. Every time she saw Juan Carlos, she felt like the fourteen-year old slave girl sneaking out to Santo Domingo to flirt with the sailors. She felt confused. Could she give Jean-Michel and the *Marée Rouge* the loyalty they needed? Did she really want to win this fight? "You're not the only target," she said to Jean-Michel. "I'm not going back to El Morro."

That seemed to satisfy him. It didn't satisfy Isabella.

24

A flame burst from one of the *Marée Rouge*'s forward cannons as her sights trained on the Spanish brig. The shot fell short. Another shot flew over the deck of the *Grenada.*

"Jean-Michel," said Isabella in mock surprise, trying to cover her own fears about the coming duel.

"A rifled twelve-pound cannon can do better than that," he yelled toward the gunner's crew. The *Grenada's* guns remained silent, unsettling Isabella even more. Changing battle plans now would spell disaster. Stay the course. That's what Jacob would do, she told herself. That's what Juan Carlos would do on the battlefield. What if the Spaniards had a better strategy? What if Juan Carlos had purposely steered her toward this course? What if he anticipated they would face off like this? Sweat broke out over Isabella's entire body at the thought. What if...?

Stay the course, she ordered herself, wiping the sweat with her sleeve.

The boom of another cannon rang down the main deck. Orange and yellow ignited on the Spanish ship, sending a loud crack across the water. A hit!

"Jean-Michel?" Isabella asked, noticing an odd silence.

"The Dagos are trimming their sails. They'll fire any minute."

Isabella drew in a breath, closed her eyes, and let the air ebb. "*Bien sur, mon ami.* I won't question your loyalties. Or your faith." She looked at him, hoping her smile would reassure him. "You're a good friend."

"And a talented lieutenant?"

"Aye," she smiled, giving his shoulder a light-hearted slap. "Lieutenants aren't given the credit due. We both know who the real captain is aboard the *Marée Rouge*. If nothing else, this fight has shown that."

One hundred yards. The imposing, well-armed bulk of the *Grenada* loomed in front of them. For the first time, Jean-Michel seemed to hesitate.

"Donc, mon capitaine, quand sera t'il arrête?" Jean-Michel's said, his voice sympathetic again. Jean-Michel started toward the ladder to orchestrate the broadsides. "It will stop when we give the order, *mon capitaine.* The crew stands ready at your command."

"Captain!" The voice came from a stout man now standing at midships. His thick eyebrows gave him a seasoned stare, enhanced even more by long bushy hair dipping below his shoulders.

"Mr. Washington?"

"At your command."

"Thank you, Mr. Washington," Isabella said without turning. "Jean-Michel?" She looked at him as if asking for permission. Jean-Michel nodded.

There was no turning back. She would not go back to El Morro, no matter what the cost. She was relaxed. She felt strong again. Focused. Excited. Her emotions had splintered. She had glued them together again, making a strong yoke. She was sure of it. "Fire on Jean-Michel's order."

Isabella drew her sword, and the men below instantly sprang to their stations. Buccaneers floated and hovered over their cannon, as their snouts thrust through the gun portals. "Jean-Michel?"

"Aye, Captain." Jean-Michel pulled his blade from its sheath.

"Merci et bon chance."

Jean-Michel shrugged, smiled, and disappeared toward the bow.

Isabella turned to the Spanish brig for the last time. Now, they would show them their teeth and their gut. The only hope for the *Marée Rouge* was a series of three accurate broadsides. They had to cripple the *Grenada* before she could regroup. Two fires were now burning on the *Grenada*—a good sign. Why did they still wait? She had never seen a Spanish captain so patient. It didn't make sense. He was giving her the advantage. Was this arrogance or confidence?

A trap? Perhaps another brig, or schooner, was ready to pounce around the cay. Isabella scoured the horizon for signs of other masts. Nothing. Were legions of soldiers below deck, waiting to board the *Marée Rouge*? That would be ideal—Juan Carlos could recapture her easily if that happened. Could Juan Carlos do that, knowing what El Morro had done to her?

No, she quickly convinced herself, trying to push her feelings for Juan Carlos far from her mind. They couldn't hold that many marines and sailors below deck for long. Isabella caught Jean-Michel watching her from the forecastle. At a hundred paces, he still knew by the feverish twitch of her hands that something was amiss.

"Captain?" came a voice from the main deck, again.

"Yes, Mr. Washington."

"Orders?"

What were her orders? She had to show Jean-Michel she could do this. *Stay the course,* she told herself, *aggressively.* Isabella looked down at Washington. "Standard orders, Mr. Washington. Arm the men with extra daggers and pistols—in case they try to board."

"Aye, Captain." Isabella looked at Jean-Michel. Could he tell she needed him, now more than ever? Jacob was gone. Juan Carlos was nothing but a mirage. The decks went eerily quiet. As the waves beat against the hull, scenario after scenario clicked through her brain, as she pondered every possibility and its response. Her men were ready. She was ready. "Now," she muttered to herself, "we'll see whether you'll get what you bargained for."

Power and decisiveness surged through her body. She hadn't felt such energy since the slave revolt. She gave Jean-Michel the signal. Jean-Michel raised his saber. The ship rumbled with the thunderous flare of cannon as the *Marée Rouge*'s shot seared through the afternoon air.

25

The bow of the *Marée Rouge* shuddered as cannon carriages rocked in unison. The cannon careened back on their runners, pulling the barrels inside the ship. One broadside down, two more to go.

Isabella kept her eyes focused on the *Grenada*. Where was Juan Carlos? What was he doing? What was he telling the captain of the *Grenada*? Was he telling him of her tears in El Morro? Was he plotting her death with the same comforting hand that kneaded her shoulders as they bled from the lashes of the boatswain's whip? She struggled to keep tears from blurring her eyes. She needed to stay focused on the battle.

Like a well-greased wheel, the crew of the *Marée Rouge* worked coolly, methodically, and efficiently. They jammed wet swabs down the barrels. Steam spewed from their open holes. Others turned toward the powder boxes, lifting heavy, neatly packed charges. Still others chased the charges down the barrels with cannon balls. They pushed the cannon through the gun ports, and waited for Jean-Michel's signal.

The *Marée Rouge* lurched out of the water as a deafening roar engulfed the ship. The *Grenada's* first broadside pierced through deck and rigging with deadly accuracy. Ropes, blocks, and splintered wood cascaded down onto the main deck. Small fires burst out on the forecastle and around the main mast. A yard cut loose, sending up a twisting, falling roar that momentarily drowned out all human sounds. The sails ripped from their rings, sending canvass floating toward the deck.

Isabella's insides reeled. She now knew they would duel to the death.

The buccaneers huddled near their guns, waiting for orders. Jean-Michel's saber arced toward the deck; the *Marée Rouge* shuddered as another broadside leapt toward the *Grenada.*

Isabella peered through the telescope, hoping for a glimpse of the *Grenada's* main deck. "My God," she gasped. Disciplined rows of uniformed Spanish marines loaded their muskets and drew their sabers. They were preparing to board the *Marée Rouge*. How could this be? Two broadsides should have devastated their ranks!

Isabella's eyes raked the *Grenada's* deck for a sign. Deep in her chest, she knew the answer. She had to be sure. There, in a hole in the mist. She saw him. Juan Carlos was rallying the Spanish marines, like ghosts in the bubbling smoke. Saber in hand, he ran down their ranks as muskets lowered and fired at the *Marée Rouge*. Isabella ducked, and looked at her crew. Sabers clattered as musket balls hit their marks and crewmen dropped listlessly to the deck.

Isabella climbed the ropes of what was left of the aft mast, straining through the sounds of the battle. She watched in awe as Juan Carlos orchestrated the crisp orderliness of the marines. He was everything she had remembered. They would board within minutes, unless she did something. A pall of smoke filled the hole, and Juan Carlos, her ghost, was gone. Anger flooded her head. How could he do this to her?

Another broadside from the *Marée Rouge* ripped into the *Grenada*. Musket balls whistled through the air around her, but none could force her back to the main deck. The *Marée Rouge* shuddered as a broadside from the *Grenada* pierced her wooden decks. How much longer could this go on? How long could Juan Carlos punish her? Isabella relaxed as she saw another flash of Jean-Michel's saber. Another broadside burst from the hull of the *Marée Rouge*. The ships pounded each other with broadside after broadside. Each ship seemed to withstand the rain of cannon balls that shredded rigging and crew.

Then, as Isabella peered into the thick haze of battle, the top portion of the *Grenada's* masts disappeared into the mist. An unsettling silence seized the ships and their crews. For an instant, Isabella wondered if they had unknowingly drifted away from each other.

A breeze swept the haze from the ships. Fires smoldered on both decks. The *Grenada* listed slightly seaward, its rigging loose and undisciplined, sails shredded by shot, barely able to hold a breeze. Men lay writhing and motionless; the marines had scattered.

The *Marée Rouge* was scarcely in better shape. Cannon balls had sliced the forward mast in half, its crow's nest leaning clumsily over the port side in the water. The mizzenmast was barely standing; the topsail shot away, with the crow's nest and the mizzen sail a tattered remnant. More than a dozen of her pirate crew lay strewn across deck, two cannons blown from their carriages. The *Marée Rouge* was still afloat, even stable, but Isabella sensed the end was near. Both ships laid dead in the water, battered. Neither could make sail and gain any meaningful speed, let alone maneuver for advantage. Neither crew knew if they would be victor or vanquished.

Isabella looked toward the *Grenada* again. Both sides seemed to have grown tired and weary, too worn to go on.

Isabella walked over to the railing, and watched. She looked up at the flag, Jacob's flag, as it fluttered in the wind. Its scarlet background was clear and defiant, but the embroidered panther was weakened by smoke and shot. She smiled—Jacob would not let this fight end now. He would finish it, even if it meant sinking the *Marée Rouge*. That was the honorable course.

She began to turn toward the quarterdeck but stopped. Spain's flag still flew. Like Jacob's, it had weathered the battle.

The *Grenada's* men weren't moving with the urgency of battle. She slapped the telescope to her eye and watched more closely. Juan Carlos was on deck. So was a young officer. They were launching a long boat. Isabella scanned what was left of the masts of her brig. What was Juan Carlos doing?

26

Isabella and Jean-Michel met at midship, still befuddled by the actions on the *Grenada.* What was Juan Carlos Lopez de Santa Ana, Counsel to the Viceroy of the West Indies, up to now? Four Spanish seamen pulled at the long boat's oars, pushing it sluggishly toward the *Marée Rouge* under a white flag. Three other Spanish naval officers were in the boat. Juan Carlos's well-mannered clothes and military figure stood out. The *Grenada's* gun ports remained open, but her cannons pulled inside. Marines stood at their stations, but they held their rifles at their sides. Surely, Santa Ana was not going to ask for their surrender. Surely, he knew Isabella better than that. Surely, he knew Jean-Michel better than that. The pieces of the puzzle didn't fit. Isabella began to worry.

Hours seemed to pass before Juan Carlos's head rose above the gunwales (although Isabella knew it was more likely just a quarter of an hour). He pulled himself over the railing and onto the deck. Isabella's heart skipped; she began to breathe more heavily. She had to control herself. This was a life or death struggle. She could not go back to El Morro. All she wanted to do was rush into his arms.

How selfish, she thought. *And stupid.*

A quick look at Juan Carlos's face showed little emotion. She regrouped, trying to push her feelings far below her skin. She tried to convince herself that she had to deal with him for the filth he was: an emissary of the Spanish Empire, working for the corrupt Viceroy of the West Indies. A Spanish officer, a lieutenant, followed Juan Carlos. A third Spaniard, of lower rank, followed the lieutenant.

Isabella recognized the Spanish boatswain. The scars on her back seemed to cry out. Her fingers fidgeted with the hilt of her saber. She stared as her hand closed around the grip. How could Juan Carlos allow this man to step onto his ship? Jean-Michel moved closer, gently holding her arm as if to say, "Patience, my Captain. There will be time, soon enough, to take revenge."

"Buenos dias," Juan Carlos said. He took his hat off, respectfully, and looked at the deck and crew. He seemed to be logging the casualties and damage. Isabella and Jean-Michel remained silent, refusing to bow.

Isabella fumed. She could feel the blood rush through her veins. Carl was right. Jean-Michel was right. Juan Carlos had only one loyalty—to King and Empire. Isabella shifted her glare to Juan Carlos. His face seemed to soften ever so slightly when their eyes met. His eyes became dark and cold again. Damn his God, Isabella cursed. How could she have felt anything for him? Had El Morro weakened her so much she had given up all that she cared about? Had this man been so cunning, so devious, that he could take a surgeon's knife to her heart, let it smolder for so many weeks, and then rip it out with the coldness of the devil?

Isabella's anger strengthened her; she could feel it. Surrender? No. She would die first, with Jean-Michel and her crew. These men were loyal and committed. They were patient. This morning, they had seen their opportunity; they seized it, and they had retaken the *Marée Rouge*. They weren't going to lose her again, not as long as one deckhand, one gunner, or one officer still lived.

A resolute calm overtook Isabella. That was it. This was it. The prophecy. This battle, the sinking of the *Marée Rouge*, was not a defeat at all. It was vindication.

"State your business," Jean-Michel said.

"I want to discuss terms," Juan Carlos said. His tone was smooth, like silk, just what Isabella expected from a well-groomed colonial administrator. Her free hand coiled around her waist to the small of her back: The pistol was there. All she had to do was cock it, pull it, and fire. Juan Carlos would not be able to react. A quick death like that seemed charitable.

"Terms for what?" Jean-Michel said. "This ship and crew will not surrender to you. Given the choice between dying here, off this point, or from a noose at San Cristóbal, we'll take the pirate's choice."

Juan Carlos looked around at the ship and crew again, nodding his head.

"Of all people," Jean-Michel said, "you should know that."

The comment shook Juan Carlos. Isabella saw it in his eyes when they darted to the two men beside him.

"You've got fifteen minutes to get back to your ship," Jean-Michel said. "Then we open fire."

"That's fool's talk," the lieutenant said. "You'll die."

"We die either way," Isabella said. "In this fight, we serve a higher purpose. If we surrender, we have none."

Jean-Michel cast a curious side-glance to Isabella. Juan Carlos's eyes hinted of panic.

"You'll die," grumbled the boatswain. His tone had an angry bitterness that reminded Isabella of a slow burning wick leading into a powder box. Now, more than ever, she wanted the keg to explode—to give her an excuse. She pulled the saber slightly from its sheath; it moved cleanly and smoothly.

Jean-Michel looked out over the bay. The Spanish schooner was on fire, dead in the water. The sloops seemed evenly matched. The *Grenada* listed slightly, but she was seaworthy enough to finish off the *Marée Rouge*. It was a stalemate. "I like our odds."

Juan Carlos shifted his weight. "I don't think this is the best place to discuss a proposal. Why don't we go someplace private? Some place with fewer distractions."

Jean-Michel looked at Isabella. Isabella's heart missed a beat. She liked the security of the gun deck. "I don't know what we could discuss."

"This isn't the best place," Juan Carlos insisted. "I suggest the captain's quarters. At least the breeze might keep the talk tolerable."

"Aren't you worried you won't come back?" Isabella said, half-heartedly.

"The *Grenada* has orders to fire at the first sign of trouble. I will leave Lieutenant Gonzalez on the main deck. If he is killed, or gives any sign that I have been harmed, or that your crew intends to resume the fight, the *Grenada* will open fire. Boatswain Perez will come with me. We're prepared to finish this now."

Isabella looked at Jean-Michel. Jean-Michel nodded. She turned, and the four descended into the captain's quarters below.

27

The stairs were familiar. The smell wasn't. The hallway reeked of mold and rotten food despite the intensity of the battle on the deck above. Small furry animals squealed in the darkness, and then scampered out of the way. Condensation left a slick, damp sheen on the ceiling beams. Isabella felt caught, trapped, in her own ship.

She opened the door to the captain's cabin, unsure of what to expect. Stiles had done nothing to it, physically. The mirror, her mirror, still hung over the washbasin. The large desk still sat at the center of the room, a foot-long gash in its top. The cot sat in the back, its bedding as stark as when she had left it. She shivered at the thought of Stiles sleeping in her bed. She would burn it before nightfall. Only the windowpanes were new.

The door slammed closed, and the foursome took up positions. Isabella stood behind the desk. Jean-Michel stood at her side. Juan Carlos and Perez stood in front of the desk.

"*Sientese, por favor,*" Isabella said, waving toward one of the two chairs sitting in front of the desk. She could barely contain her anger. She held the grip of her saber firmly.

Juan Carlos laughed. "*No, muchas gracias,*" he said, smiling as he put his hand on the back of one of the chairs. "The last time I sat in that chair… let's just say… I'm in a stronger negotiating position. I'll stand."

The tension in the room seemed to disappear as everyone, save Perez, smiled. Why did he have to laugh that way? A humble laugh, not the arrogant one she expected.

Isabella was surprised at herself. Where had the anger gone? It was as if a witch had lifted a curse. She found herself struggling to keep her anger. She wanted to close the doors and windows to keep it from escaping. She needed her anger.

Jean-Michel looked at Juan Carlos and Perez. "You have a proposal?" he said briskly, bringing everyone back to the seriousness of their plight.

Juan Carlos nodded. "We're at a stalemate." Perez shifted his weight, catching Isabella's attention. She wasn't angry with Juan Carlos, but she wanted to kill Perez. She wished he would draw his sword, or even a pistol. "The *Grenada* will sink you with one more broadside—"

"Don't place your bets," Isabella blurted. "Our crew is more seasoned than the best crew of a Spanish man-of-war. You fear a victory—our victory; not yours, your viceroy's, or your King's."

Juan Carlos looked at Isabella, somewhat surprised by her outburst. Jean-Michel looked at Isabella, too.

"I doubt you could deliver another broadside," Jean-Michel said, in a more level voice. Isabella was embarrassed. Why was she so brash? Why couldn't she be as calm, as patient, as Jean-Michel could? She watched Perez and Juan Carlos. Juan Carlos wasn't looking at her. He waited patiently to hear Jean-Michel's point. Perez fidgeted, keeping his eyes trained on Isabella. She didn't like the way he held the grip of his blade, or the way he looked at her.

"The *Marée Rouge* would turtle you with one more broadside," Jean-Michel said confidently. "You've already got a bad list to windward. We can see your water line."

Juan Carlos nodded. "Perhaps, Jean-Michel." Perez fidgeted some more, letting his cutlass tip dip toward the floor. "But, you're operating with a skeleton crew. You've lost at least a dozen already. I doubt you could muster two full broadsides. The wind has picked up. We would be close enough to board by the time the second one fired."

Isabella looked down at the table, thinking through different scenarios. Each one left both ships destroyed. Juan Carlos was right. She looked at Jean-Michel; his face was expressionless. He knew Juan Carlos was right, too. "We die here," she said, "or in one of Rodriguez's nooses. I choose to die here."

The choice seemed clear. She knew her neck in the noose in San Juan would not fulfill the prophecy. Only here, at Privateer Pointe, could her destiny be fulfilled.

Juan Carlos's eyes glistened in the dim light. They betrayed the same compassion she felt when his hands touched her in the cell in El

Morro. She blushed, praying the others couldn't see her well enough to notice.

"I have a proposal," Juan Carlos said. His voice had lost its bureaucratic edge. "Rodriguez—"

"His Excellency," Perez corrected.

Juan Carlos blinked, as if to check an instinct to slap Perez across the head.

"Losing a squadron of ships and more than 300 sailors and marines does not serve the purpose of King Charles or the Empire," Juan Carlos continued. "Re-engaging the fight cripples us both. Possibly destroys us both. We can end our skirmish here. We can settle this war on another day."

Jean-Michel and Isabella stood, puzzled by the proposal's pragmatism.

"Your captain has agreed to this?" Jean-Michel asked suspiciously. Juan Carlos nodded, but Perez was now swaying uneasily. Perez pulled the tip of his cutlass up. Isabella stepped back, her hand steady on her sword's hilt.

"I don't believe you," she said, looking at Perez.

"Perez!" Juan Carlos scolded.

Perez had already started around the table. Isabella drew her saber and pointed the tip defensively at his chest.

"Stand back," she ordered.

Jean-Michel pulled his saber.

"No!" Juan Carlos yelled. "Perez! Stand back. What are you doing? I order you to stand back."

"I followed your orders once," Perez rumbled, "and it destroyed my ship and my captain."

What did he mean by that? thought Isabella. What had Juan Carlos done on the *Ana Maria*? All Isabella could focus on now was the boatswain pointing his cutlass at her throat.

"Don't be stupid," she warned.

"This isn't over," Perez said, bringing his blade toward her head. Isabella lifted her saber, deflecting Perez's deadly arc. She parried, pulling her saber up. Their blades locked.

"You idiot!" Juan Carlos yelled.

"This wench killed my captain and most of my crew. I'm going to finish this now if you don't."

Perez lunged. Isabella parried downward, deflecting the cutlass. She jerked her blade up under Perez's cutlass, pulling it cleanly from his hands. Perez stood, stunned and helpless. She stepped toward him. Perez's eyes widened. He stepped back toward the wall.

"Isabella—" Juan Carlos said in the soothing voice of a negotiator.

"Quiet," Jean-Michel said softly. "This is her fight. Let it be done."

"But—" Juan Carlos protested.

"Shut up."

Isabella stepped closer to Perez. Perez retreated.

"What's wrong?" she taunted. "Need your whip? Can't do much without chains binding me to a wall, can you?"

Fresh sweat soaked through Perez's shirt. His knees quivered with each backward step. Perez stopped with a thud as he backed into the hull of the ship. The mirror on the wall clinked. Perez dropped his hand to the washbasin, gripping it so hard his hands became white.

"Cat's got your tongue, eh?" Isabella circled the tip in front of his face, watching his panicked eyes follow it. He seemed to have stopped breathing. Isabella nudged the tip of her saber into a button on Perez's shirt. The button flicked off, dropping to the floor. She pushed the tip through the cotton and into his skin. Perez winced as a speck of blood oozed into his shirt.

"Isabella," Juan Carlos said softly.

"This is my fight," Isabella insisted. "You saw what he did to me. What better justice than this?"

"For the love of God."

"Whose God? Yours? What has he ever given me? Lashes from the overseer's whip, a mutinous first mate, and El Morro. I don't believe in your God. I'm going to finish this."

"You know more about my God than my King," Juan Carlos pleaded. "What kind of judgment is this?"

Isabella hesitated. She looked at Perez. He had closed his eyes. His lips twitched nervously. Saliva drooled down his chin.

Isabella caught a glimpse of her disheveled self in the mirror. She was tired, but her eyes held a fierceness she hadn't seen before. Is this what El Morro had done to her? She blinked, hoping the image would clear itself. What had she become? She had killed Stiles. She had to. It was the Law. But Perez? What was his crime? She had captured his ship and killed his captain. She could see her death in his eyes—they sparkled with hatred and vengeance.

Was this the fulfillment of the prophecy? Killing some weak, vindictive Spanish seaman? Everything seemed wrong.

Isabella pulled back as she felt a calm overwhelm her. Her body relaxed. Her thoughts were loose and her mind seemed to open. Revenge. Was that good enough to justify killing Perez? Did the injustices of the plantations and El Morro leave her with nothing more than a thirst for revenge? They would be enough for Perez. He lost his ship, his captain, his life, to her purpose. Perez was pitiful. He was sure he would die because only one kind of justice drove him—revenge.

Isabella stepped backward, letting her tip drop. This was not the fight to fulfill the prophecy. Not yet.

"Open your eyes." The command was soft, hard. Perez shut his eyes even tighter. She thumped his chest with the dull side of the saber. "Open your eyes." Perez opened his eyes, surely expecting his last living sight to be Isabella's face as she rammed her blade through his heart.

"I have every reason to kill you. You have attacked me even as we were negotiating for a cease-fire in good faith. My Creed would justify your death. Some would even say I must kill you." She brought her face close to his. Panic glistened around the whites of his eyes. "I want to kill you." She stepped back. "I choose to spare your life." These last words caught her by surprise. The words "I choose" excited her. They gave her a strength and purpose she had never felt before. They were cathartic.

Perez's body slipped to the floor.

Isabella turned toward Jean-Michel. "You said, 'It will stop when we say it can stop.' I am stopping it now." Jean-Michel looked at her and nodded a smile.

"You trust him?" he asked, casting a look over to Juan Carlos.

"He's practical," she said, looking at Juan Carlos. "He wants to win. As we do. He won't get a win today. We can finish this another day." She turned back toward Perez. "Now, get this pathetic coward out of my cabin."

"Aye, Captain," Jean-Michel said. He walked over to Perez, leaned down, and pulled his body through the doors and up the stairs without even casting a sideways glance toward Juan Carlos.

Juan Carlos and Isabella stood in the cabin for a few silent moments.

"Gracias," Juan Carlos said, giving her a respectful bow.

"I didn't do it for you." Isabella bent down and picked up the button she had plucked from Perez's coat. "I did it for me."

"Souvenir?"

Isabella looked at the button resting in her hand, and turned it over. She looked over to the drawer under the washbasin. "At least it's not a tombstone." She cocked her hand and threw the button out into the sea. "It had to stop."

"It can stop now. All of it can stop; if you want it to."

"Do you really think Rodriguez would let me roam the waters freely?"

"If you stopped raiding Spain's ships..."

"Don't be a fool. Rodriguez can't afford to let me roam these waters."

Juan Carlos stepped closer and gently reached for Isabella's arm. His grip was gentle and comforting. She longed for the touch she had felt inside the cells of El Morro. Isabella turned and looked into his eyes. They were soft and moist. She stepped closer. Their bodies touched, her hips against his, her breasts against his chest. She reached for his hand and pulled it to her face. His palm cradled her cheek. His hands were warm and soft. She closed her eyes and let herself drift. Each breath seemed to unleash a new wave of comfort. She felt herself drawn closer to him. His arm wrapped around her waist. She slipped her arms under his. She pulled herself firmly into his chest, resting her head.

They stood holding each other, listening to the water lap against the hull of the *Marée Rouge*. The thud of patient footsteps above told them nothing was urgent. She felt secure; she felt settled. She couldn't remember feeling this way, even with Jacob. The mood felt natural, like long-lost pieces of a puzzle finally coming together after a life-long search. They savored each moment as if they could never recapture it.

"Juan Carlos," Isabella whispered.

"Yes."

"What are we going to do?"

Juan Carlos lifted her head with his hand. He looked into her eyes, and they kissed. They kissed for what seemed like a long, soothing island night. How could she have doubted him? Why had she struggled for so long to deny her feelings for him?

"I don't know," he admitted.

"Come with me," she said. "Join us. You don't have to sail with us. Stay on Saint John. Be there when I return."

Juan Carlos chuckled. "The dreams of a girl. You know as well as I that can't happen. I have to go back to San Juan. I have to face Rodriguez. It is my duty."

"Duty? Duty to whom? Your King? The Empire? Your God?"

"Isabella," Juan Carlos said, frustration growing in his tone. "I can't leave God or my King. My life has been dedicated to serving him."

"You mean them." Isabella pushed herself away from Juan Carlos and rested on the edge of the table. "Who are you loyal to? God or your King?"

"The two are one."

Isabella shook her head in disgust. "Do you really think your God would tolerate the plantations? People like Stiles, Smith, and Rodriguez?"

"They are servants of my King and God."

"They are servants to themselves." Juan Carlos turned away from Isabella.

"We can't work. How can it possibly work?"

"I don't know." Isabella shook her head. "All I know is that I think of you all the time. I struggle to keep from thinking of you, and it exhausts me."

Juan Carlos pulled Isabella close again. He kissed her, even more passionately. "No one has ever meant as much to me as you."

"Rosa?"

"Rosa is beautiful and clever, but she is more loyal to the Empire than her father. Her principles are first to herself."

"Then, we need a plan." Juan Carlos nodded.

"*Si,* a plan. I don't think I can go on without you near me."

Isabella pushed herself from his arms. "What does Rodriguez expect of you?"

"I'm his counsel," Juan Carlos said, confused.

"Why were you on the *Grenada?"*

"My orders were to bring you back to San Juan."

"Your orders put you on board a ship?"

"*Si,*" Juan Carlos confirmed. "How else could I capture pirates?"

"Then you will be traveling through the West Indies." Isabella could see her plan begin to form in Juan Carlos's mind.

Juan Carlos nodded. "We make port every three weeks."

"Jean-Michel and I have many friends throughout the West Indies. As long as you are true to us, they will help us."

"I don't know if I can go two weeks without you in my arms."

Isabella stepped closer to him. She lifted her face to his and kissed him. "We don't have a choice."

"No," Juan Carlos agreed, "I suppose we don't." They embraced again.

"What will Jean-Michel think?"

"Jean-Michel believes in actions, not words," Isabella said. "If you are true to your words in your deeds, Jean-Michel will accept us. I'm sure of it. I need you to swear to me and my friends."

"I swear my loyalty to you before my God."

"I can think of no better promise." They stood, holding hands, looking into each other's eyes. Outside, the light began to fade. A sole star twinkled brightly through the dusk. Although Isabella couldn't see it, something in her let her feel it. For the first time in two years, Isabella didn't think about Jacob.

About the Author

SR Staley (www.srstaley.com) is an award-winning novelist, economist, and public policy analyst living in Tallahassee, Florida. He is also on the full-time faculty of the College of Social Sciences and Public Policy at Florida State University.

He is the author of five nonfiction books, and three other novels, including *St. Nic, Inc.*, a re-imagination of the legend of Santa Clause around global capitalism and rogue drug enforcement agents. Southern Yellow Pine Publishing will publish *Tortuga Bay,* the sequel to *The Pirate of Panther Bay,* in 2015.

He earned his B.A. in economics from Colby College, M.S. in applied economics from Wright State University, and Ph.D. in public administration from The Ohio State University.